James Patterson

RUN
FOR YOUR LIFE

& Michael Ledwidge

arrow books

Published in the United Kingdom by Arrow Books in 2009

5 7 9 10 8 6 4

First published in Great Britain in 2009 by
Century

Arrow Books
Random House, 20 Vauxhall Bridge Road,
London SW1V 2SA

www.rbooks.co.uk

Addresses for companies within The Random House Group Limited can be found
at: www.randomhouse.co.uk

The Random House Group Limited Reg. No. 954009

A CIP catalogue record for this book
is available from the British Library

Penguin Random House is committed to a sustainable future for
our business, our readers and our planet. This book is made from
Forest Stewardship Council® certified paper.

MIX
Paper from
responsible sources
FSC® C018179

Printed and bound in Great Britain by Clays Ltd, St Ives plc

For Kathy, Eileen, and Jean

DETECTIVE
MICHAEL BENNETT

Prologue

FIGHT THE POWER

One

GETTING STUCK ON a bus in New York City, even under normal circumstances, is a lesson in frustration.

But when the bus belongs to the NYPD Tactical Assistance Response Unit, and it's parked at a barricade that's swarming with cops, and you're there because you're the only person in the world who might have a chance at keeping several hostages from being killed, you can cancel your dinner plans.

I wasn't going anywhere on that Monday night. Much worse, I wasn't *getting* anywhere.

"Where's my money, Bennett?" an angry voice shouted through my headset.

I'd gotten to know that voice really well over the past seven and a half hours. It came from a nineteen-year-old gang hit man known as D-Ray—his real name was

Kenneth Robinson—who was the main suspect in a triple drug murder. In truth, he was the only suspect. When police had come after him earlier today, he'd holed up in a Harlem brownstone, now behind police barricades, threatening to kill five members of his own family.

"The money's coming, D-Ray," I said, speaking gently into the headset. "Like I told you, I got Wells Fargo to send an armored truck up from Brooklyn. A hundred thousand dollars in unmarked twenties, sitting on the front seat."

"You keep saying that, but I don't see no truck!"

"It's not as easy as it sounds," I lied. "They run on bank schedules. You can't just call them like a taxi. They don't carry that kind of cash around, either—they've got to go through a complicated procedure to get it. And drive through traffic, just like everybody else."

Hostage situations call for measured calm, something I'm actually pretty good at faking. If it weren't for the dozen uniformed Emergency Service Unit and Manhattan North Task Force cops listening in, you might have thought I was a priest hearing a confession.

In fact, the Wells Fargo truck had arrived a good two hours ago and was parked out of sight nearby. I was fighting with everything I had to keep it there. If it drove these last few blocks, that meant I'd failed.

"You playin' me?" D-Ray barked. "*Nobody* plays me, cop. You think I don't know I'm already lookin' at life in prison? What I got to lose if I kill somebody else?"

"I know you're not playing, D-Ray," I said. "I'm not,

4

either—that's the last thing I want to do. The money's on its way. Meantime, you need anything else? More pizza, soda pop, anything like that? Hey, it must be hot in there—how about some ice cream for your niece and nephew?"

"*Ice* cream?" he yelled with a fury that made me wince. "You better get your shit together, Bennett! I don't see no armored truck in five minutes, you gonna see a body come rolling down that stoop."

The line went dead. Wiping sweat from my face, I pulled off the headset and stepped to the window of the NYPD bus. It was parked with a clear view of D-Ray's brown-stone, on 131st Street near Frederick Douglass Boulevard. I raised my binoculars and panned the kitchen window. I swallowed as I spotted an Eracism magnet holding up children's drawings and a picture of Maya Angelou on the fridge. His niece and nephew were six and eight years old. I had kids those same ages.

At first, I'd hoped that the situation would be easier because his hostages were his own flesh and blood. A lot of criminals might make this kind of desperate bluff, but they'd back down before they'd harm someone close to them, especially little kids. D-Ray's eighty-three-year-old grandmother, Miss Carol, was also in there with them, and she was a neighborhood institution, a powerful and respected woman who ran the rec center and the commu-nity garden. If anybody could make him listen, it was Miss Carol.

But she hadn't, which was a very bad sign. D-Ray had

already proved that he was a killer, and during the hours I'd spent talking to him, I'd sensed his rage rising and his control slipping. I was sure that all along he'd been getting higher on crack or meth or whatever, and by now he was half insane. He was clinging to a fantasy of escape, and he was ready to kill for it.

I had helped him build that fantasy, and I'd used every trick I knew to keep it going so we could get those people out of there alive—tried to create a bond, talked like a sympathetic friend, even told him my name. But I was out of both tricks and time.

I lowered the binoculars and scanned the scene outside the bus windows. Behind the sawhorses and the flashing lights of the gathered police vehicles, there were several news vans and maybe sixty or seventy spectators. Some were eating Chinese take-out or holding up cell phone cameras. There were school-age kids zipping around on Razor scooters. The crowd seemed anxious, impatient, like picnickers disappointed that the fireworks hadn't started yet.

I turned away from them just as Joe Hunt, the Manhattan North borough commander, sagged back in the office chair beside me and let out a long, deflated breath.

"Just heard from ESU," he said. "Snipers think they got a pretty good bead on him through one of the back windows."

I didn't say anything, but Joe knew what I was thinking. He stared at me with his almost sad, world-weary brown eyes.

"Kid or not, we're dealing with a violent sociopath," he went on. "We need to give this to Tactical while those poor people inside still have a chance. I'm calling in the Wells Fargo truck. I want you to get D-Ray back on the phone and tell him to watch for it. Then Con Ed's going to cut the power, and the snipers will drop him with night vision." Joe heaved himself to his feet and gave me a rough pat on the shoulder. "Sorry, Mike. You did better than anyone has any right to expect, but the kid flat-out refuses to live."

I passed my hands through my hair and scrubbed my own tired eyes. New York City has one of the best reputations in the world for resolving hostage situations nonviolently, and I hated like hell to be a part of changing that fine tradition. But I couldn't argue with Hunt's logic. D-Ray definitely wasn't even trying to help me save him.

I nodded, defeated. We had to think about his family now. There was no other way.

I listened to Joe Hunt call the armored truck and order it to start moving toward us. As soon as it came into sight, I'd be talking to D-Ray for the last time.

We stepped out of the bus for a breath of fresh air while we waited.

Two

AS I CLIMBED OUTSIDE, the first thing I noticed was the chanting from a different crowd—at the far end of the block, in front of a housing project over on Frederick Douglass Boulevard.

It took my brain a second to decipher the words: "Fight the power!"

Hunt and I exchanged stunned looks. We cops were there to save the lives of their friends and neighbors—including two little children and the much-loved Miss Carol—and we were the bad guys? Talk about a neighborhood in need of some new role models.

"Fight the power! Fight the power!" The roar kept coming at me while I anxiously searched for the armored truck.

New role models! my brain yelled back.

Then, out of nowhere, the two thoughts connected.

"Hold that truck, Chief!" I hollered at Hunt. I rushed back onto the bus and snatched up my headset, nodding to a uniformed TARU tech to patch me into the brownstone again.

"D-Ray, it's Mike Bennett," I said when he picked up.

"You got two minutes, cop!" He was practically frothing with agitation.

"Whoa, whoa," I said. "Listen to the crowd outside, will you? They're rooting for you. You're their hero."

"What kind of bullshit you pullin' now, Bennett?"

"This isn't bullshit, D-Ray. Open up a window and listen. You think you've got nothing left to live for, but you're wrong."

All the cops and techs on the bus stopped what they were doing and watched the brownstone. After a very long thirty seconds, one of the window sashes rose a few inches. We couldn't see D-Ray—he was beside or below it—but he was there, listening.

"Hear that?" I said into the headset. "*Fight the power.* They're talking to you, D-Ray. They think you're a badass for holding us off. Not only that, you know what one of your grandmother's church-lady friends just told me? You've done this neighborhood a great service by getting rid of the Drew Boyz and all their dope-dealing and violence. People hated them, were terrified of them, and you took them out."

"Ohhh, man! You serious?" For the first time, D-Ray

sounded like what he was, a scared, confused nineteen-year-old kid.

"I'm damn serious, and I feel the same way they do," I said. It was another bald-faced lie, but I'd sell him both the George Washington and the Brooklyn bridges if it meant saving lives.

The crew on the bus were staring at me now. I swabbed my sleeve across my sweaty face and took the next risk.

"Now, there's two ways left you can play this, D-Ray," I said. "You can keep your hostages and try to get away with the money. But you won't get far, and you know it. Probably you'll get yourself killed, and maybe your grandma and the little kids, too. Or you can stand up like the hero these people believe you are, and let everybody go."

It felt like my heart stopped, and maybe time itself, as D-Ray suddenly cut the connection.

"D-Ray!" I yelled. "D-Ray, come back, goddammit!"

The line stayed dead. I tore off the headset and burst out of the hot, bright bus into the cool darkness of the street.

Three

I RAN TO THE BARRICADES in front of the brownstone, tensed for the hollow popping sound of gunshots from inside, then the sickening thud of a body being shoved out onto the steps. The crowds at both ends of the block hushed, as if they sensed that this was a critical moment.

The door at the top of the building's stoop opened slowly. The first person I saw was a large elderly woman. It was D-Ray's grandmother, Miss Carol, and she was walking on her own! Better yet, the two other adults—D-Ray's grand-aunt and -uncle—were flanking her, and I could just make out the small shapes of the niece and nephew behind them. My ruse had worked—they were all alive, and he was releasing them!

My breath had been locked in my throat. I let it out with a whoosh and started sucking air into my starving lungs. But my joy warped into shock when I realized that they all had their arms linked to form a circle.

They were making themselves into a protective human shield, with D-Ray crouching in the center.

"Don't you shoot my baby!" Miss Carol screeched, loud and clear in the sudden stillness.

Unreal—even more unreal than the crowd making a hero of D-Ray! His hostages were actually *protecting* him. First, insane role models, and now, double-insane Stockholm syndrome.

I gestured toward Commander Hunt to stand down the rooftop snipers as I shoved my radio earphone in place and hurried toward the bizarre human chain making its way along the brownstone steps.

"It's me, D-Ray, I'm Mike Bennett," I called to them. "You're doing the right thing, D-Ray. You're making everybody *proud* of you. Now we need your family to move aside."

"Don't you hurt him!" Miss Carol cried out again. I could see the glimmer of tears in her eyes.

"He'll be safe with me, I promise." I held my hands up high and open to show that they were empty, and as I lowered them, I repeated my stand-down gesture to the nervous cops. "D-Ray, if you have any guns, throw them out on the ground," I said, putting a little more authority in my voice. "You'll be fine, don't worry."

There was another pause that seemed endless before a flat gray pistol clattered out from inside the human circle and onto the sidewalk. It looked like a Glock, probably a .40 or .45 caliber, with a ten- to thirteen-round clip—a whole lot of death in a package smaller than a paperback.

"Good man, D-Ray," I said. "Now I'm coming in there to you, and we're going to walk together to a car."

Miss Carol and the others unlinked their arms and parted, revealing a stocky young man wearing below-the-knee athletic shorts and a baseball cap turned to the side. I stepped over the barricade sawhorse and walked toward him.

Then came a terrible sound that almost made me jump out of my shoes: the *boom* of a gunshot from somewhere behind me.

D-Ray fell into the gutter like a chainsawed tree while his family watched, frozen with horror.

In the next instant, everything changed. Cops tackled asphalt with their weapons ready, and the crowds started milling and shoving in panic.

"Cease fire!" I yelled, and I piled into Miss Carol, knocking her back into the others so they all went down like dominoes. Then I scrambled on my knees to D-Ray.

But neither I nor anybody else would be able to help him. There was a bullet hole, trickling blood, neatly centered between his open eyes.

"*Not us*, Mike! Stay down!" It was Lieutenant Steve Reno from the ESU tactical squad, calling into my radio earphone.

"Then who?!" I shouted back.

"We think it came from the crowd near Frederick Douglass. We're sending a team in there now."

A sniper in the crowd—not a cop? Christ! What was going on?

"Get EMS over here," I told Reno over the radio squawk. Then I stood up. I knew he was right, that the sniper might be looking for more targets, but I couldn't just lie there with the chaos erupting around me.

Instantly I felt like I was swimming in quicksand. The crowd had seen D-Ray fall, and they assumed that the police had shot him. They were turning ugly, jamming up against the barricades, their faces contorted in rage. Other cops were on their feet now, too, running to this area and forming a line to hold them back.

"They killed that boy! They *murdered* him!" some woman kept screaming.

A surge of human beings sent one of the sawhorses tumbling over, knocking down a female NYPD officer. Her partners leaped in to drag her to safety, while others charged along beside them, swinging nightsticks. The ear-splitting chatter of sirens ripped through the air as two squad cars drove up onto the sidewalk to reinforce the barrier between us and the mushrooming riot closing in on us.

I was keeping tabs on that, while also scanning the rooftops, in dread of more gunfire. Then, what felt like a baseball bat with knuckles slammed into the back of my head. It sent me reeling and spun me clear around.

"You lyin' pig, you killed my baby!" Miss Carol screamed. She came after me, moving very fast for a woman of her age and size, and rammed another punch into my chest, knocking the breath out of me.

"No, we didn't do it," I croaked out, but she was already winding up for a haymaker that would have knocked me silly. I managed to duck that one, only to have D-Ray's emaciated uncle grab my lapels and try to head-butt me. As I pried off his hands, his equally fragile-looking wife walloped me across the shoulders with her cane. I'd taken some thumpings in my life, but this set a new record for bizarre.

As I backpedaled frantically, I realized that the news camera lights weren't on the crowd anymore, but now were spotlighting my geriatric ass-whooping. That inflamed the crowd further, and people at both ends of the block started to converge, tearing down the barricades and leaping over the hoods of the patrol cars. A couple of uniforms came to my rescue, forcing my attackers aside, and Joe Hunt grabbed my arm and yanked me along with him in retreat to the TARU bus.

"Call for backup!" he was yelling. "Get the Two-five, the Two-six and the Three-oh over here. I mean everybody, and I mean yesterday!"

In the distance, I could hear the wail of the reinforcement sirens already starting.

DETECTIVE
MICHAEL BENNETT

Part One

THE TEACHER

Chapter 1

IT WAS COMING on three a.m. when I finally managed to get myself smuggled out of Harlem by a uniform who owed me a favor.

As we negotiated the gridlock maze of news satellite vans, barricades, and mounted crowd-control cops, there still wasn't the slightest hint about who had killed D-Ray.

Any standoff that led to a death would have been bad enough, but this bizarre shooting was the department's worst nightmare come true. No matter how much evidence suggested that the NYPD wasn't responsible, it *looked* like we were. The rabble-rousers, conspiracy theorists, and their many friends in the New York City media were going to have a field day.

And if that wasn't enough to make me rip into a blister pack of Prilosec, there was the mountain of reports and other red tape I'd be facing come morning. I'd have gladly accepted another caning from D-Ray's grandaunt instead.

When the cop dropped me off in front of my West End Avenue apartment building, I was so burnt out from fatigue, unresolved tension, and worry about what lay ahead that I almost stumbled to the door. I craved a few hours of peaceful sleep as a man who'd been crawling for days through the desert craves an oasis.

But the oasis turned out to be a mirage. Right off the bat, my crazy Dominican doorman, Ralph, seemed pissed off that I had to wake him up. I liked Ralph, but I was in no mood for petty surliness, and I gave him a look that told him so.

"Any time you want to trade jobs, Ralph, just let me know," I said.

He lowered his eyes apologetically. "Rough night, Mr. Bennett?"

"You'll read about it tomorrow in the *Times*."

When I finally made it into my darkened apartment, the Crayola products and Polly Pocket debris that crunched underfoot was actually welcoming. I mustered up enough energy to lock up my service weapon and ammo in the pistol safe in my front hall closet. Then, totally wiped, I collapsed onto one of the high stools at the kitchen island.

If my wife, Maeve, were still here, she'd be standing at the stove right now, handing me an icy Bud while something wonderful fried—chicken wings or a cheeseburger, heavy on the bacon. With divinely sent, cop-wife wisdom, she knew that the only panaceas for the grim reality of the streets were grease, cold beer, a shower, and bed, with her warm beside me.

A strange moment of clarity pierced my weariness, and I realized that she hadn't just been my love—she'd been my life support. On nights like this, the really bad ones, she'd listen for hours if I needed to talk, and understand completely when I couldn't.

Right then, more than anything in the world, I longed to feel her fingers caress the back of my neck as she told me that I'd tried my best. That sometimes there's nothing we can do. I would circle her waist with my hands, and her magic would make all my doubts and guilt and stress disappear.

Maeve had been dead for almost a year now, and in all that time, I hadn't found any new ways to cope with it—only new ways to miss her.

I'd been at the funeral of a homicide victim one time and heard his mother quote a poem by Edna St. Vincent Millay. It kept ringing in my ears lately, like a song you can't get out of your head.

Gently they go, the beautiful, the tender, the kind...

I know. But I do not approve. And I am not resigned.

I don't know how much longer I can live without you, Maeve, I thought. My head sagged, and I leaned my forearms on the counter for support.

But I jerked back upright when I noticed that my left hand was resting in a pool of something sticky. I examined the stuff, sniffed it, then tasted it: grape jelly, Welch's finest, covering not just my hand, but my whole suit jacket sleeve.

Living without you isn't the only thing that's impossible, I told Maeve while I stood up on tired legs to search for a paper towel.

How can I take care of all our kids the way only you could?

Chapter 2

I WAS HOPELESS on the domestic front, all right. I couldn't even find a paper towel. I rinsed off the jelly with water as well as I could, and put the suit coat in a closet with some other clothes that were waiting to be dry-cleaned. My luck started looking better when I poked around inside the fridge. There was a Saran-wrapped plate of baked ziti on a shelf, and I dug up a can of Coors Light buried beneath half a case of Capri Suns in the drink drawer. I set the microwave humming, and I was just crunching open my Silver Bullet when a hair-raising sound emanated from the dark interior of my apartment—a sort of howling moan followed by a long, unholy splatter. Then it happened again, only in a different tone.

As I slowly lowered my untouched brew, I was visited by one of those blink moments I'd read about. Though my conscious mind wasn't sure what was causing those noises, some deeper instinct warned me that it signaled a danger that any sane person would flee with all his might.

Against my better judgment, I staggered down the hall in that direction. Peering around a corner, I spotted a bar of light under the rear bathroom door. I tiptoed to it and slowly twisted the knob.

I stood rooted there, speechless with visceral horror. My instincts had been all too correct. I should have fled when I had the chance.

Not one, not two, but three of my children were projectile-vomiting into the tub. It was like looking at an outtake from *The Exorcist* while you were seeing triple. I reared back as Ricky, Bridget, and Chrissy hurled again, each one's upchuck triggered by the previous one, like they were trying to puke a campfire round. Think Vesuvius, Krakatoa, and Mount Saint Helens all going off in musical succession.

Before I could catch myself, I made the mistake of breathing through my nose. My stomach lurched precariously. I blessed my stars that I hadn't had a chance to eat during the Harlem siege, or to get started on the ziti. Otherwise, yours truly would have chimed in a fourth eruption of his own.

My Irish nanny, Mary Catherine, was right beside the kids, her golden ringlets bouncing out from beneath a red bandanna as she mopped furiously at the blowback they left. She had wisely put on elbow-length, industrial rubber gloves and covered her face with another bandanna, but I could see from her eyes—usually crisp blue, but now damp and faded—that she was as exhausted as I was.

She gave me a quick wave, then pulled off the bandanna and said, in her lilting brogue, "Mike, remember before you left for work, I told you Chrissy was looking a little green?"

I nodded mutely, still struggling to absorb the enormity of the situation.

"I think that flu that's been going around school has arrived," Mary Catherine said. "Repent, for the plague is upon us."

I crossed myself solemnly, trying to pick up her joke to make us both feel a little better. But a nervous part of me wasn't entirely kidding. The way things had been going, maybe this *was* the plague.

"I've got it from here, Mary," I said, taking the mop from her. "You're officially off duty."

"That, I most certainly am not," she said indignantly. "Now, the Tylenol is in the cabinet over the sink, but we're running out of cough syrup, and—"

"And enough," I said, pointing toward the stairs to her upstairs apartment, formerly the maid's quarters. "I don't need any more patients to take care of."

"Oh? What makes you think *you* won't get sick?" She folded her arms in stubborn loyalty, which I'd come to know well. "Because you're a big tough copper?"

I sighed. "No—because I don't have time to. Get some

sleep and you can take over in the morning, okay? That's what I'm going to need."

She wavered, then gave me a weary but sweet smile.

"You're not fooling anybody," Mary Catherine said. "But okay."

Chapter 3

I MOANED along with the kids as the front door closed behind Mary Catherine.

It's not that I don't love my children. I really do. But I'm the guardian of the kind of brood that would send Mother Teresa doctor-shopping for pharmaceutical assistance.

How's this for the Bennett lineup? Juliana, thirteen; Brian, twelve; Jane, eleven; Ricky, ten; Eddie, nine; twins Fiona and Bridget, eight; Trent, six; Shawna, five; and Chrissy, four. A total of ten, count them: two Hispanic, two black, one Asian, and the rest white. All of them are adopted. Pretty impressive, I know. Not many families can field a multicultural baseball team, plus a bench player.

It was primarily Maeve's idea. We started taking in her "stray angels," as she called our gang way back before Brangelina got into the act. How could either of us have foreseen the nightmare of her death from cancer at the age of thirty-eight?

I wasn't completely alone, thank God. Mary Catherine had appeared like a gift from heaven while Maeve was dying, and for some unfathomably merciful reason, she still hadn't fled screaming. My crotchety grandfather-turned-priest, Seamus, was pastor of Holy Name Church, just around the corner. He'd wangled the job so he could help with the kids and disapprove of me, but the disapproval was a small price to pay for his help.

But it had been nearly impossible to take care of my young ones even when their mother was still alive and they were perfectly healthy. What was I going to do with the apartment transformed into a children's ward at a hospital?

A thousand worries sprang up in my already stress-racked head. How was I going to get the well kids to school? What about taking the sick ones to a doctor's office? How much sick leave did I have left? Had I paid this month's health insurance premium on time? And what about the missed schoolwork? An image of the kids' strong-willed, meticulous principal, Sister Sheilah, loomed in my mind like a specter.

I palmed my forehead and took a deep breath. I was a trained problem solver, I reminded myself. I could get us through this. It was temporary—a rough spot for sure, but a brief one. Like in any survival situation, the worst thing I could do was panic.

Run for Your Life

I bent down over Chrissy, my youngest, as she began to wail at the tippity-top of her lungs. Through her thin Backyardigans pj top, I could feel her burning up with fever. So were her copatients, Ricky and Bridget. They all started whining for ginger ale.

Me, too, I thought, searching around frantically for Mary Catherine's spare bandanna. And let's not spare the Jack Daniel's.

Chapter 4

THE MAN IN the beautifully tailored, two-button Givenchy suit had finished his morning's work with his usual expertise and speed. Many things in his life had changed since he had seen the truth — he was a new man now — but his superior intelligence and skills remained intact.

As he stepped into the garage of the stately Locust Valley home, he heard the lawn sprinklers kick on. He glanced at the black dial of his stainless-steel Rolex Explorer. Seven a.m. sharp. Excellent: he was running ahead of schedule, just the way he liked it.

He opened the gleaming door of the BMW 720Li, placed his Vuitton briefcase on the passenger seat, and swung his long, muscular legs under the steering wheel. As he adjusted the rearview mirror, he caught his own reflection. With his lean, brutally chiseled features, his razor-straight, collar-length black hair, and piercing, almost royal blue eyes, he looked like a model in a *Vanity Fair* ad. He smiled, showing himself his dimples and his perfect, gleaming white teeth.

He had it all, didn't he? he thought.

The V12 engine of the luxury BMW sedan came to life with an elegant explosion when he turned the key.

Too bad "it all" wasn't nearly enough.

While the engine warmed, the New Man took a Palm Treo 750 smart phone from his silk-lined inside jacket pocket. The little gadget could do everything: phone, e-mail, surf the Web. He clicked on Microsoft Tasks and opened the file he'd been working on.

It was a mission statement, a brief written summary of his goals, philosophy, and ambitions. He'd actually gotten the idea from the movie *Jerry Maguire,* of all places. In it, Tom Cruise's character sends out a mission statement that gets everyone all riled up.

That was precisely what the New Man was going to do today.

Except this was no movie.

He still liked Cruise, even though Cruise had made a fool of himself on *Oprah* with his couch-jumping antics. Maybe it was the slight resemblance they shared, but the New Man considered him a kind of a role model, almost a psychic brother. Cruise was a perfectionist, a peerless professional, a winner—just like himself.

Rereading the document for the hundredth time, he

knew it was complete. The only problem that remained was how to sign it. There was no way he could use his real name, and the "New Man" wasn't distinguished enough. He could feel the true name hovering at the edge of his mind, but he couldn't quite reel it in. Well, it would come, he thought, closing the Treo down and tucking it back into his jacket. The important things always did.

He jauntily tapped the garage door opener on the Beemer's visor, and backed out smoothly toward the daylight flooding in through the rising door.

Then his passing glance caught the rearview mirror again—just in time to see the immense grille of a Lincoln Navigator, parked in the driveway directly in his path.

He slammed on the brakes barely in time to keep from ramming the Navigator and turning the shiny, showy grille into a twisted chunk of metal.

He exhaled a seething breath through his gritted teeth and wrenched the gearshift into park. Goddamn Erica! She had to leave her monster SUV right *there,* didn't she? *Exactly* in the one spot where he couldn't get around it. Now he'd have to go back inside the house, find the keys, move it, *then* start all over again in the Beemer. Like he wasn't in a distinct rush here. Like he didn't have important things to do. Erica wouldn't understand that—she'd *never* had anything important to do.

And now, she never would.

That thought made him feel a little better, but when

he strode back to the Navigator three minutes later, his annoyance erupted all over again. This was cutting into his comfortable extra margin of time.

He twisted the key in the ignition so hard it bent, floored the accelerator, and threw the tranny into reverse. The SUV's seventeen-inch tires screamed as it rocketed backward, streaking rubber down the length of the herringbone-patterned limestone driveway. Instead of curving along with it, he kept going straight, onto the immaculate lawn. The spinning tires tore deep gouges and threw up tufts of shining green grass.

Leaving the Navigator's engine running, he parked the BMW, much more carefully, on the deserted suburban street. He was feeling a little calmer now. He was almost done with this crap, almost back where he'd started, and still ahead of schedule.

Then, as he was getting into the Navigator to return it to where it had been, a cold jet of water from a sprinkler pop-up lashed across the back of his designer suit from his shoulders to his waist.

His blue eyes practically smoked with fury, and he almost started pounding on the steering wheel with the heels of his hands. But a memory cut in, from an anger management therapy session he'd been ordered to take part in several years before. The therapist had concentrated on techniques to ratchet down his destructive rage: count backward from ten, breathe deeply, clench his fists, and pretend he was squeezing oranges.

Squeeze your oranges, he could almost hear her soothing voice saying to him. *Then flick, flick, flick off the juice.*

He gave it a try. Squeeze and flick. Squeeze and flick.

The sprinkler jet shot across the Navigator again, pissing into his face through the open window.

"I'll show you anger management, you idiot bitch!" he snarled, and stomped on the accelerator.

Spraying grass and chunks of limestone, the SUV hurtled straight through the garage and into the back wall at thirty-five miles per hour. The crash was like a bomb going off in a phone booth, with studs splintering and clouds of drywall dust billowing through the air.

He managed to switch off the ignition around the deployed air bag, then squeezed himself out of the seat. Things were nice and quiet now, except for the hiss of the cracked radiator and the soft spattering of the lawn pop-ups.

"That'll teach her," he said.

Then he stopped dead.

Teach her. Teacher.

That was it—the perfect name he'd been looking for!

"Erica, you finally did one useful thing," he said softly.

He shook the Treo out of his damp suit coat and blooped it on.

At the bottom of his mission statement, below "Best Wishes," he typed across the glowing screen: "The Teacher."

One last time, he checked the recipient box to make sure the address for the *New York Times* was correct.

Then he hit Send.

He tucked the Treo into his pocket and jogged along the elegantly sweeping drive toward the waiting BMW.

He could hardly believe it. Finally, the deed was done.

He was the Teacher; the world was his students, and class was about to begin.

Chapter 5

THE TEACHER ZIPPED the 720Li into the resident parking section of the Locust Valley, Long Island Rail Road station, between a Mercedes SL600 convertible and a Range Rover HSE. Even the cars in Locust Valley insisted on expensive neighbors, he thought.

He cut the engine and checked his suit coat, which he'd spread out on the back seat to dry. With the warm, sunny weather helping, the fine fabric had recovered nicely. No one would notice the slight dampness that remained.

His good mood had returned. In fact, he was feeling great. Things were going his way again. He was on top of the world. Whistling the first aria from Mozart's *Idomeneo*, he lifted the butter-soft Vuitton briefcase off the passenger seat and got out of the car.

As he approached the platform, he noticed a tall pregnant woman struggling with a baby stroller on the platform steps.

"Here, let me help you with that," he said. He gripped the stroller's front axle with his free hand and helped her boost it the rest of the way up the stairs. It was one of those complicated-looking Bugaboo models—expensive, like everything else around here. Including the mother. She was in her early thirties, a head-turning blonde with a diamond tennis bracelet blazing like an electrical fire around her right wrist. Did she notice that her breasts were practically popping out of her skintight lace cami above her swollen belly? he wondered, and decided, Yes. The package was very tantalizing in a kinky way—a way he liked.

He smiled as she appreciatively sized up his Givenchy suit, Prada shoes, and tanned, chiseled face. Of course she was impressed. He had looks, the kind of high sheen polish that came only from money, and unerring taste, and balls. The combination wasn't all that common.

"Thanks so much," she said, then rolled her eyes at her sleeping, angelic little boy. "Wouldn't you know it—we flew back from the Maldives yesterday, I have a lunch date at Jean Georges today that I simply *can't* break, and on the flight, our nanny quit. I should have left her there." She lowered her voice to a teasing, conspiratorial tone. "You wouldn't want to buy a one-year-old, would you?"

The Teacher gazed into her eyes for a long, leisurely moment, the kind of look that told her he was everything she imagined, and much, much more besides. Her lips parted a little as she stared back at him, rapt.

"I'd certainly rent him for an hour or two if the mom came with him," he said.

The full-bodied stunner arched herself like a cat, giving him a sly smile of her own.

"You're naughty *and* sexy, aren't you?" she said. "I go into the city two or three days a week, usually about this time—and I'm usually alone. Maybe we'll bump into each other again, naughty man." The bastion of elite modern motherhood winked, then sashayed away on her Chanel peep-toe pumps, giving him a show of her long, firm calves and rolling hips.

The Teacher stood there, puzzled. *Naughty?* He'd meant his remark to *insult* the whore, to shame her by letting her know how much her assault on human dignity disgusted him. Hadn't his sarcasm been clear? Obviously, it had gone right by her.

But he'd been plenty clear enough. The problem was that you couldn't possibly shame someone who had none.

There had been a time in the not-so-distant past when he would have used his formidable charm to get her "digits," as they said—a time when he'd have taken her to a hotel and let his sadistic lust, inflamed by her pregnancy, run rampant.

But that man was someone he had once been and no longer was—someone he'd left behind in the dust as he trod the path that had made him the Teacher.

Now he could vividly imagine beating her to death with the Bugaboo stroller.

The roar of the arriving New York City–bound train mounted in the Teacher's ears, and its weight subtly tilted the concrete platform beneath his feet.

"All aboard!" the conductor called from the ringing doors.

Next stop, the Teacher thought, as he joined the other passengers stepping onto the train: Revelation.

Chapter 6

ABOUT AN HOUR LATER, the Teacher stepped onto the 34th Street subway platform for the 2 and 3 trains. It was eight thirty-five a.m., the height of rush hour, and the strip of cement was jam-packed with all stripes of humanity from one grimy end to the other.

He walked to the platform edge's warning line, near the southern end of the downtown side. On his right was a homeless man who smelled like an open sewer, and on his left, a young female strap hanger, talking loudly on her cell phone.

The Teacher tried to ignore them both. He had tremendously important things to think about. But while he succeeded with the homeless man, it was impossible to shut out the brazen young hussy who was punishing everyone within earshot with the details of her boring, pointless life.

He watched her out of his peripheral vision. She was eighteen or nineteen, tall and thin, and, like her squawking voice, her appearance was all about calling attention to herself—dark tan set off by hair bleached an unnatural white, oversized shades, and a pink cutoff designer hoodie that revealed a diamond belly stud in front and one of those oh-so-original, above-the-butt, slut tattoos in the back.

Forced to hear her rant about her purebred dachshund's hernia operation through mouthfuls of her onion bagel, he actually found himself leaning more and more toward the reeking Dumpster diver.

The dime-sized lights of an approaching train appeared in the distance of the far tunnel. The Teacher relaxed—relief from this petty torment was on its way.

But the human Bratz doll stepped closer to the platform's edge, brushing past him as she moved. A blob of cream cheese fell from her breakfast and plopped onto the toe cap of his Prada shoe.

He stared in disbelief, first at his six-hundred-dollar footwear, then at her, as he waited for an apology. But so entrenched was she in the profane hollowness she called her life that she either hadn't noticed or didn't care that she had offended a fellow human being.

He felt a sudden lightness in his belly—a hatred and contempt that went far beyond mere anger.

But just as swiftly, it turned to pity. People like her were the very ones that he had come to educate.

Do it now! It's the perfect opportunity. Start the mission! came a barrage of voices in his head.

But the Plan, he protested. Don't I have to stick to the Plan?

Can't you take a fucking bonus when you see one, you anal prick? Improvise, overcome, remember? Now!

The Teacher closed his eyes, as a purpose that he could describe only as holy descended upon him.

Very well, he thought. So be it.

The girl weighed barely a hundred pounds. It took him only a slight hip-check to send her over the edge of the platform.

Too shocked even to scream, she clawed at empty air as she plunged the four feet onto the tracks and landed spread-eagled on her tattooed ass. With beautiful symmetry, her cell phone landed at the exact same instant and clattered along the rails toward the oncoming train.

Yes! the Teacher thought. It was a sign—a perfect beginning!

Now she was screaming. Her mouth was open wide enough to stuff in a tennis ball. For once in her life, instead of drivel, something genuine and human was coming out of it. Congratulations, he thought. I didn't think you had it in you.

But it wouldn't do to let his amusement show. "Oh, my God! She jumped!" he called out.

She was trying to drag herself off the track with her

hands, as if her legs wouldn't move. Maybe her spine had been injured in the fall. He could just hear her words before they were drowned out by the roar of the approaching train: "Help me! Somebody, please, God—"

Too bad you lost your cell phone, you could call for help on that! he felt like yelling at her. He knew he should leave, but her pitiful crawling and the freaked-out crowd were too delicious a sight.

Then out of nowhere, a neatly dressed, middle-aged Hispanic man shoved people aside and leaped down onto the tracks. He scooped up the girl in a fireman's carry, as naturally as if he'd been doing it all his life.

Which meant he just might be a cop.

At the same instant, someone in the crowd yelled, "She not jump—he push! Him, in suit!"

The Teacher's head jerked toward the voice. A gnarled, stooped old woman wearing a babushka was pointing at him.

People on the platform had dropped to the floor, reaching down to the hero and the girl. The train's horn blared and the sparking brakes shrieked as it tried to make the impossible stop in time. It wasn't more than twenty feet away when the helping hands from the crowd hauled the pair back to the safety of the platform.

"You! You push her!" the old lady cried, still pointing at the Teacher. You've got to be kidding, the Teacher thought, furious. Not only did the White Knight appear out of nowhere and save her, some old bag lady had seen him. His fingers itched to grab *her* and throw her under the still-moving train.

But with the danger past, other heads were turning toward him. He put on his best charming smile and tapped his temple with his forefinger.

"She's crazy," he said, edging backward. "Wacko." Instead of boarding the subway car, he turned and walked away casually. People still watched him, but no one was going to challenge a man who looked like him, on the word of a woman who looked like her.

But when he got to the stairs, he went up them fast and kept a watch for pursuers, just to be sure. Unbelievable, he thought, shaking his head. Whatever happened to good old-fashioned New York apathy? *What a pain in my ass!*

Still, there was always something to be learned from experiments. He knew now never to veer from the Plan, no matter how tempting.

He blinked as he stepped out into the different world above ground. The light-and-shadow-striped gully of Seventh Avenue was crammed with people—thousands, *tens* of thousands of them.

Good morning, class, he said silently, as he pointed himself toward the geyser of lights in Times Square.

Chapter 7

GETTING MY KIDS CLEANED UP, hydrated, medicated, and back into their beds took me over an hour. I wasn't able to tuck myself in until after four a.m. Outside my bedroom window, the sky was actually beginning to lighten above the East Side.

Hadn't pulling an all-nighter once been fun? was my last thought before I fell unconscious.

It seemed like just a finger snap later when my eyes shot open again. The sonata of coughing, sneezing, and wailing that had awakened me continued at full pitch through my open bedroom door. Who needed an alarm clock?

Being a single parent was tough in a lot of ways, but as I lay there staring up at the ceiling, I decided on the absolute worst one: there was nobody beside me to nudge with an elbow, and mumble, "Your turn."

Somehow I managed to get to my feet. Two more of the kids were down: Jane and Fiona in the bathroom, taking turns at the Bennett vomitorium. A dizzy, pleasant fantasy suddenly occurred to me—maybe I was just having a nightmare.

But it lasted only a couple of nanoseconds before I heard my six-year-old, Trent, moan from his bedroom. Then he uttered a chilling premonition, another thing that fell into the worst-possible category for parents.

"I think I'm going to be sick," his little voice quavered.

My bathrobe wafted out behind me like Batman's cape as I hightailed it to the kitchen. I ripped the garbage bag out of the pail, sprinted back to Trent's room with the empty barrel—and threw open his door just in time to watch him lose it from the top bunk.

Trent's guess had been right, and then some. I stood there helplessly, wondering which was worse. That the thick rope of his projectile vomit had demolished his pajamas, his sheets, and the carpet. Or that I'd been forced to witness another scene straight out of *The Exorcist*.

I gingerly picked him up under his arms and lifted him out of bed, shaking the excess vomit off him into the mess on the floor. Then I carried him, crying, toward my shower. At that point, I was seriously considering taking up crying myself. It wouldn't help, but if I wailed along with everybody else, maybe at least I wouldn't have felt so alone.

For the next half hour, while dispensing children's

Tylenol, ginger ale, and puke buckets, I wondered what the procedure was for getting a national disaster declared. I knew it usually applied to geographical areas, but my family's population was almost up there with Rhode Island's.

I'd been checking on our baby, Chrissy, every few minutes. She was still giving off more heat than the radiator. That was good, wasn't it? The body was fighting the virus or something? Or was it the other way around—the higher the fever got, the more you had to worry?

Where was Maeve, to tell me in her sweet but no-nonsense way exactly how much of an idiot I was?

Chrissy's hacking, crushed-glass cough sounded as loud as thunder to my ears, but when she tried to talk, her voice was just a weak whisper.

"I want my mommy," she cried.

So do I, honey, I thought, as I did the only thing I could think of, cradle her in my arms. *I want your mommy, too.*

Chapter 8

"DADDY?"

The speaker was my five-year-old, Shawna, watching me from the kitchen doorway. She'd been following me around all morning, a faithful lieutenant delivering front-line dispatches to a doomed general. "Daddy, we're out of orange juice." "Daddy, Eddie doesn't like peanut butter."

I raised my hand in a wait gesture as I squinted at the microscopic Sanskrit on a bottle of children's cough syrup. Which patient was this for? I tried to remember. Ah, yes, Chrissy. One teaspoon for somebody two to five years and under forty-seven pounds, I managed to decipher. I didn't have any clear idea of how much she weighed, but she was four and normal size, so I decided to go with it.

"Daddy?" Shawna inquired again, as the microwave

timer behind me started beeping like a nuclear reactor approaching meltdown. Between tending to the sick kids and getting the well ones ready for school, our household had now apparently entered DEFCON 3.

"Yes, baby?" I yelled above the din, now looking around for the medicine bottle's plastic measuring cup, which had gone AWOL.

"Eddie's wearing two different-colored socks," she said solemnly.

I almost dropped the cough syrup and collapsed in laughter. But she looked so concerned that I managed to keep a straight face.

"What two colors?" I said.

"Black and blue."

Finally, a no-brainer. "That's okay," I said. "Cool, in fact. He's a trendsetter."

I gave up on trying to find the measuring cup—it could be anywhere on the planet by now—and started looking for an alternative. My roving gaze landed on my oldest son, Brian, eating Cap'n Crunch at the kitchen table just three feet away.

"Hey!" he said as I snatched his spoon out of his hand.

"All's fair in love and especially war," I said, drying the spoon off on my bathrobe.

"War? Jeez, Dad, I'm just trying to eat breakfast."

"Slurping works pretty good with cereal," I said. "Try it."

I was tilting out the dose of cough syrup when I noticed that a pregnant silence had taken over the kitchen.

Uh-oh.

"Well, good morning, Mike," Mary Catherine said behind me. "What do you *think* you're doing with that spoon?"

I tried giving her my warmest smile while I groped for an answer.

"Uhh—a teaspoon's a teaspoon, right?" I said.

"Not with medicine, it's not." Mary Catherine set a shopping bag on the counter and took out a fresh new package of Vicks children's cough syrup. "This is what civilized humans use," she said, producing the bottle's plastic measuring cup and holding it up.

"Daddy?" It was Shawna again.

"Yes, Shawna?" I said, for the thousandth time that morning.

"You're totally busted!" She ran away down the hall, giggling.

Busted or not, I didn't think I'd ever been so glad to see anybody in my life as I was to see Mary Catherine just then.

"You take over the brain work," I said, and picked up a vomit pail. "I'll go back to swamping."

"Right," she said, pouring the dose of cough syrup carefully into the cup. Then, impishly, she offered it to me. "Care for a shot of this to brace you up?"

"You bet. Neat, with a beer back."

"Sorry, too early for beer. But I'll make some coffee."

"You're a miracle, Mary," I said.

As I squeezed past her in the tight kitchen aisle, it suddenly struck me that she was a very warm and lovely miracle. Maybe she read my mind, because I thought I saw her start to blush before she turned hastily away.

She'd brought a bunch of other supplies, too, including a packet of Flents ear-loop surgical masks. We armored ourselves with them and spent the rest of the hour treating the sick. And by *we*, I really mean her. While I stayed on relatively undemanding bucket-emptying and sheet-changing patrol, she took care of dispensing medicine and getting the survivors ready for school.

Within twenty minutes, the moans of the dying had stopped, and the living were in the front hall, lined up, scrubbed, combed, and even wearing correct socks. My private Florence Nightingale had done the impossible. The insanity was almost under control.

Almost. On the way out the door, Brian, my oldest boy, suddenly bent double, clutching his belly.

"Ohhhh, I don't feel so hot," he groaned.

Mary Catherine didn't hesitate a second. She pressed the back of her hand against his forehead to feel his temperature, then lightly swatted her fingers against the side of his ear.

"The 'didn't-study' flu is what you've got, as if I didn't

know about your math test," she said. "Get moving, you malingerer. I've well enough to do around this house than to deal with your messin'."

As they left, I did something I'd written off for this morning. I smiled with genuine good humor.

Cancel the National Guard, I thought. All this situation required was one petite young Irish lass.

Chapter 9

THE TEACHER WALKED into Bryant Park, behind the New York Public Library, at eleven a.m.—still ahead of schedule. He'd stopped by his headquarters, a rented apartment in Hell's Kitchen, and changed his appearance from head to toe. The Rolex was gone, replaced by a Casio sports watch. So was the Givenchy suit. Now he was wearing wraparound shades, a Jets cap, a traffic-cone-orange Mets spring training jersey, and baggy yellow basketball shorts.

No one could possibly have recognized him as the elegant businessman who'd pushed that worthless bitch in front of the train—which was precisely the point. To make the mission succeed, speed and surprise were key. He needed to strike like a cobra, get in and back out again before anyone even knew he'd been there. Melt into the crowds and use them as human shields. Exploit the multilevel, mazelike streetscape of Manhattan. Totally change his appearance — then strike again.

He found an empty folding chair in the park, removed his Palm Treo from his fanny pack, and brought up the other vital document it contained. To accompany his mission statement, the Plan was a fourteen-page blueprint for what he needed to accomplish. He scrolled to its last and most important page, a long bullet-pointed list. Almost in a trance, he read it over slowly, mentally rehearsing each and every possibility as he went along, visualizing how he would perform every act with calm, serious perfection.

He'd first learned about the power of visualization when he was a pitcher on the baseball team at Princeton. He wasn't especially gifted — just a basic power righty, with a fastball in the low nineties. But his coach had taught him to go over the lineup of the opposing team before every game, imagining each strikeout in detail.

That coach had taught him a couple of more down-to-earth techniques, too. One was a velvety smooth delivery that made him seem faster. Another was to throw inside, which led to his well-deserved reputation as a headhunter.

And that was what had gotten him kicked off the team in his junior year. He'd plunked some blond pansy from Dartmouth so hard that the baseball cracked his helmet and gave him a concussion. The Dartmouth team assumed that he'd done it on purpose, because the asshole had gone three for three against him. The field had erupted in a bench-clearing brawl.

They were right that the Teacher had thrown the beaner deliberately, but wrong about the reason. What had pissed him off was the other guy's hot girlfriend, sitting in the front row of the stands, who jumped up and cheered every time he was at bat. No way did that faggot deserve a girl like her. So the Teacher had decided to show her what a real man was all about.

He smiled at the memory. It had been his last game, but far and away the best of his life. He'd broken the Dartmouth third-base coach's nose and all but spiked the ear off their catcher. If you had to go out, that was the way to do it. Too bad he'd never seen the girl again. But she'd remember him for the rest of her life.

The Teacher shook away the reverie and tucked the Treo safely back into his fanny pack. He stood, spent a moment stretching, then lowered himself to a runner's on-your-mark stance, fingers digging into the gravel path.

He had his game face on now. It was time to get to work.

Bang! went an imaginary starting pistol in his head.

With his strong legs churning and gravel flying behind him, he bolted into a sprint.

Chapter 10

STEP ONE OF THE PLAN was to create a smoke screen. The Teacher was racing along the pavement between 41st and 40th when he spotted a perfect opportunity—a middle-aged businessman jaywalking across Sixth Avenue.

Strike like a cobra, he thought, instantly changing the course of his pounding footsteps.

He crashed into the suit like a linebacker, catching him in a headlock and dragging him to the curb.

"Hey! What the hell?" the guy gasped, struggling feebly.

"Cross on the green, not in between," the Teacher sang, and spilled him to the pavement. "Like a human being—not a worthless animal."

He spun away, and within seconds he was back at full

speed, arms pumping, alert for his next target. He spotted it in an Asian restaurant deliveryman who was rushing south down the opposite sidewalk, jostling other pedestrians as he wove in and out of the crowd.

The Teacher made another instant turn, dashing out in front of the oncoming traffic and across the street, accompanied by a symphony of blaring horns, screeching brakes, and shouted curses.

Take-out food bags flew into the air like startled pigeons as he clotheslined the deliveryman with a forearm across the throat.

"Where's the fire, buddy?" the Teacher roared. "This is a sidewalk, not a racetrack. Show some fucking *courtesy*, you got me?"

He took off again, his flying feet barely touching the pavement. He felt incredible, invincible. He could run straight up the fronts of the glass canyon office towers and down the backs of them. He could run *forever*.

"WE WILL, WE WILL, ROCK YOU!" he screamed into startled faces. He'd always hated that song, but damn if it didn't feel spot-on right now.

People stopped and stared. The street-smart ones, hot dog vendors and waiting radio car drivers and bike messengers, were wisely getting the hell out of his way.

It was hard to rouse attention on the jaded streets of Manhattan, but he was doing a bang-up job.

The light bouncing off the dark glass curtains of the

monstrous buildings poured down on him like a holy baptism. His face split into a huge grin, and his eyes filled with happy tears.

He was actually doing it. After all the planning, all the obstacles, it was showtime.

He jumped out into the curb lane of the wide avenue and sprinted full bore toward the trees of Central Park.

Chapter 11

TWENTY MINUTES LATER, the Teacher emerged from Central Park on the Upper East Side. Though he'd run more than thirty blocks, he hardly noticed it. He wasn't even winded. He raced out across tony Fifth Avenue and kept going east down 72nd.

Then he finally slowed to a halt, in front of a fabulously ornate four-story French château-style building on the southeast corner of 72nd and Madison — the flagship Ralph Lauren store.

The first target that really counted.

The Teacher glanced at his watch to make sure he was still on schedule, then took a long look up and down both the side street and the avenue. There were no cops in sight, which wasn't surprising. This store sat smack-dab in the middle of the city's most populated precinct. Roughly fifty officers, probably fewer counting sick days and vacation, were supposed to protect more than two hundred thousand people. Good luck, the Teacher thought. He pulled open the store's shining brass door and stepped inside.

He gazed around, taking in the Persian rugs, chandeliers, and oil paintings on the fifteen-foot mahogany-paneled walls. Not exactly your local Kmart. Among the antiques and flower arrangements, piles of cashmere cable knits and oxford-cloth button-downs were distributed with artful casualness. The overall impression was that you'd walked in and caught the Vanderbilts unpacking from a summer in Europe.

In other words, it was disgusting. He jogged up the wide mahogany stairs to the men's shop.

A slick-haired man in an impeccably tailored three-piece suit stood behind an antique glass display case filled with neckties. One of his eyebrows rose just enough to signify his contempt for the slovenly buffoon he saw approaching.

"May I help you?" he said with a condescension that bordered on vicious. The Teacher knew that if he answered "yes," the salesman would laugh out loud.

So he just smiled.

"Are we a trifle language-challenged, *sir*?" the malicious bastard crooned. Then he dropped the polished pretense and spoke in much coarser, and much more natural-sounding, Brooklynese. "We're all outta fanny packs today. Maybe you better go to Mo's instead."

The Teacher still didn't speak. Instead, he unzipped the little pack and took out a pair of objects that looked like Cheez Doodles. They were actually firing-range earplugs. Without hurrying, he pressed one of them into his left ear.

The haberdasher started to look flustered, and took on his piss-elegant tone again.

"I beg your pardon, sir, I didn't realize you needed hearing aids. Still, if you're not here to purchase something, I'm afraid I'll have to ask you to leave."

The Teacher paused, with the second earplug still between his fingers, and finally spoke.

"I'm really here to give you a lesson," he said.

"Give *me* a lesson?"

"In salesmanship," the Teacher said, mimicking the prick's supercilious tone. "You'll be *sew* much more successful if you learn to treat all your customers with respect. Watch how it should be done."

He pushed in the second earplug, then reached into the fanny pack again and drew out an oiled pistol.

"And here," he said, with his words muffled in his own ears, "we have the Colt M1911 semiautomatic in .45 caliber. Would you care to try it, sir? I *dew* believe you'll be impressed by its performance." He flicked off the safety and put the hammer on full cock.

The clerk's mouth opened in an O. His lips moved as he stammered words that the Teacher could barely hear. "Oh, my God...terribly s-sorry..." One soft, manicured hand flew to the cash register and punched open the drawer. "Please, take everything..."

But his other hand moved, too, dropping under the counter, no doubt to reach for a hidden alarm button.

The Teacher was expecting that. His finger twitched, and the first big .45-caliber round boomed like a stick of dynamite, blowing the display case into a cymbal crash of shattering glass. The clerk screamed, staggering backward, clutching at his mangled, bloody hand.

"I'm not here to take," the Teacher said quietly. "I'm here to give you something you've wanted your whole life, but were afraid to ask for.

"Redemption." He emptied the rest of the clip point-blank into the salesman's chest.

Watching him careen backward, limbs flopping spastically like he'd been hit by a giant sledgehammer, was the most electrically satisfying moment of the Teacher's life.

There were going to be more of those soon.

He reloaded the Colt with smooth, practiced motions as he hurried back down the steps. As he got to the door, he noticed another suave clerk, crouched beside a cashmere upholstered club chair. This man was shivering in shock, too terrified even to scream for help.

The Teacher paused long enough to press the Colt's barrel against his cheek. Then he spun the big gun off his finger, caught it in the air, and stuffed it back into his fanny pack.

"You are the witness to history," the Teacher said, patting the sniveling fop on the head. "I envy you."

He opened the door enough to scan the streets again, then stepped out of the store and blended in with the passersby on 72nd—once again, just another anonymous guy in the crowd. But he headed straight for the west-bound side of the street and hailed the first cab he saw. He instructed the turbaned driver to take him to the Port Authority Bus Terminal, then settled back in the seat and took out the Treo.

"Ralph Lauren Clerk" was the first item that came up on the screen. He deleted it from the list and checked his watch. The operation had taken just two minutes from start to finish, plus he'd caught a cab right off the bat—all even smoother than he could have hoped.

He wasn't just the Teacher. He was the *man*.

Chapter 12

AT NINE THAT MORNING, I called my office to take a personal day. It was another no-brainer. If half a dozen sick kids wasn't a personal crisis, what was? Then, after Mary Catherine and I made sure the troops were accounted for and tended to, I did something I hadn't done in over a week. I pulled on my FULL BLOODED IRISH T-shirt and a pair of sweats and went for a run.

As usual, I huffed it up to Grant's Tomb at 122nd and Riverside to pay my respects to the general. It would have taken magic to make me resemble the lean Manhattan College Jasper center fielder I'd once been, but I managed to keep a steady, strong pace the entire way.

I studiously avoided newspaper stands that would have thrown last night's debacle in my face, and not a single person started shooting at me. It was by far the nicest morning I'd had in recent memory.

When I got back home, I started at the top of my priority list—substituting a dollar bill for the tooth that Fiona had lost and left under her pillow. In the confusion last night, I'd forgotten all about it. The tooth fairy's job performance ratings, like a lot of other things around this place, had gone way downhill since we'd lost Maeve.

With that taken care of, I brewed a pot of coffee and went on to less important tasks, like paying bills online. I took my time, letting my thoughts wander as I poked along. It felt great playing a little hooky for a change. Maybe I should have felt guilty about all those DD5 incident reports I needed to file, but they could write themselves as far as I was concerned. I was home with my own crew, feeling the love, and especially ecstatic to be taking care of people who weren't trying to kill me for it.

For about the billionth time, I found myself thinking about how I'd been burning myself at both ends lately—burning myself out, really. That, in turn, led me to contemplate some of the job offers I'd gotten in the past few months, since a major hostage incident at St. Patrick's Cathedral had made me into a sort of celebrity cop.

The best prospect was a corporate security management position at ABC. The job consisted of coordinating security at the local news studios they had over on Columbus Avenue in the Sixties. The commute was easy, the hours were human, and it paid about twice my current salary.

But I still had five years to go until my twenty-year pension, and frankly I wasn't at all sure I wanted to hand in my shield just yet. The main problem was that I loved being a cop, especially a homicide detective. It was who I was.

Then again, I also loved my family, who needed me more now than ever. A job where I could count on being home every evening and weekend would be a godsend, and so would the extra money. What to do?

As usual, no clear, easy decision came to me. When I finished with the bills and some other busywork, I rounded up my sick kids and sat everybody down in front of the TV for a game of Harry Potter: Scene It?

Then my cell phone rang. I had a feeling it wasn't going to be good news. Still, I couldn't ignore it.

"Mike Bennett," I said.

"Hi, Mike. This is Marissa Wyatt. Would you hold for Commissioner Daly?"

I sat up, blinking. I knew that calling in for a personal, after the chaos of last night, might cause a few grumbles. But a call from the commissioner's office? What did he want with me? Had the Harlem fiasco turned that bad that fast?

"Mike?" Daly said.

I'd met Daly at a couple of upper-level meetings I'd been invited to. He seemed like a straight shooter, at least as straight a shooter as could be found in the puzzle palace that was One Police Plaza. I decided I might as well make my case right away.

"Hi, Commissioner," I said. "I can't tell you how sorry I am about the way things went last night—"

He cut me off brusquely. "We'll talk about that later. I need you on the bricks, right *now*. Strange things going down this fair morning. A couple of psycho assaults, including somebody pushing a young woman in front of a subway. Then an ugly shooting at the Polo store on Madison about fifteen minutes ago. Since today looks like a catastrophe in the making, and you happen to be the department's only former CRU section chief, I'm hand-picking you to coordinate our team."

Damn, I thought. Not fair. The commissioner must have been looking through my personnel file. In another life, back when I was single, I'd spent some time work-ing for the CRU, or Catastrophic Response Unit, a federal forward-response team that helped out and investigated disasters, especially ones that seemed to have a criminal element.

But to call me a section chief was ridiculous. Because of my Irish gift o' the gab, they just put me out in front to dis-tract everyone while the real heroes—my team of foren-sic anthropologists, environmental engineers, and clinical psychologists—made me look good.

"C'mon, Commissioner. That was a long time ago. I'll admit it. I lost my head and worked for the Feds for a few years. You can't use that against me," I said. *Besides doesn't the Nineteenth Precinct have detectives anymore?*

"Oh, yes, I can. You're my star, Mike, like it or not. And this one's a big red ball. Make me look good, okay? There's a payoff for you, too—you're on assignment, so you don't have to write reports about the Harlem thing, or deal with the media jackals. The office of information has just about lit on fire with requests to interview you."

The truth, I knew perfectly well, was that Daly didn't want anybody talking to the media about last night until all the facts were in. But he was using it to make me think he was doing me a favor. Add public relations savvy to his skill set, I thought.

"Get on your horse and go straight to Seventy-second, ASAP," he finished. "Chief of Detectives McGinnis will fill you in."

Get on my what? I thought, listening to the dial tone. No wonder he was commissioner. The man was a professional manipulator. Not only did he show no respect for my personal day, he hadn't even given me a chance to tell him about my sick kids.

I put the phone away, pissed off at Daly and at all the idiots out there who used guns to solve their problems, but mostly heartbroken because my rare quality time with my kids was ruined. At least Mary Catherine was here to take over, and they'd probably have more fun with her, anyway. I was the big loser.

I decided I'd better take a quick shower. I hadn't washed

off the sweat from my run, and I might not get another chance for a couple of days. Distracted by thoughts of the crime scene I was about to face, I stepped into the bathtub without looking—until my toes squished in the vomit-choked drain.

I'd failed at playing hooky from work, and I couldn't even get away with it here at home, I thought, reaching for the toilet paper.

Chapter 13

STRADDLING HIS FREJUS ten-speed, the Teacher clung with one hand to the rear fender of a number 5 city bus barreling along Fifth Avenue. Just as it got to 52nd, he let go and peeled off down the side street. Legs already pumping, he was just able to thread the bike between a town car and the huge wooden wheels of a Central Park buggy.

After being dropped at the Port Authority, he had jogged back to his apartment and changed into another, entirely different outfit—frayed Bianchi bike shorts, faded Motta top, and bike helmet—and picked up the ten-speed. Now he looked like any other low-rent, imitation Lance Armstrong bike messenger.

Stick and move, he thought, wrenching the ten-speed high into the air to bunny-hop a construction plate.

And this disguise had another beauty of its own. It was

bursting with irony and symbolism. Because he was delivering one mother of a message this morning.

To: World

From: The Teacher

Subject: Existence, the Universe, the Meaninglessness of Life

Like background music to his thoughts, a cacophony of car horns on full blast rose from the vehicles clogged motionless in the narrow trench of the street, as a delivery truck tried to parallel-park.

"Shaddup, ya dirty scumbags!" the truck's ape-faced driver was yelling out the window.

You have a nice day, too, the Teacher thought, lasering the bike through the mess.

The stink of garbage and piss assaulted his nostrils as he sailed past a waist-high line of black Hefty trash bags piled along the curb. Or was it coming from the hot dog cart beside them? Hard to tell. He spotted a parking sign with the pleasant greeting DON'T EVEN THINK OF PARKING HERE! Jesus—why not just cut to the chase and say, COMMIT SUICIDE?

He gaped in disbelief at the gutless herds of secretaries and businesspeople milling around on the corners, waiting like sheep for the stoplights that controlled their lives. How could they even pretend that this living hell they were zombie-shuffling through was acceptable? Legions of the walking dead, with a brainlessness that defied reason.

But wait. They weren't necessarily brainless, or even

stupid—that was a bit harsh. They were ignorant. Uninstructed.

And that was where he came in: to show them the way.

He brought the bike to a skidding, tire-squealing stop in front of a restaurant on the north side of the street.

This morning's second lesson was going to be even more impressive than the first one.

The line of jockey statues on the 21 Club's balcony looked down arrogantly as he slipped his OnGuard lock over his head and chained the Frejus to the wrought-iron railing. As he maneuvered through the throng of well-dressed businesspeople under the awning, a barrage of new scents wafted to him—this time, rich cigar smoke, succulent steak, and expensive perfume. Stepping inside the place was like entering another dimension, one of muted lighting and classy jazz, of fireplaces and draperies and wingback chairs.

For just a second, his will wavered. For the slightest of moments, he was tempted to keep on walking to the dark wood-paneled bar in the back—to order a cold, stiff, alcoholic drink, to lay down his burden at one of the plush red leather banquettes, to put aside the mighty cup of his destiny.

He steeled himself. The cup was heavy, yes—it would crush most men. Only an equally strong resolve, like his own, could bear it. That resolve would not fail.

"Excuse me! Whoa!" a voice said. The Teacher turned to see a tall maître d' zeroing in on him like a smart bomb.

"Jackets are required and restrooms are for customers only. If you're making a delivery, use the service entrance."

"This is the Twenty-one Club, right?" the Teacher said.

The maître d's lips curved in an icy smile. "Very good. What company do you work for? I'll be sure to use it next time I need a very clever delivery boy."

The Teacher ignored the sneer as if he didn't notice it. "Package for a Mr. Joe Miller," he said, opening the flap of his Chrome courier bag.

"I'm Joe Miller. You sure? I'm not expecting anything."

"Maybe somebody wants to surprise you." The Teacher winked as he lifted a large envelope from the pouch. "Maybe you impressed one of your lady customers more than you know."

Miller obviously found that an interesting thought. "All right, thanks. But next time, the service entrance, got it?"

The Teacher nodded solemnly. "Without a doubt." *You bet, buddy. As if there was going to be a next time.*

"Here you go," Miller said, thumbing a couple of dollar bills out of his wallet.

"Oh, no, I can't take tips," the Teacher said. "But I'm supposed to wait for a response." He winked again as he handed Miller the envelope. "You might not want to open this in front of all those people, if you know what I mean."

The maître d' glanced around. The crowd waiting to be seated was growing. But his curiosity won out. Impatiently, he stepped into a small anteroom beside the reservation desk. The Teacher followed him, waiting at the doorway.

James Patterson

He watched as Miller tore open the envelope and stared at the letter it held. The maître d's haughty face looked puzzled.

"'Your blood is my paint'?" he said. "'Your flesh is my clay'? What the hell is this crap?" He looked up at the Teacher, getting angry now. "Who sent this?"

The Teacher stepped into the room with him.

"Actually," he said, pulling a silenced .22-caliber Colt Woodsman pistol from his bag and placing the barrel against the sycophant's empty heart, "I did."

He waited the split second it took for comprehension to dawn in the other man's eyes. Then, before Miller could so much as blink, the Teacher pulled the trigger twice.

Even in the small room, the sound was inconsequential, like someone clearing his throat.

As the maître d' collapsed in a heap of dead flesh, the Teacher eased him into a chair, then quickly righted a sheaf of menus that had started spilling off a shelf. He tucked the bloody missive between the man's shoes. Anyone who glanced in would think that Miller had sat down for a moment to read.

Shielding the gun from sight, the Teacher turned to the open doorway and scanned the scene outside. He preferred stealth, but he was more than happy to shoot his way out if he had to.

But in both the crowded dining room and bar, people continued to laugh and drink, talk and eat, like the pointless animatronic jackasses they were. The carnival wheel

74

continued to spin. Nobody had noticed a thing. What else was new?

He slipped the warm gun into his bag, and a few steps later he was back outside, straddling his ten-speed. There was still nobody paying any attention to him. He shrugged. Might as well update the list. He took out his Treo, brought up the Plan on its glowing screen, and deleted "Self-satisfied Prick at 21."

"Hey, is that the 750?" a man's voice said. A sleek, dressed-to-the-nines Wall Street type, jawing a hundred-dollar Havana, pulled out his own smart phone from his pin-striped jacket. "Treos kick ass, boyeee," he said.

Boyeee? Even *Wall Street Journal*–reading, Ivy League bond traders were talking like crack dealers these days. It was bad enough that society had become a bunch of amoral, money-grubbing shitheads, but how had it turned into gangsta wannabes, too?

"Yeah, um, word to your moms, home slice," the Teacher said, and gave the asshole a thumbs-up as he rolled the Frejus out into the street.

Chapter 14

MY OFFICIAL NYPD VEHICLE was in the shop for repairs, so I was reduced to the family car. It was a sturdy, battle-tested Dodge van, bought used a few months ago, although the way my luck was running, the horn would go any second now, like on the VW in *Little Miss Sunshine*.

I was on my way to 72nd Street, steering with one hand and knotting my tie with the other, when Chief of Detectives McGinnis called my cell.

"Where the hell are you, Bennett?" His voice was forceful enough to burst a blood vessel.

"Moving as fast as I can, Chief," I said. "I'll be there within five. What's up?"

"The maître d' at the Twenty-one Club just got popped!"

I felt an all-too-familiar twisting in the pit of my stomach. The Polo store and now 21? Two murders, at two of the city's highest-profile places, within an hour of each other? This was starting to look as bad as last night, and maybe worse.

"You got any take on it?" I said.

"Maybe Donald Trump finally went postal. Maybe there's a roving shooter, maybe a couple of them and it's a coincidence. We've mobilized the Counter-Terror Unit, just in case that's involved. That's your specialty, right—terrorism? No, I'm sorry, catastrophes."

I shook my head. The cat was all the way out of the bag about my working for the CRU, wasn't it? Pretty soon the whole NYPD would learn my dirty little secret. Michael Bennett had once been a *Fed*.

"I wouldn't call it a specialty," I said.

"I don't care what you call it. You're the commissioner's handpicked expert. Now get your ass over here and figure it all out for me, huh?"

So *that* was why McGinnis's britches were in a knot, I thought. I wasn't his first choice to handle this, but he'd been overridden by Commissioner Daly.

"You think I volunteered for this, Chief?" I shot back. But he'd already hung up.

I stomped down on the Dodge's gas pedal, sending a tangle of errant soccer cleats and Happy Meal castoffs rattling around in the passenger-seat footwell.

Chapter 15

THE FRONT OF THE MADISON AVENUE Polo store looked like a police vehicle sales auction. There were cop motorcycles, Emergency Service Unit heavy rescue trucks, dozens of blue-and-whites.

I'd seen hot crime scenes before, but this was way over the top. Then I realized it must have been part of the NYPD Counter-Terror Unit's new surge tactic, which I'd heard about but hadn't yet seen. At the first hint of a threat, as many as two hundred cops would be sent in to blanket an area with an overwhelming shock-and-awe presence.

Maybe Daly was right, I thought for a moment. The lights and cops and chaos, the adrenaline rush stiffening my spine. What I was seeing was definitely reminding me of the disaster scenes I once worked.

It was impressive, all right. As I badged my way past the Emergency Service Unit guys on the sidewalk, I blinked warily at the cut-down M16s they were strapping on. Those had been issued after 9/11, but I still couldn't get used to them, and I probably never would. If we could just go back to the good old days when only the drug dealers had assault rifles, I thought.

The inside of Polo's flagship store looked satanically plush, especially to a guy who did most of his shopping at Old Navy and the Children's Place. A sandy-haired man at the top of the mahogany staircase came forward to meet me — Terry Lavery, a very competent Nineteenth Precinct detective. I was glad to see somebody who I knew I could get along with, and who was smart, to boot.

"What do you think of the army out there, Mikey?" he said. "I haven't seen this much NYPD blue since the DC convention."

I snapped my fingers, like a lightbulb in my head had just gone on.

"So that's why I want to get naked and slide down this banister," I said. "Hey, right off, I just want to let you know that it wasn't my idea to come tromping on your turf. I actually called in for a personal today. But the PC insisted. He wants me out of the way, so I can't be questioned about that debacle up in Harlem last night."

"Sure, sure," Lavery said, rolling his eyes. "Just tell the Commish I said hi, next time you meet him for lunch at Elaine's."

With the ritual chop-busting out of the way, Lavery flipped opened his notepad.

"Here's what we got so far," he said. "Victim's name is Kyle Devens. He was forty-six, gay, lived in Brooklyn, been working here eleven years. There was one witness to the actual incident, another clerk. He managed to whisper about a dozen words to us, then he went catatonic, so we don't have a description of the shooter yet.

"Near as we can put it all together, he walked in here before noon, pulled out a semiautomatic pistol, pumped a full clip into our boy, then walked back out."

"That's it?" I said. "No robbery, no struggle, nothing else?"

"If he was trying to hold the place up, he really botched it, because absolutely nothing's missing. If there's another reason, we don't know it."

"Did Devens have a boyfriend?" I said. Despite the anti-terror response, we had to treat this as a regular murder until we knew otherwise.

"The manager said he lived with a guy a couple of years ago, but it didn't work out, so he moved back in with his mother. We're still trying to contact her. But there didn't seem to be anything in the wind like a lovers' quarrel, and he got along with his coworkers. No priors or indications that he might have hung out with bad guys."

My lousy luck was holding. It was already clear that this wasn't going to be an easy case.

My gaze moved to the scattered cuff links in a crime

scene cop's camera FlashPack, sparkling like ornaments on the expensive rug—except that mixed in with them were several fat .45-caliber brass shell casings.

The Crime Scene Unit tech, an old friend named John Cleary, caught me eyeing them. "Don't get your hopes up, Mike," he said. "We already dusted them. No prints. And if that's not good enough news, no exit wounds, from a .45 at point-blank range. I'm not the ME, but my guess is that means hollow points."

More good news, all right. Not just a murderous psycho, but one who was locked and loaded with especially lethal ammo.

Kyle Devens's body was still lying on the fancy rug, too. He'd fallen in such a way that he was reflected in the ten-foot-high corner try-on mirror—a composition of blood, death, and broken glass, multiplied by three. I stared down at the gaping wounds in his chest.

"Yeah, when you're up against unarmed tie salesmen, everyone knows it's all about stopping power."

But almost more unsettling than the degree of violence was the shooter's meticulousness. Not only had he been quick and efficient, he'd used gloves when he loaded his gun.

I thought of the 21 Club killing and I started to get the vague, uneasy hunch that we were dealing with the same man.

There was nothing vague about my feeling that this was going to be one heck of a long day. That settled down on me like a soggy raincoat.

Chapter 16

A MINOR COMMOTION at the store's ground-floor entrance signaled the arrival of the medical examiner. I got out of his way and put in a call to Midtown South to find out if any more information had come to light about the other assaults that Commissioner Daly had mentioned.

The detective who'd caught the case was a newly promoted woman named Beth Peters, whom I'd never met before.

"The girl in the subway says somebody shoved her. She wasn't paying attention, so she didn't see who. But a dozen witnesses saw a man standing right beside her. One elderly lady swears he bumped her deliberately with his hip, and several others think he might have."

"Description of the guy?" I said.

"Not anything like you'd think. A businessman, very well groomed, wearing a quote unquote 'gorgeous' tailored gray suit. White male, around thirty. Black hair, six two, two hundred pounds. In other words, a metro-sexual sociopath. Very twenty-first-century, right?"

Detective Peters was crisp, clear, and sardonic. I decided I was going to get along fine with her.

"Just right, unfortunately," I said. "Anything on video, like which direction he headed?"

"We collected surveillance tapes from Macy's and a few other places around Herald Square. The witnesses are viewing them as we speak, but I'm not holding my breath. Thirty-fourth and Seventh at morning rush, it looks like outside Yankee Stadium after a play-off game."

A possible correspondence ticked in my brain— between a man who was beautifully dressed and groomed, and the ultra-high-fashion men's store where I was standing. Was there some kind of upper-class angle?

"At least we'll have your witnesses to ID this maniac once we catch him," I said. "Thanks, Beth. Let's keep each other posted."

When I finished the call, I granted myself a sixty-second time-out to take a leak. The manager's men's room, though small, was almost as luxurious as the rest of the store. And it didn't smell like puke. I gave it four stars.

I took the opportunity to phone back home.

"I'm really sorry," I told Mary Catherine when she answered. "You know I wanted to take today off to give you a hand, but there's this wacko—or maybe wackos—running around and…anyway, suffice it to say, I'm not going to be home for a while."

"I'm doing fine, Mike. Truth is, I'm glad to get you out from underneath me feet," she said.

I wasn't sure that was a compliment, but I was damn sure that the lass was a trouper.

"Thanks a million, Mary," I said. "I'll check in again when I get a chance."

"Wait, someone here wants to talk to you," she said.

"Daddy?" It was Chrissy, my youngest. Her 'sore froath,' as she called it, actually sounded a little better. Thank God for small mercies.

"Daddy, please tell Ricky to stop bothering me," she said. "It's my turn to watch TV."

Yet another bonus to being a widower, I thought. Oh, the joys of teleparenting.

"Put him on, Peep," I said.

That's when somebody else tried to walk into the small bathroom, and opened the door so hard it crashed into my back. I fumbled for my flying phone and managed to save it from the urinal by sheer luck.

"*Ocupado,* you moron," I yelled, kick-slamming the door closed behind me.

What a day, I thought. Then—day? What the hell was I saying? What a *lifetime.*

Chapter 17

THE NEXT PRIORITY ON MY LIST was to start comparing descriptions of the suspects in the different incidents. The problem was, I had only the one that Beth Peters had given me. That kind of information from the 21 Club hadn't gotten to me yet. I'd learned from Lavery that the street search and canvass of local doormen around the Polo store had produced nothing. And we were still waiting for a coherent statement from the men's shop clerk who'd watched his coworker get gunned down.

I decided it was time for some coaxing.

His name was Patrick Cardone. He was being cared for by EMTs in an ambulance that was still outside, double-parked on Madison Avenue. As I walked up to it, I saw him through the open rear door, sitting on a stretcher and crying.

I didn't like intruding on people who'd just experienced a tragedy, but it had to be done, and doing it was my job. I tried to handle it as gently as I knew how.

I waited until he was between sobbing spells, then tapped on the door of the ambulance, at the same time giving the paramedics the high sign that I was taking over.

"Hi, Patrick? My name's Mike," I said, flashing my badge as I climbed in and quietly closed the door behind me. "I can only imagine how awful you're feeling. You went through a terrible, traumatic experience, and the last thing I want to do is make it worse. But I need your help—me, and all the other people in this city. Do you feel up to talking for a minute?"

The clerk wiped his tearful face with his hands, too distraught to pay attention to the box of tissues beside him.

"Here," I said, setting the box on his knees. He gave me a grateful look.

"Tell me about Kyle," I said. "Was he a friend?"

"Oh, yes," Cardone said emphatically, dabbing at his eyes. "We used to ride in to work together on Saturday mornings, and when he picked me up at my place in Brooklyn Heights, he'd have a coffee for me. You know how many kind people like him there are in this city? I'll tell you—exactly zero. And that...that *bastard* in the Mets jersey just shot him. Just came in and shot him and—"

"Whoa, wait," I said. "The man who shot him was wearing *what*?"

"An orange Mets jersey. 'Wright,' it said across the back,

and these atrocious basketball shorts and a…a green Jets cap."

"This is very important," I said. "Are you absolutely sure?"

"One thing I know, it's clothes," Cardone said, with a trace of wounded dignity. "His were ridiculous. Like a comic advertisement for the Sports Authority."

So we had men wearing completely different outfits. Well, the incident in the subway and the Polo shooting had taken place hours apart. It was conceivable that it was the same guy, and he'd changed clothes. Or were there two psychos? A tag team? Maybe there was a terrorist angle after all. As Mary Catherine liked to say, *Shite*.

"What else did you notice?" I said. "His hair color, all that?"

"He had big sunglasses, and the cap was pulled low. His hair was darkish, and he was white, fairly tall. Everything else about him was a haze. Except his clothes, of course. And the gun he put to my head. It was square and silver."

White, darkish hair, fairly tall—that jibed with the subway suspect.

"Did he say anything?" I asked.

Patrick Cardone closed his eyes as he nodded.

"He said, 'You are the witness to history, I envy you.'"

That unsettling sensation came back again—that we were dealing with a maniac, and maybe a smart one.

I stood up to go, and patted Cardone's back.

"You did great, Patrick. I'm not kidding—the best

possible way to help your buddy Kyle. We're going to catch this guy, okay? I'm going to leave my card right here next to you. If you think of anything else, you call me, I don't care what time it is."

I thanked him again and hopped down into the street, already opening my cell phone.

"Chief, I just got a description of the Polo shooter," I said when McGinnis answered. "Same physical type as the subway guy, but he was wearing an orange Mets jersey."

"An orange *what*?" McGinnis fumed. "I just heard from the Twenty-one Club scene, and they're saying that the shooter was dressed like a bike messenger and actually left on a ten-speed. But otherwise, he looked like the subway guy, too."

"It gets worse, Chief," I said. "He spoke to one of the other clerks here, and told him that he was a quote 'witness to history' unquote."

"Christ on a cross! Okay, I'll put all that out over the wire. You triple-check the details there, then get down to the clambake at Twenty-one and see if you can make any sense of it."

Now we were getting into the realm of nightmare, I thought.

DETECTIVE
MICHAEL BENNETT

Part Two

PUKE BY THE GALLON

Chapter 18

IN THE SMALL, blessedly quiet foyer outside the Bennett apartment, Mary Catherine picked up the day's mail, and then paused for a moment. What a nice little space, she thought, lingering before the framed architectural drawings, the antique light fixture, the tarnished copper umbrella stand. The next-door neighbors, the Underhills, had arranged a cornucopia of golden leaves, baby pumpkins, and squash on the mail table.

But the pleasant tour ended all too soon, as she came back to the Bennett apartment. She took a deep breath, bracing herself, and opened the door.

Sound slammed into her like a collapsed wall as she stepped inside. In the living room, Trent and Ricky were still loudly squabbling over PlayStation rights. Not to be outdone, Chrissy and Fiona had become locked in a DVD death match at their bedroom computer. The old, over-worked washing machine accompanied the yells, thundering from the kitchen as if a full rehearsal of the musical *Stomp* was under way.

Mary Catherine jumped back as a small, yowling, vomit-colored object streaked between her feet. She stared at it, refusing to believe her eyes. But it was true.

Somebody had just thrown up on Socky, the cat.

Amid all the clamor, she could hardly hear the phone ringing. Her first thought was to let the machine pick it up. The last thing she needed was another hassle. But then she decided, The heck with it. Things couldn't get worse. She stepped over to the wall phone and lifted it off the hook.

"Bennett residence," she half screamed.

The caller was a woman who spoke in a clipped, no-nonsense tone. "This is Sister Sheilah from Holy Name."

Oh, Lord, Mary Catherine thought—the kids' principal. This was not going to be good news. Well, it served her right for taunting fate.

The din seemed, if anything, to be getting even louder. She glanced around, trying to think of a quick way to quiet it. Then inspiration hit.

"Yes, Sister. This is Mary Catherine, the children's au pair. Could you hold on one second?"

She calmly set down the phone, got the stepladder out of the pantry, and climbed up to the electrical box on the wall beside the door. As she unscrewed each of the four fuses, the noise abruptly stopped — the TV, the computer game, the washing machine, and finally, the voices.

Mary Catherine picked up the phone again and said, "Sorry, Sister. I've a bit of a mutiny on my hands here. What can I do for you?"

She closed her eyes as the principal curtly informed her that Shawna and Brian, half of the Bennett faction that Mary Catherine had managed to get out the door this morning, had "become ill." They were in the school nurse's office and had to be picked up immediately.

Perfect, she thought. Mike was involved in something too serious to break away from, and she couldn't leave the little ones here alone.

She assured Sister Sheilah that she'd have someone pick up the latest casualties as soon as humanly possible, and she called Mike's grandfather, Seamus. This time, fate relented. He was available to go get them right away.

Mary Catherine had just finished talking to him when Ricky, Trent, Fiona, and Chrissy wandered into the kitchen with a chorus of complaints.

"The TV stopped!"

"So'd my computer!"

"Yeah, like — *everything*."

"Must be a power blackout," Mary Catherine said, shrugging. "Nothing to be done about it." She rummaged in the utility drawer and took out a deck of cards. "Have you guys ever played blackjack?"

Ten minutes later, the kitchen island had become a card table with Trent as the dealer and the others squinting at their hands. The noise level was reduced to the little guys counting out loud and grappling with the rules. Mary Catherine smiled. She wasn't one to encourage gambling, but she was pleased to see them having fun without batteries. She decided to make sure the entertainment devices were turned off, then screw the fuses back in so she could finish the laundry and make soup. They'd be too absorbed to notice.

But first, there was an important matter to take care of. Socky was still complaining piteously and trying to rub its vomit-stained coat against her ankles. She gingerly lifted the cat by the back of the neck.

"You'll thank me in the long run," she said, and carried it, clawing the air in furious protest, to the kitchen sink.

Chapter 19

"YOU MUST BE A COP, because you certainly don't look like a customer," a young woman called to me as I was exiting the Polo store.

Well, if it isn't Cathy Calvin, intrepid *Times* police reporter and all around pain in the ass, I thought.

She wasn't somebody I wanted to talk to right now. On top of all the problems I was facing, I was still very annoyed at how distinctly unhelpful she'd been at the St. Pat's Cathedral siege.

But I put a smile on my face and walked over to the barricade where she was standing. The enemies we cannot kill, we must caress, and deception is the art of war, I remembered. Thank God for the classical education I'd received from the Jesuits at Regis High. You needed to brush up on your Machiavelli *and* Sun Tzu to survive an encounter with this lady.

"Why is it every time we meet, it's over police saw-horses and crime scene tape?" she said with a big bright grin of her own.

"Good fences make good neighbors, I guess, Cathy," I said. "I'd love to chat, but I'm really busy."

"Aw, come on, Mike. How about a quick statement, at least?" She said as she turned on her digital recorder. She was giving me some pretty intense eye contact. For the first time, I noticed that hers were green—striking, and actually kind of playful. She smelled good, too. What was it she'd just said? Oh yeah, she wanted a statement.

I kept it as by-the-book vague and as short as possible. A store clerk had been shot, I told her, and we were with-holding his name pending notification of his family.

"Wow, you're a font of information just like always, Detective Bennett. What about the shooting at Twenty-one? Is it related?"

"We can't speculate at this time."

"What's that mean, really? Chief McGinnis isn't letting you in on that one?"

"Off the record?" I asked.

"Of course," Cathy said, clicking off her recorder as I leaned in.

"No comment," I whispered.

Her emerald eyes didn't look so frolicsome anymore as she clicked the recorder back on.

"Let's talk about last night, up in Harlem," she said, totally switching tracks. "Witnesses say police snipers shot an unarmed man. You were right next to the victim. What did you see?"

I was used to aggressive reporting before, but I was starting to wonder where I'd left my pepper spray.

"Cathy, I'd just love to relive that experience, especially with you," I said. "But as you can see, I'm in the middle of an investigation, so if you'll excuse me."

"Why don't you tell me about it over lunch? You have to eat, right? My treat. And no tape recorder."

I snapped my fingers in fake disappointment. "Wouldn't you know it? I already have a reservation at Twenty-one."

"Very funny," she said with a wry look. Then she shrugged. "Oh, well. A girl has to try. I probably shouldn't tell you this—it'll go to your head—but I could think of worse lunch dates. If you ever put an ad in the personals, I'll give you a couple of tips on what to say. Tall, nice build, thick brown hair, definitely cute."

I was startled that she thought that about me. Maybe she was just flattering me to get more information, but she seemed like she meant it.

"I don't have any plans to," I said. "But thanks."

"And that crack I made about you not looking like a Polo customer was below the belt. You're actually a very sharp dresser."

My hand rose automatically to smooth my tie. Christ, was she really hitting on me? Or was I a total fool to even imagine it? Cathy was damned nice-looking herself, and in the kind of outfit she was wearing right now—short, tight black skirt, tighter blouse, and patent leather pumps—she was flat-out hot. As long as you could ignore her being a bitch on Rollerblades.

But was she even such a bitch? I started wondering. Or just a hard-driving professional trying to do her job, with a brassy style of flirting, and I was a hopelessly grumpy old bastard who'd been taking it all wrong?

I backed away, as confused as a schoolboy. She was watching me with her hands on her hips and her head cocked a little to one side, like she'd challenged me to a duel and was waiting for my response.

"Don't let it go to your head, Cathy," I said, "but I could think of worse lunch dates, too."

Chapter 20

I SPENT THE REST OF THAT AFTERNOON at the 21 Club, mostly interviewing witnesses who had been there when the maître d', Joe Miller, was shot. When I finished, I sank into a red leather banquette in the back bar and yawned. There'd been a lot of them.

No one here had seen the actual killing, but there didn't seem any doubt that the shooter was a bike messenger, who had come in and left again quickly at just that time. Miller had been found with the bloody message tucked between his shoes. There was also a general consensus that the messenger was a fairly tall, white male, probably around thirty years old.

From there, it was a good news/bad news scenario. Every single person I'd talked to, from the high-powered executive customers to the busboys, confirmed that he'd been wearing a light, uniform-style shirt—not an orange Mets jersey. But he'd also had on a helmet and sunglasses. Like at the Polo store, nobody had gotten a clear look at his face, or even his hair color. Which left us still without any details for matching the suspects in the various assaults.

Along with that little problem, there was another troubling mystery. The bullets that had killed the maître d' were .22 caliber, very different from the .45s that were used on Kyle Devens. Then again, they were also clean of fingerprints.

There were still a ton of possibilities. But in spite of the contradictions, my increasingly queasy gut pushed me more and more toward thinking that the two shootings, at least, were related. The suspects' ages and general physical descriptions were similar. Both crimes had occurred at high-end establishments.

But most important was the text of the typed message found with the maître d's body. I lifted up the evidence bag and read it again.

Your blood is my paint. Your flesh is my clay.

It had a creepy similarity to what the Polo clerk shooter had said to Patrick Cardone.

You are the witness to history. I envy you.

My hunch was that we were talking about a guy who'd gotten an A in Crackpot Composition 101, and wanted people to know it—wanted them to buy into his delusions of grandeur. But the only way he could get that kind of attention was through vicious, cold-blooded murder.

Unfortunately, if I was right, he *was* smart, and also careful. Different outfits, different guns, face hard to see, no fingerprints.

Then there was the question of whether he was the same wacko who'd pushed the girl in front of the 3 train, down at Penn Station. No weapon, no coy message, and he'd let himself be seen. But again, the overall physical description fit.

Well, at least there hadn't been any more Manhattan killings in the last few hours. Maybe we'd get lucky and find out that our nutburger shot himself. But probably not. This guy seemed too organized to be a suicide. And besides, my birthday wasn't until next month.

I closed my notebook and scanned the football helmets, musical instruments, and kitschy knickknacks hanging from 21's famous bar ceiling. The bartender had told me that the toys, as they called them, had been donated over the last hundred years by movie stars and gangsters and presidents.

The thought that Bogie might have tied one on with Hemingway at the very table where I was sitting made me consider having a quick burger before I left. I lifted the menu. I had to read the prices twice before realizing I wasn't hallucinating.

Thirty bucks?

"Here's lookin' at you, kid," I mumbled as I stood.

On my way out, I studied the wall of photographs behind the reservation book. In each one, the deceased maître d', "Nice Guy" Joe Miller, was smiling with an A-list celebrity. Ronald Reagan, Johnny Carson, Tom Cruise, Shaq, Derek Jeter. "Any good maître d' can get you to sit where he wants you to sit," the manager had told me. "Joe had that rare ability to actually convince you that his choice was better than yours."

Miller hadn't missed a day's work since he'd started as a busboy thirty-three years ago. Thirty-three years, and tonight, his two girls at Columbia and his widow got to ask themselves, What the hell do we do now?

Outside, 52nd Street had become dark. Worn out though I was, I couldn't believe the miserable day had flown by so fast. Time can also fly when you're *not* having fun, apparently.

I couldn't believe, either, that the 21 Club intended to stay open for business tonight. A line of well-heeled, beautiful people filled the sidewalk, impatiently waiting to get in. Maybe the murder was an extra attraction.

The manager waved at me anxiously from the doorway, awaiting my signal that he could remove the crime scene tape. His slain employee's moment of silence had lasted a New York minute. So much for any dignity about being dead, I thought. A fat cop in a Tyvek suit hauled your carcass out of the way, and, with depressingly little trouble, the world moved on.

I watched the manager balling the yellow tape in his hands as he hurried back under the awning. Maybe they'd string it up above the bar with the other toys, was my merry parting thought—the NYPD's contribution to lifestyles of the rich and famous.

I started walking, trying to remember where I'd parked my van.

Chapter 21

EVER SINCE COMMISSIONER Daly's phone call earlier today, the fact that he'd handpicked me for this assignment had been in the back of my mind. As I drove home, it surfaced for the thousandth time. I was as nervous as hell about this case—I admitted it. In all likelihood, we would catch this guy, especially if he kept on going.

But that was precisely the problem. How many more people might he kill before we did catch him?

It was a tough spot for me to be in. So far, I had very little to work with. But I couldn't let the commissioner, or the city, down.

When I opened my apartment door, I was greeted by the strong waft of Lysol. With it came the memory of all the problems that awaited me in this world, too.

"Daddy, Daddy, look!" Fiona cried out. Her pigtails

whipped around as she ran toward me, waving the dollar bill I'd left under her pillow. Her hug-tackle almost knocked me down. "The Tooth Fairy didn't forget! She came after all!"

I'd read somewhere that eight-year-old girls couldn't care less about toys or other childish things any more—just makeup, clothes, and electronics. But I was blessed with one who still believed in magic. I returned her hug, with all my anxiousness shedding off me like old skin. At least I was doing something right.

As Fiona tugged me into the living room, I spotted a mop and plastic pail, and I started thinking about how Mary Catherine must have spent *her* day. Who was I to complain? As bad as mine had been, hers had to have been worse.

A moment later, she came hurrying in for the mop. I grabbed it at the same instant she did, and with my other hand I pointed to the stairs to the third floor, Mary Catherine's apartment.

"Out you go, Mary," I said. "Whatever needs doing here, I'm all over it. You go have fun with somebody who's old enough to vote. That's an order."

"Mike, you just got in, you need to relax a bit," she said. "I can stay for a few more minutes."

She pulled at the mop, but I held on to it. In the tug of war that followed, the water-filled pail went over with a splash, flooding across the hardwood.

I don't know which of us started giggling first, but after a second, we were both full out belly laughing.

"The floor needed a mop anyway," I finally said. "Now for the last time, I'm giving you a police order to remove yourself from these premises. I have handcuffs, and I'll use them on you."

Mary Catherine stopped laughing abruptly. She let go of the mop and turned away hastily, like she'd done when we'd brushed against each other in the kitchen. This time, there was no doubt that she was blushing.

"I didn't mean...*that*," I said warily. "I..."

"It's been a long day, Mike. There'll be another tomorrow, so let's both get some rest." With her face still averted, she started to leave, pausing to tap a sheaf of paper on the coffee table. "This'll be useful to you. Good night."

I was setting a personal-best record for the number of times I'd put my foot in my mouth with women in one day, I thought. I decided to blame it on exhaustion. Or maybe I was coming down with the flu, too.

I looked at the papers she'd left me—a detailed computer printout, a medical chart of my quarantined family. Who needed which medicine, how much of it, and when. I shook my head in disbelief. This woman could do the impossible.

I should have asked her where the psycho killer was.

Chapter 22

THE TEACHER SCRUBBED his wet hair with a towel as he came out of the bathroom in his apartment. He stopped when he heard a strange sound outside the bedroom window. He hooked a finger to the drawn shade and peeked out.

Down on West 38th, a buggy driver was walking a beaten-down looking gray horse into the tenement-turned-stable next door. His other neighbors included a greasy taxi garage and a check-cashing place with a steel grille over the windows and a perpetual litter of broken glass on the sidewalk out front.

He chuckled to himself. The corner of 38th and Eleventh Avenue was exceedingly crappy and run-down, even for Hell's Kitchen. Maybe he was crazy, but he loved it anyway. At least it was authentic.

Still amped to the gills from the day's adrenaline rush, he lay down on the weight bench beside his bed. The bar held two hundred-and-eighty pounders. He lifted it easily off its brackets, lowered it to touch his chest, and raised it back up until his elbows locked at full extension. He did this ten times with an exquisite slowness that burned through his throbbing muscles and brought tears to his eyes.

Much better, he thought, sitting up. *What a day. What a freaking day.*

He wetted a rag, put it on his forehead, and lay back on the bench. He had downtime now—time for everybody to catch up, like putting on the ol' boob tube while waiting for mom and pop to get home from work.

The workout had helped to burn off some of his wired energy, and the cool damp cloth was soothing. He let his eyes shut. A little nap before dinner would be sweet. He'd wake up fresh and ready for the next phase.

But just as he was drifting off, a burst of loud laughter and the heavy, thumping bass of rap music made him sit up again. Angrily, he strode across the room and twitched the window shade aside. In the brightly lit, curtainless window of a loft across the street, a little Asian guy was taking pictures of two tall, anorexic white girls in long gowns. The girls started dancing like jackasses to the brainless noise of 50 Cent, bragging that he was a P-I-M-P.

What the hell? Last time he'd noticed, that building was a warehouse where some legless fat guy named Manny stored hot dog carts. Now it was some kind of fashion studio bullshit? There went the goddamn neighborhood.

In Iraq One, he'd been in a marine recon unit that had been given an experimental bazooka-like weapon called a SMAW. The SMAW had been outfitted with a new explosive thermobaric round. Leaking a fine mist of gas in the air microseconds before ignition, a thermobaric was capable not only of vaporizing masonry structures, but it actually ignited the oxygen within its blast zone.

He'd have given anything he had for one of those right now. His trigger finger actually tingled as he remembered the feeling of touching off one of those megarounds. His imagination kicked in, substituting the building across the street for the ones he'd destroyed back then, throwing a fireball and shock wave that would have torn off the top several floors.

He had plenty of other weapons on hand, though — half a dozen pistols, a Mac-9, a sawed-off tactical shotgun, a Colt AR-15 with an M203 grenade launcher, a selection of silencers. Behind them, appropriate cardboard ammunition boxes were stacked and arrayed in orderly little rows. A half-dozen each of fragmentation, smoke, and flash-bang grenades sat in a Crate and Barrel carton beneath his worktable like an oversized container of lethal eggs.

But no. Trying to kill every annoying fool would be like

pissing into a live volcano. He had to stick to the Plan and kill the ones who counted.

He stalked into the room he'd outfitted as an office, sat in a Pottery Barn retro office chair, and clicked on a green-shaded banker's desk lamp. Every inch of the wall above the desk was covered. There were subway and street maps, photos of building lobbies and subway stations, and a framed poster of Tom Cruise from *Top Gun* in the center. More portraits of Marcus Aurelius, Henry David Thoreau, and Travis Bickle from *Taxi Driver* were taped over the credits. The desk itself was covered with worn marble notebooks, a laptop, and a police scanner connected to a tape recorder. Alongside it was a heavy worktable that looked like one of those bust pictures cops took after a raid.

His telephone and answering machine sat on top of it. Lately, he'd hardly been bothering to check his messages. But when he glanced at the machine, he blinked in astonishment. Thirty-six messages? That couldn't be right.

Then he remembered where he was supposed to have been earlier that morning. Ah, yes, it made sense now. That appointment had seemed so infinitely important when he'd first made it. But since he'd had his Epiphany, he couldn't have cared less about it.

That thought improved his mood. Smiling, he deleted the messages without listening to them and stepped back into his bedroom. He popped a relaxation CD into the player beside the weight bench and hit Play.

Run for Your Life

The sound of waves washing gently against the shore and the soft caw of seagulls drowned out the rap from across the street. He stretched out on the bench again, jerked up the crushing weight, and lowered it toward his chest.

Chapter 23

THE TEACHER AWOKE, completely starved, a little after ten p.m. He went into the kitchen, turned on the oven, and took a brown paper–wrapped package out of the fridge.

Twenty minutes later, baby lamb chops were sizzling in a port-rosemary demi-glace. He touched the hot meat with a fingertip to test it and smiled at the just-so give. Almost there, he thought. He drained the pommes frites and drizzled them with truffle oil.

After plating, he brought the steaming dish to the linen-covered table in the apartment's small dining room. He opened the $450 bottle of '95 Château Mouton Rothschild with a pop, chucked the cork over his shoulder, and poured himself a healthy glass.

The lamb practically melted in his mouth as he slowly chewed the first bite, then chased it with a sip of the exquisite Bordeaux. Tight tannins, floral nose, tastes of cassis and licorice in the finish. It probably could have used another six months to mellow to absolute perfection, but he couldn't wait another six months.

He closed his eyes as he ate, savoring the truffle oil and Parmesan fries, the succulent meat, the kick-ass Cab. He'd eaten at pretty much every fine restaurant in New York and Paris, and this was as good a meal as he'd ever had. Or was it because of all the work he'd accomplished today? Did it matter? This was gastronomic nirvana. He'd truly nailed it.

He stretched the meal out as long as he could, but at last, regrettably, it was done. He drained the wine bottle into his balloon glass and took that into the darkened living room. There, he dropped onto the couch, found the remote, and flipped on the sixty-inch Sony plasma on the wall.

The crystal-clear image of a CNN anchor, Roz Abrams, appeared with her mouth going at full speed. There was a flu going around the city, she informed her audience. *No shit. As if he cared.*

He put up with a couple more minutes of inanities and commercials before she came back to the day's main story.

There was also a killer on the loose.

Really, Rozzy baby? You don't fucking say. How's that for some real *news?*

He leaned forward as she spoke and listened intently

to the coverage. There was still confusion about the two shootings. The police weren't sure if they were related, either to each other or to a bizarre incident where a young woman had been pushed in front of a subway. They didn't know if they were looking for a single suspect or more than one. They were fearful that terrorists might be to blame.

The Teacher sat back and relaxed, smiling. The police and the media were still scratching their heads—exactly how he wanted it.

There was no mention of the mission statement that he'd sent to the *Times*. He wondered if that was a cop trick—withholding information from the public for some reason—or if there was some other explanation. Maybe the newspapers simply hadn't made the connection yet. No matter. They would, soon enough.

When the report about the killings was over, and Roz Abrams went back to more banal bullshit that would interest only the herds of human cattle out on the streets, the Teacher turned off the TV set and stood. Carrying the glass with the last of the Bordeaux, he stepped into the apartment's spare room and clicked on the wall switch, bathing the room in bright incandescent light.

There was a human shape on the guest bed, like someone sleeping. Except it was entirely covered by a sheet.

The Teacher gently lifted the sheet off the shape's face.

"It's starting, buddy," he said.

A dead man stared back, his features masked by caked

blood. A small bullet hole was visible in his right temple, and a much larger exit wound in his left.

"To getting their attention," the Teacher said, winking and raising the glass of ruby wine over the body. "And to tomorrow, when we turn it up to eleven."

Chapter 24

AT SIX THIRTY IN THE MORNING, the pews of Holy Name Church on the Upper West Side were silent and empty. With its still-dark stained-glass windows, it might have been the most solemn spot in all of Manhattan.

Which was precisely the problem, Father Seamus Bennett thought, as he sat hidden underneath the altar.

This was not some new form of devotional activity. Far from it—he was on a stakeout. For the past two weeks, a thief had been stealing from the poor boxes at the front of the church, and Seamus was determined to catch the culprit red-handed.

He parted the altar cloth and peered out, frowning, through his binoculars. In another couple of hours, the church would be filled with glorious light, pouring through the multicolored windows. But right now, it was so dim he could barely see the front doors. He'd been watching for almost an hour, with no sign of activity.

But this individual was clever. He, or she, always left some money in the boxes, probably thinking that the pilferage wouldn't be noticed. Seamus knew damned well that it was going on — the usual daily take had dropped by more than half. Still, that suggested that the thief was also stealthy, and probably could sneak in and out of the dim building without Seamus even knowing it. He didn't want to turn on the church's electric lights, which ordinarily weren't used in the mornings. Any change in routine like that might red-flag the stakeout.

He lowered his — what was the cop lingo for binoculars again? oh, yeah, "eyes" — and poured himself some coffee from the thermos he'd brought. There had to be a better way to handle this. He was going to bring a fan next time. It was stifling inside the tiny, covered space. And a cushion, maybe even a beach chair. His legs and butt were past numb from sitting cross-legged on the cold marble floor. A partner would help, too — someone to take turns with him. Maybe one of the deacons.

This was all the fault of his uncooperative grandson, Seamus thought grumpily. Mike had refused to arrange for an NYPD crime scene analysis, and an FBI profile. In fact, he'd seemed quite amused at the thought, adding insult to injury. Was that so much to ask for the glory of God?

"You'd think having a cop in the family might come in handy," Seamus mumbled through a sip of the steaming coffee.

The ring of his cell phone startled him, and he banged his head on the underside of the altar as he groped for it in his pocket.

The caller was none other than Mike. How do you like that? Seamus thought. Speak of the...

"I need you, monsignor," Mike said. "Here. Now. Please and thank you."

"Oh, I see," Seamus began. "When I needed a bit of help from you, it was 'Sorry, Father.' But now that you need *me*—"

But Mike had already hung up.

Seamus closed his phone with a sharp snap. "You think you can get away with it by being polite," he griped. "But the old priest sees through to your insidious heart." He crawled out from underneath the altar, rubbing his aching lower back.

Then a voice said, "Monsignor, is that you?"

Seamus swiveled toward the figure, standing by the votives in front of the sacristy. It was Burt, the church's caretaker, staring at him in wonder.

"Don't be silly, Burt," Seamus growled. "Isn't it obvious that I'm Father Bennett's evil twin?"

Chapter 25

YOU KNOW YOU'RE IN for a rough day when, the instant you wake up, you're already overwhelmed. I stumbled out of bed and rushed deliriously through my apartment to take the body count. Moans and groans came from every corner. No doubt about it—my family had gone from bad to worse. Thinking of the place as a hospital ward no longer applied. Now it was a MASH unit under mortar fire.

Pretty soon, I had chicken soup on the stove and a Jell-O chilling in the fridge. Meantime, I ran from child to child with cold cloths in one hand, a digital ear thermometer in the other, and a five-year-old on my back—taking temperatures, hydrating the hot and sweaty victims, and trying to warm those with the shivers. Somewhere in the bunch, there might have been one or two of them who were well enough to go to school, but I was too busy to care. The healthy were on their own this morning.

Especially after only a few hours of restless half sleep, I didn't know how much more of this I could take. So, reluctantly, I'd called Seamus. I hated to bother him so early, but twenty minutes of dealing with my family's epidemic had stripped me of all my manners. Besides, didn't every battlefield need a priest?

"Dad?" Jane said, lifting a notebook from her night table as I came into her room. "Let me bounce this off you. 'The plague continued. It was looking hopeless. What had Michael, the head of the Bennett family, done to bring such misfortune upon his innocent children?'"

I shook my aching head. At eleven, Jane was the budding writer in the family, and she'd decided to use her downtime to do an in-depth biography of the Bennetts. It sounded like her style was influenced equally by gothic romances and precocious guilt-tripping.

"That's lovely, Jane," I said, closing my eyes as Trent, across the hall, sneezed and then wiped his hands on poor Socky. "But why don't you add something like, 'Then their father had an inspired idea for a last-ditch radical cure — blistering spankings for one and all!'"

Jane frowned. "Sorry, Dad, nobody'd believe it." She wetted her forefinger and flicked through pages. "I still have some background stuff I've been meaning to ask you. First off, about Grandpa Seamus. I thought priests couldn't get married. Was there some sort of juicy scandal?"

"No!" I half yelled. "There were no juicy scandals. Grandpa Seamus just came to the priesthood later in life, after he lost Grandma Eileen. *After* he had his family. Get it?"

"Are you sure that's allowed?" she said suspiciously.

"I'm sure," I said, and retreated before she could think up something else. *Jaysus,* as the old micks would say. Just what I needed—another female reporter trying to nail me.

Chapter 26

I FOUND MARY CATHERINE in the kitchen, turning off the soup just as it started to boil over. I froze as I noticed something on the island behind her.

People wonder why New Yorkers stay put, with the outrageous crime and tax rates. Well, one of the most compelling reasons was sitting on my kitchen island. *Real bagels*. Mary Catherine had gone out and picked up a dozen of them, the steam on the inside of the plastic bag the telltale sign that they were still warm. Beside them was a cardboard tray with two large coffees.

I squinted warily. I'd given up on the idea of breakfast five minutes after waking up. Desperate as I'd become, this all very well could have been a mirage.

"Reinforcements?" I said.

"And supplies." She handed me a coffee and gave me

a brave smile. But as I bit into a butter-drenched poppy seed, I noticed the bags under Mary's eyes. She was looking as peaked as I felt.

Why was she still here? I thought for the thousandth time since she'd arrived. I knew that several of my much wealthier neighbors, seeing the impossibly professional job she did with my mob of kids, had offered her almost blank checks to steal her away. Nannies were big business in Manhattan. Perks like expense accounts, cars, and summers in Europe weren't unheard of. And most of those millionaire children were onlies. I wouldn't have blamed Mary one bit for taking the money and running. Considering the pittance I was paying her, she'd certainly put in her charity time with our eleven sorry butts.

Did she feel some sort of obligation? I knew she'd come here at the behest of Maeve's family to help out while she was dying. But Maeve was gone now. Mary Catherine was what? Twenty-six, twenty-seven? She had the rest of her life to pick up crushing responsibilities all her own.

I was trying to phrase my concern to her when the walking wounded flooded into the kitchen, and surrounded her with a big cheer of affection. As sick as my kids were, they weren't stupid—they appreciated somebody who actually knew what she was doing. When Shawna climbed down off my back and attached herself to Mary's leg like a tick, I wasn't offended in the slightest.

Then, as she laughed and joked with them, I noticed something perplexing. Weary though Mary Catherine looked, there was new color in her cheeks and a new determination in her blue eyes. I stood there speechless, a little stunned. She actually seemed to be right where she wanted to be.

I felt overwhelmed all over again, but suddenly in a good way. *How could anybody be so wonderful?* I thought.

My brief moment of elation ended when my grandfather, Seamus, burst in through the front door.

"I just heard from the church caretaker," he cried into the crowded kitchen. "The thief hit the poor box again! Is nothing sacred?"

"Absolutely nothing," I told him with a mock frown. "Now hurry up and snarf a bagel, then grab a mop and swab the deck in the kids' bathroom, Monsignor."

Chapter 27

WITH THE ARRIVAL OF THE CAVALRY, I was actually able to shower *and* shave. I grabbed another bagel on my way out, egg this time, and almost knocked down my neighbor, Camille Underhill, waiting for the elevator in the foyer we shared.

Our large, actually quite luxurious apartment had been a bequest to my deceased wife, Maeve, who had been the nurse of the previous millionaire owner. Ms. Underhill, a senior editor for *W* magazine, had tried hard to block our occupancy. So I guess it wasn't that surprising that I'd yet to be invited to one of her "Page Six" cocktail parties.

Although her snobbery hadn't stopped her from knocking on my door at three in the morning a couple of years ago because she thought she saw a prowler on her fire escape. Go figure.

"Morning, Camille," I grunted around my breakfast. The elegant lady ignored me as if she hadn't heard me, and just hit the elevator call button again.

I almost said, *No prowlers lately, huh?* But I had enough troubles without starting an in-house skirmish.

I picked up the *Times* from my doormat, a ploy to avoid sharing a ride down with her. It worked beautifully. When the elevator arrived, she was gone like a shot.

The front page of the Metro section was wrinkled, and someone had circled the lead article, entitled "Manhattan Spree Killing." Scrawled in the margin with a black pen was a note from my ever-helpful grandfather, Seamus: *FYI—I'd be concerned about this if I were you.*

Thanks, Monsignor, I thought, and scanned the article while I waited for the elevator to return.

When I was about halfway down the page, my bagel dropped from my open mouth. The reporter stated that "a source close to the case" had confirmed that the push attempt and two shootings were directly related, and that the killer was using more than one gun and disguises to "elude capture."

I didn't even have to look at the byline to know that my favorite journalist, Cathy Calvin, had struck again with her poison pen.

Christ! Bad enough she wanted to incite panic, but why did she have to keep dragging me in? "A source close to the case"—she might as well have printed my name in giant red letters. Besides, while it was true that I'd been thinking along those lines, I hadn't told her anything of the kind.

So who *had* told her that? Did we have a leak in the department? Was there somebody out there who could read minds?

The elevator arrived and I stepped in, waving the newspaper to waft away the lingering cloud of my neighbor's Chanel No. 5. How do you like that? I thought. Completely hamstrung before I was even out the door.

Wednesday was looking like a real winner, too.

Chapter 28

THE RATTLING ELEVATED number 1 train woke me up more than my second cup of coffee did as I retrieved my Chevy out in front of the Manhattan North Homicide office at 133rd and Broadway. The department mechanics had managed to get it running okay, but inexplicably had left the passenger headrest still torn up from a shotgun assault several months ago.

I decided to appreciate the fact that it started.

As I was pulling out, my cell phone went off. My mood lightened slightly when I saw that it was the commissioner's office. They had already e-mailed a request for my presence at a nine thirty a.m. meeting at headquarters. It looked like he wanted a personal briefing on the spree killer beforehand. I started to feel useful again.

I expected a secretary asking me to hold, but it was the commissioner himself. Nice.

"Bennett, is that you?"

"Yes, sir," I said. "What can I do for you?"

"Do for me?" he yelled. "For starters, how about you close your big mouth and keep it shut—especially around the *Times. I* don't even talk to the press without permission from the mayor's office. One more move like that and you'll find yourself on foot patrol in the ass end of Staten Island. Do you understand me?"

Gee, Commish, don't sugarcoat it, I thought bitterly. Tell me how you really feel.

I wanted to defend myself, but as fired up as Daly sounded, it probably just would have made things worse.

"Won't happen again, sir," I muttered.

I maneuvered the Chevy down to the street and started crawling through the morning traffic toward downtown.

Ten minutes later, as I was passing 82nd and Fifth, the phone rang again.

"Mr. Bennett?" This time it was a woman's voice I didn't recognize. Probably more press trying to get the latest on the case. Well, who could blame them? With the way Cathy Calvin had portrayed me on this morning's front page, I looked like the media's new best friend and law enforcement consultant.

"What do you want?" I barked.

There was a brief, icy silence before she said, "This is Sister Sheilah, the principal of Holy Name School."

Oh, boy.

"Sister, I'm really sorry about that," I said. "I thought you were—"

"Never mind, Mr. Bennett." Her quiet voice somehow conveyed even more distaste for me than the commissioner had.

"Yesterday, you sent in two children who turned out to be ill," she went on. "Might I refresh your memory that on page eleven of the 'Parent/Student Handbook,' it states, and I quote, 'Children who are ill should be kept home,' unquote. We here at Holy Name are doing our best to stem the effects of the citywide flu epidemic, and the flouting of our preventative measures cannot and will not be tolerated."

Again, I reached for my excuse bag. I had a good one. My kids had looked fine when we sent them in. But the negative mojo coming from the Mother Superior stopped my words like a cinder-block wall. I felt like I was back in fifth grade myself.

"Yes, Sister. It won't happen again," I mumbled.

I hadn't made it three blocks farther south in the gridlock when my cell phone rang yet again. This time, it was Chief of Detectives McGinnis.

Why do I even have one of these things? I thought, putting the phone to my ear and bracing myself for a tirade. I wasn't disappointed.

"Listen, Bennett. I just heard from Daly," McGinnis

roared. "Are you trying to get me fired? How about instead of canoodling with *Times* reporters, you do us both a favor and do what you're getting paid for? Namely, figuring out where this serial shooter is! Your la-di-da attitude toward this case is pissing me off big-time. As is the way you're handling this catastrophe, Mr. Expert. Now I'm starting to understand why people got so upset about Hurricane Katrina."

That was it—I'd had enough. Two capitulations was my morning's limit. I was also fed up with having the truly self-sacrificing professionals I used to work with at the CRU be insulted. Had McGinnis ever been a first responder at a plane crash? Had he ever had to work in a portable morgue and deal with human misery on a mass scale day in and day out? I cut sharply in front of a Liberty Lines bus and shrieked to a stop in the middle of Fifth Avenue. The rush-hour traffic behind me must have snarled clear back into Harlem, but I didn't care.

"Hey, that gives me an idea, boss," I yelled. "From here on out, I'm legally changing my name to Mike 'La-di-da' Bennett. If you don't like that and you want my resignation, you're welcome to it. Or maybe you should just go ahead and bring me up on departmental charges. Canoodling in the first degree."

I endured another icy pause before McGinnis said, "Don't tempt me, Bennett," and hung up.

I sat there for a second, my face red, my head pounding. His giving me an earful was one thing, but to imply that I'd jeopardize a case over a reporter was a really low blow. *They* asked *me* to come in on this, right? What an idiot I'd been—so proud to be handpicked, and worried sick about letting down the team. Now my team was kicking me in the teeth.

I guess William Tell's son had been handpicked, too. Right before they'd put an apple on his head.

"Yeah, yeah, yeah," I yelled to the wailing horns all around me. No wonder people in this town went nuts. I added my own horn to the chorus as I peeled out.

Chapter 29

IN A CONFERENCE ROOM on the twelfth floor of One Police Plaza, I met Detective Beth Peters face-to-face for the first time, by the coffee cups. Fortyish, petite, and fine-boned, she looked more like a news anchor than a cop. She was pleasant but sharp, with a quick smile. Again, I got the sense that we were going to get along.

But there was no time for small talk. This was an emergency task force on the shootings, put together by Chief of Detectives McGinnis. After my morning's conversation with him, I was almost surprised that I was actually allowed to take part.

There were about twenty of us crammed into the room, mostly NYPD, but I spotted a few FBI agents and civilians. Beth and I found seats at the back end of the conference table as Paul Hanbury, a young black forensic psychologist and Columbia professor, spoke first.

"I think from this person's attention to detail, we can rule out the possibility that he's a paranoid schizophrenic. If he were hearing voices, he probably would have been caught by now. However, he does seem to be somewhat delusional. And with his changing clothes and using two different weapons, I don't think I'd completely rule out that a multiple personality is involved. At this point, I can only guess at a motive, but he fits the model of a reclusive type who doesn't get along with others—maybe someone who suffered an early childhood trauma and is seeking revenge through a homicidal fantasy."

Next to give us his take was Tom Lamb, a thin, harried-looking FBI profiler from 26 Federal Plaza.

"Our shooter is almost definitely a male, probably in his thirties. I don't know if I go along with the theory that he's reclusive. He certainly has no qualms about getting up close and personal with his victims. The fact that he's using two different caliber weapons leads me to believe he's either ex-military or a gun nut. I'd lean toward the latter, so maybe we should take a look at the usual Guns and Ammo suspects."

"Do you think there could be more than one killer?" Beth Peters asked him. "Maybe a team of shooters, like the Malvo thing down in DC?"

The federal agent gripped his sharp chin in concentration. "That's an interesting idea. Let's face it. This guy isn't exactly acting in a way that fits previous homicide models. But like Paul said, all we can do so far is guess."

Then I stood up. Heads turned toward me.

"In that case, why don't we slow down a little and consider the possibility that the shooter has a personal connection to the victims?" I said. "This guy is a cool customer. Not just angry, emotionally disturbed, out of control, like a lot of them."

Paul Hanbury spoke up again. "Mass murderers often plan their crimes for years, Detective," he said. "It's what comforts them when they're stonewalled or hurt. The old 'Some day I'll come back and then I'll get the respect I deserve.' That buildup of frustration can have surprising results."

"Point taken," I said looking straight at Chief McGinnis. "Still, I'm not completely convinced yet that he's a garden-variety serial. Shouldn't he have contacted the press by now?"

"So you're saying maybe he's just *acting* like he's nuts?" Beth said to me.

"If he's just acting," Detective Lavery joined in from across the table, "I'd like to be the first to nominate him for an Academy Award."

"What I'm saying is, if this guy's got a program, maybe that gives us something to go on," I said. "Otherwise, what's our alternative? Just blanket Manhattan with cops, and cross our fingers that one's around when he goes off again?"

Then McGinnis himself stood up, glaring back at me.

"That's exactly what we're going to do, Bennett. It's called being proactive. Please explain your plan, Agent Lamb."

I sat back down as the FBI agent recommended that beefed-up patrols, and especially the Counter-Terror Unit, should be stationed at certain affluent areas—Rockefeller Center, the Harvard Club, the New York Athletic Club, Lincoln Center, Carnegie Hall, and Tiffany's.

Tiffany's, I thought. Like they needed more security! And what about MoMA and half the restaurants in the Zagat guide? This was New York. There weren't enough cops on the force to play goalie at every high-end institution.

"And let me remind everyone that this is confidential information," McGinnis finished. His hard stare returned to my face and stayed there.

I rolled my eyes, thinking again about defending myself, but decided the hell with it. Instead, I got another cup of coffee, took a hot, sour sip, and stared out the conference room window at headquarters' breathtaking view of the Brooklyn Bridge.

Maybe the killer would do me a personal favor and go terrorize one of the other boroughs today.

Chapter 30

BEHIND HIS DIESEL SUNGLASSES, the Teacher squinted into the bright sunlight that hit him as he cornered the sidewalk off Eighth Avenue and onto 42nd Street.

He was into his next chameleon act, now wearing a Piero Tucci lambskin jacket over a distressed graffiti T, Morphine jeans, and Lucchese stingray-skin boots—an outfit that looked casual, but people with eyes for that sort of thing would know it cost more than a lot of monthly paychecks. He hadn't shaved, and his fashionable stubble gave him the look of a rock or film star.

He felt like bursting into laughter as he marched toward Times Square with the mass of clueless rat-racers. The fact that he was doing all this in broad daylight was so crazy, so bold. It was like being high on the greatest drug he could possibly imagine.

Finally—being able to unload a lifetime of pent-up venom! Ever since he was little, people had tried to sell him the big lie. How great everything was, the holy privilege of being alive. Worst of all was his god-awful, annoying mother. The world is a gift from God, life is precious, count your blessings, she'd always say. He'd loved her, of course, but Christ, sometimes he'd thought her gums would never stop flapping.

She'd been gone three years now, along with her witless philosophy degree from the University of Hallmark. Near the end, at her deathbed, he'd had to restrain himself from pushing aside the IV cords that entangled her like vines in a plastic rain forest, and asking her, *If life was such a precious gift, then why the hell was* He *such a frigging Indian giver?*

He hadn't, of course. Despite her faults, she was his mother. She'd sacrificed for him. The least he could do was to let her die as deluded as she'd lived.

But now he no longer had to play charades. Let's face it, he thought—in this insanely decadent modern mess called society, being negative and antisocial was downright proper. He wanted no part of the pointless mistake that humanity had become.

Take today, for example. Wednesday—matinee day for the Broadway musicals. All around him, idiots by the busload were milling mindlessly. In from their flyspeck towns and suburbs, clamoring to pay a hundred bucks a pop to watch even bigger idiots in Halloween costumes sing trite, sappy love songs. This was art? The best that life had to offer?

And it wasn't just the hicks and suburbi-schmucks, by any stretch. Right around the corner on 40th, he'd passed the supposedly *très* hip, in-the-know *New York Times* reporters and photographers flocking into the paper's new office building for another slave shift at the Ministry of Truth. Toe that Democratic party line, comrades, he felt like yelling at them. All hail, Big Brother, and even bigger liberal government.

He slowed his pace as he came to Madame Tussauds wax museum. Crowds of tourists were swarming around a life-sized Spider-Man doll in front of the building. He shook his head in disgust. He was passing through the land of the dead.

"Fifty bucks? For a Rolex?" he heard a southern voice cry out in the crowd. "Goddamn right you got yourself a deal!"

Ten feet ahead, a skinny young man with a shaved head was about to hand over his money to the West African sitting behind a folding table of fake watches.

The Teacher smiled. So many in his old unit had been from the South—good men from small towns who still believed in simple things like patriotism and manners and doing what a man had to do.

The Teacher didn't intend to stop, but when he spotted the USMC bulldog tat on the kid's forearm, he couldn't help himself.

"Whoa there, buddy," he said to the kid. "You really think you're going to get a Rolex for fifty bucks?"

The young Marine gawked at him, half-suspicious and half-glad to be getting advice from someone who obviously knew this turf.

The Teacher slipped off his own Rolex Explorer and handed it to the kid, exchanging it for the bogus imitation.

"Feel how heavy that is?" he said. "That's real. This one"—he flicked the fake into the con man's chest—"is bullshit." The heavyset African guy started to rise up angrily, but the Teacher stared him back down into his seat.

A sheepish grin split the young southerner's face. "Lord, what an idiot I am," he said. "Just two weeks back from a year in Iraq, you'd think I'd have learned something there."

He handed back the Teacher's Rolex. But instead of taking it, the Teacher just stared at it. He remembered buying it for himself when he was twenty-eight.

Screw it, he finally thought. *You can't take it with you.*

"It's yours," the Teacher said. "Don't worry, no strings attached."

"Huh?" the young man stammered. "Well, thanks, mister, but I couldn't—"

"Listen, jarhead, I was here when they knocked down the Towers. If everyone in this city wasn't such a piece of crap, they'd celebrate you and every other soldier who lays his ass on the line in the Middle East, like the American heroes you are. Giving this dirty old town some payback is the least I can do for you."

Look at him, he thought. Mr. Generous all of a sudden, acting like a Boy Scout.

He was tempted to upend the table of watches into the glowering con man's lap, but now was the wrong time. Maybe he'd come back this way again, he thought as he strode on.

Chapter 31

TWENTY MINUTES LATER, holding a freshly bought, hundred-seventy-five dollar bouquet of pink and yellow roses, the Teacher entered the vast lobby of the Platinum Star Hotel on Sixth Avenue.

He almost stopped to genuflect toward the quarry loads of glowing white marble that covered the floors and the thirty-foot walls. The ceiling was graced by a Renaissance-inspired painted canvas, along with sparkling crystal chandeliers the size of tugboats. He shook his head in awe at the crown moldings that looked like they were made of gold.

Once in a while, the assholes got things right.

He hurried to the check-in desk, looking flustered, and placed the flower arrangement on the marble counter right in front of the cute brunette clerk. He could see that she was impressed.

"Please tell me I'm not too late," he begged her with clasped hands. "They're for Martine Broussard. She hasn't checked out yet, has she?"

The young woman smiled at his nervous suitor act, and tapped at the keyboard in front of her.

"You're in luck," she said. "Ms. Broussard is still here."

The Teacher put on a look of ecstatic relief. "Thank God." Then he asked her earnestly, "Do you think she'll like them? Too over the top? I don't want to come off as desperate."

"She'll like them, believe me," the clerk said. "They're gorgeous."

The Teacher bit at his thumbnail anxiously.

"We only met two days ago, and I know it's crazy, but this morning I woke up certain that if I let her leave without telling her how I truly feel, I'd never forgive myself. But I want to surprise her. Where would be the best place to wait so I don't miss her?"

The clerk's smile widened. She was in on this with him now, happy to be part of true love in the making.

"The couches over by the elevator," she said, pointing at them. "Good luck."

The Teacher took a seat, with the bouquet in his lap. His hand edged inside his jacket to the small of his back, where both of his pistols were holstered inside his belt. He chose the .22 Colt and eased it around to his front.

Less than five minutes later, a musical ding signaled an arriving elevator, and one of the gleaming brass doors opened. The Teacher stood as five stewardesses stepped out, all with Air France logos on their knotted blue silk scarves. They could have been models. Or maybe actresses from the kind of movies the hotel made you pay extra for.

The sight of them made him feel like his stomach was filled with helium. He was dizzy at the thought of what he was about to pull.

Martine Broussard was in the lead. Six feet tall, aggressively beautiful, with long hair trailing behind her like blond satin as she stalked, preening, out onto the marble as if it were a Victoria's Secret runway.

The Teacher stood and rushed to meet her, thrusting the flowers forward.

"Martine! Here, I got these for your birthday!"

The statuesque blonde stopped, eyeing the bouquet in confusion.

"My birthday?" she said, pronouncing it "birzday." "What are you talking about? That is not for three months more." Her gaze shifted to the Teacher's face. "Do I know you, monsieur?" But a flirtatious look came into her eyes. Same as the desk clerk, she liked what she saw.

The Teacher held his breath while his hand snaked the .22, barrel-first, into the bouquet. Everything was suddenly quieter, slower, incredibly peaceful. Had he ever felt this untroubled? This free? He felt like a fetus floating weightlessly in its mother's womb.

Flower petals exploded into the air as he squeezed the pistol's trigger. The bullet hit her just below her left eye.

She dropped to the marble floor without even a twitch, blood pouring down her face.

"Did I just say your *birthday*?" the Teacher growled. "I'm sorry. I meant your *funeral*." He fired twice more into her exquisite bosom.

The other flight attendants stampeded away, screaming. He tossed the flowers onto Martine's corpse, reholstered the .22, and backed toward the lobby door.

Chapter 32

THE HOTEL DOORMAN, at his post outside, actually held the door open as the Teacher strode through it. Obviously, he hadn't heard the muffled shots, but now he paused and stared in at the panicked, screaming Frenchwomen.

"Call the cops quick!" the Teacher yelled at him. "Some nutcase in there has a gun."

The doorman took off running into the building. The Teacher walked fast but smoothly, covering ground but not attracting attention. As he passed the fountain outside the hotel, he took the Treo from the pocket of his jeans and brought up his list.

"Air France Stewardess" disappeared with a peppy little press of his thumb.

Then, out of nowhere, he heard the shriek of brakes

behind him. Car doors thunked open, along with the unmistakable static burst of police radio chatter.

Don't even turn around, he told himself. Keep moving. Blend with the crowd. No way could the cops have a description of him yet.

"That's him!" somebody screamed.

The Teacher tossed a quick glance over his shoulder. Across the plaza, the hotel doorman was pointing directly at him. The two uniformed NYPD cops climbing out of their radio car drew their guns.

Damn! He'd figured the doorman, like all the others, would be too stunned to move that fast. Okay, no biggie. Escape Plan Two coming right up—the Rockefeller Center subway entrance at the southern end of the block. He broke into a sprint.

Suddenly, from everywhere at once, dozens of police vehicles were converging, cutting off both ends of the street. Off to his right, a heavy Emergency Service Unit truck slammed, fishtailing, up onto the sidewalk. A SWAT cop jumped out and dropped to one knee, throwing his M16 to his shoulder.

Son of a bitch! It was like they were appearing out of thin air. Then he suddenly realized it was because of 9/11. He'd never thought about how much that had changed cop response.

He forced his pumping legs to their maximum speed and did the only thing he could—dove headfirst right into the pit of the subway stairs.

Luck was with him. Instead of landing on the descending concrete stairs, he collided with an elderly couple who were coming up. His momentum flattened them to a backward sprawl; and he used them like a human toboggan to ride to the bottom. He got up running, grinding his boots into their wailing, pathetically thrashing bodies as he took off. He rounded a corner, hopped a turnstile, and sprinted across a platform.

The Rockefeller Center station, one of the largest in the entire subway system, was a virtual catacomb of passageways and exits. It had four tracks, two island platforms, and more than fourteen exits to the street. As a special bonus, there were also entryways into the Rockefeller Center concourse, an underground maze lined with shops that stretched for blocks in every direction.

As he ran, the Teacher yanked his T-shirt out of his jeans to cover his pistols, then ripped off his Tucci jacket and tossed it by one of the exits. There was no worry about leaving a trail—someone would grab it and be gone within seconds. He hit another flight of stairs and lunged down them four at a time, racing toward the metallic screech of an approaching V train.

He got to the second car just as the doors bonged open. Yes! he thought, jumping on.

But a sudden thunder of footfalls down the stairwell he'd just exited made his head swivel.

"Stop that train!" he heard a cop yelling. More voices joined in. "Yo! Yo! Driver, stop! Stop!"

Bing bong. The subway's driver, sitting in his compartment at the front of the train, closed the doors as if absolutely nothing was out of the ordinary. You had to love this goddam city. Everybody was insane. The train pulled forward, humming.

The Teacher wiped sweat from his eyes and looked at the passengers in the half-full car. Every single one of them had their heads buried in a newspaper or a paperback. Never get involved. Damn right. He turned to stare at the tunnel lights that flashed outside the windows as the subway whizzed past, constellations of blue shooting stars.

Unbelievable—he was free again. Unstoppable! The hand of Destiny itself really was guiding him. There was simply no other explanation.

Just as he'd decided that, the door at the rear end of the car rattled opened. Two transit cops stood there, breathing heavily. One was a heavyset, older white man, the other a black female so young she had to be a rookie. Both had their hands on the butts of their Glocks, but the weapons were still undrawn.

"Freeze!" the old flatfoot yelled, but he still didn't draw. What the hell was he waiting for? An engraved invite?

It took the Teacher less than a second to draw both of his own guns simultaneously from the small of his back, the .22 in his right hand and the .45 in his left.

Now the passengers paid attention to him. Wide-eyed, some shrieking, they flattened themselves down onto the seats or dove to the floor.

"Listen to me," the Teacher yelled across the car. "I like cops, I swear. I've got no beef with you, and I don't want to hurt you. Let me go. That's all I want."

The train was coming into the 51st and Lex station. Maybe the driver finally realized that something was up, because it made a sudden lurch. Thrown off balance, the two uniforms reacted by finally going for their Glocks.

"I said *no*, damn it!" the Teacher roared. Left-handed, with the .45, he shot the male officer in the knee, then the groin, and then the head. At the same time, with his right hand, he emptied the last four rounds of the .22 into the space just above the female cop's Sam Browne belt. Had to get around those pesky Kevlar vests.

His eardrums felt like they were bleeding from the thunder of the unsilenced .45, like a pack of cherry bombs had gone off inside his head. But a blizzard of endorphins whirled through his skull as well. What a rush! Like nothing in the world.

The train came to a shuddering halt, its doors opening automatically. A businessman waiting on the platform started to step into the car, but stopped dead at what he saw, then scurried away.

The Teacher was about to do the same, when a gunshot exploded behind him, and a stinging sound whipped past his left ear. He spun back around and stared in disbelief.

It was the lady cop. She was down on the floor of the train with Swiss cheese for a tummy, yet still trying to line him up in her shaking gun sights. What courage under fire!

"That's magnificent," he said to her sincerely. "You should get a medal. I'm really sorry I have to do this."

He raised the .45 and aimed it at her terrified face.

"I really am," he said, and pulled the trigger.

Chapter 33

I COULDN'T BELIEVE IT! What the hell was going on in this world? As we were wrapping up the task force meeting, we got word that there'd been not one, but *two* more shootings in midtown. Preliminary reports said that a civilian and two transit cops had been shot, around Rockefeller Center, by the same assailant.

Our assailant. There wasn't much doubt about it by now.

Even with my siren cranked, it took me most of forty minutes to get through the gridlock from headquarters to the frantic crime scene at 51st and Lexington.

Right off the top, it was impossible not to notice the NYPD chopper hovering above the Citicorp building. The throb of its rotors seemed to keep time with my heart as I waded through the crowd that was seething around a completely blocked-off 51st Street.

A sergeant let me under the yellow tape beside the 51st Street subway stairs. His serious-as-cancer face told me something I didn't want to know. The echoing metallic squawk of police radios and sirens seemed to be coming from everywhere at once as I descended into the hot, narrow stairwell.

A train was stopped in the tunnel. There were maybe two dozen cops standing on the platform alongside one of the front cars. Inside it, I saw spent shell casings on the bloodstained floor. I could tell at a glance that several rounds had been fired.

The crowd of cops parted as a team of paramedics wheeled a stretcher out of the train car. Hats were quickly taken off. A hulking Emergency Service cop next to me blessed himself. When the stretcher neared, I followed his example, shaking my head hard to fight the sudden numbness in my chest.

The victim was the female rookie transit cop. All I knew about her was that her name was Tonya Griffith, and that she was dead. I couldn't even see her face because of all the blood.

I asked another transit cop about Tonya's partner, and found out that he was en route to Bellevue.

"Likely?" the big ESU guy inquired. As in, likely to die?

The transit cop didn't answer. That meant, *affirmative*.

"Son of a bitch," the ESU cop said, clenching his fists violently. "Son of a fucking bitch."

I couldn't have said it better myself.

Everything had changed from an hour ago. The shooter had killed one, probably two, of our own. The stakes had skyrocketed.

Now it was personal.

Chapter 34

I FOLLOWED THE STRETCHER up to the street as the EMTs carried Tonya Griffith to an ambulance and put her inside. The driver slammed the rear metal doors, climbed in, and hit the roof lights. Then he seemed to think better of it, and turned them off before slowly pulling out into traffic. There was no rush on the way to the morgue.

As I watched the ambulance roll toward the Chrysler Building, I found myself thinking about taking that job at ABC. I'd had enough of shootings and death. At least, that was sure how I felt at that moment.

Detective Terry Lavery came stomping up the stairs behind me.

"Just spoke to the precinct captain, Mike," he said. "The shooter disappeared. They scoured the area under- and aboveground, stopped buses and taxis on Lex and 51st, but not a trace."

The ESU cop had said it all. Son of a bitch.

"Witnesses?" I said.

"About a dozen. Mostly they glued themselves to the car walls when the shooting started, but their descriptions match closely. Tall Caucasian male with black hair and dark sunglasses, wearing jeans and a graffiti T. He actually used two guns, a .45 and a .22. One in each hand like Jesse James."

I shook my head in amazement. One man takes down two trained, armed officers at the same time, with two different guns? Outside of a spaghetti western or a John Woo movie, that didn't happen. Drawing, aiming, and shooting with just a single weapon while under fire took an incredible level of skill and training.

"This guy's either got some kind of special ops military background, or he's the luckiest idiot in the world," I said. "Let's pray it's the latter."

"Oh, and get this," Lavery said. "He yelled out that he *liked* cops, right before he opened up on them. Tried to warn them off, even apologized to Tonya Griffith."

Christ, on top of everything else, he was a cop lover?

"With friends like that, who needs enemies," I muttered. "Okay, round up any video you can get from the token booth or the street. I'll head over to the other crime scene."

As I walked to the corner, I saw an old Jamaican hot

dog guy behind the tape waving at me. I changed direction and went to him, thinking he might have some information, but it turned out he was just handing out free water and sodas to all the responding emergency personnel.

"My daughter's an EMT in the Bronx, mon," he said with a contagious grin. "Least I could do for all you good folks."

He refused to take my money, but finally accepted the PBA card I gave him. Maybe it would get him out of a ticket.

As I went through the familiar ritual of looking for my car, it struck me that every time I was ready to throw in the towel as a cop, I bumped face-first into the reason why I did what I did.

Chapter 35

THE PLATINUM STAR HOTEL was just five blocks west on Sixth. Rolling over there, I constructed a mental outline of my impressions so far.

The most obvious pattern emerging was that after each murder, the killer hid out, then popped up again—wearing different clothes—and committed another murder. He must have a hiding place somewhere in the area. An apartment? A hotel room?

Then there were the words he'd yelled, according to witnesses, about liking cops. Maybe that was just raving. But as cool and organized as this guy was, I had the feeling he knew what he was saying. He'd shot them only because he felt he had to, in order to escape.

That meant he wasn't just out killing randomly—he

was choosing his targets. Further, the Platinum Star Hotel was the third high-end establishment out of three.

My early guess was looking strong. He had an agenda, and it had something to do with wealth.

And unlike typical serial killers, this shooter didn't operate in secret. He worked in broad daylight, and let himself be seen. Was he trying to send a message? Those kinds of guys were usually out to prove that they were smarter than the police. They wanted to taunt us, let us know that they could kill with impunity and never be caught. So why hadn't he contacted us or the press?

That was as far as I'd taken those thoughts when I pulled up in front of the hotel.

At least a hundred cops were milling inside a crooked yellow line of crime scene tape that threaded two full city blocks around the hotel. Office workers on the other side of it just stood there, silent and gaping, shell-shocked, braced for whatever was going to happen next. I found myself actually preferring the manic looky-loo curiosity that was the usual at crime scenes.

People were definitely starting to get freaked. And why shouldn't they? Even by New York standards, the body count was alarming.

I found Detective Beth Peters inside by the check-in desk. She was still cool and crisp, but subdued.

She led me across the white marble lobby to the

elevators. The body was covered with a sheet. I crouched down and lifted it away.

The woman lying there was still beautiful, with a mane of blond hair spread out around her head—except for the small black entry wounds in her face and chest, and the sticky pool of blood that had seeped out onto the floor around her.

I stared at the bouquet of flowers on her chest. The fallen petals on the marble around her seemed like offerings in a human sacrifice.

The typed message from the 21 Club crime scene appeared in my mind like a computer pop-up.

Your blood is my paint.

Your flesh is my clay.

"Are you getting anything from this, Mike, about what he's trying to say?" Beth asked. "Because I'm not."

I replaced the sheet.

"I'm pretty sure he's saying, 'Catch me,'" I said.

Chapter 36

"HER NAME WAS MARTINE BROUSSARD," Beth Peters said as we huddled together by the check-in desk. "She was an Air France flight attendant, due out on today's two p.m. to Paris. Around eleven this morning, a tall guy with black hair comes into the hotel with a bouquet of flowers. The desk clerk tells him he can wait on the couch by the elevator. When Martine comes out, he shoots her point-blank with a gun that was hidden in the roses. Once in the head, twice in the chest. Real charmer."

I let out a long, tired breath.

"But there's some good news," Beth said. "Come on."

She led me into the large back office behind the check-in desk and introduced me to the hotel security chief, a white-haired ex–FBI agent named Brian Navril. He looked pretty nervous as he shook my hand. After what had just happened, I guess he was worried that he was about to become an ex–hotel security head, too.

"I think I found something that might be useful to you," he said, motioning us over to his desk. "At least I hope so."

He brought up the video feed of the hotel's various surveillance cameras on his laptop and quickly clicked on the square that showed the registration desk. When the screen popped up, he hit Zoom and then Pause.

A relatively clear image appeared of a man in sunglasses and an expensive leather jacket. He was holding a bouquet of roses and grinning, apparently chatting with the check-in clerk.

Beth and I exchanged satisfied looks. Bingo! Finally, a solid lead! With the sunglasses it wasn't the best of pictures, but not the worst either by any stretch. He had a stack of the already printed photos on the desk, ready for distribution.

"Where's the clerk?" I said. "I need to talk with her."

Her name was Angie Hamilton. She was a petite, attractive brunette in her midtwenties, who still looked shaken up as Beth brought her into the office.

"Hi, Angie," I said. "I'm Detective Bennett. I know this is tough for you right now, but we need to know everything you can tell us about the man who shot Ms. Broussard. You talked to him, right?"

"He asked if Martine Broussard had left yet," Angie Hamilton said. "He told me they'd just met, and he was bringing her flowers because…because…" She was starting to cry. Beth put an arm around her, murmured sympathetically, and fished a tissue out of her pocket. Angie dried her tears and continued stammering.

"He said he'd never forgive himself if he didn't let her know how he felt. I thought it was so romantic."

Double score, I thought, catching Beth's eye. She nodded back. The shooter had asked specifically for Martine Broussard. He *had* known the victim. Now, for the first time, it was certain that we were looking at a nonrandom shooting. And the odds were greatly increased that this was connected to the other incidents.

We'd caught another break, and it gave us another avenue to run down.

"How did he act, Angie? Did he seem nervous? Cocky?"

"Not cocky," the desk clerk said. "A little nervous, but sweet…kind of charming, really. That's what made it even more awful. I told him to go to wait on the couch so he wouldn't miss her when she came out of the elevator. But—but I *killed* her." Angie broke into tears again, bending forward with deep wracking sobs.

This time I joined with Beth in putting an arm around her.

"You didn't do anything wrong at all, Angie," I said. "You were just trying to be decent. The only one who did wrong is this madman who's going around shooting innocent people."

Chapter 37

THE FIRST COPS ON THE SCENE had transported the victim's fellow flight attendants to Midtown North. The Air France women were hysterical—so freaked out, in fact, that the first responding detectives couldn't get anything but French from them. Being typical cops, their mastery of French began and ended with *Voulez-vous coucher avec moi ce soir.* They'd sent for a translator, but nobody had shown up yet.

Fortunately, I wasn't a completely typical cop.

"Je suis vraiment désolé pour votre amie," I said to the ladies as I entered the upstairs interview room. *"Je suis ici pour trouver le responsable, mais je vais avoir besoin de votre aide."*

Basically, that told them that I needed their help in finding the killer. At least, I *thought* that's what I was saying. Years ago, my French had been pretty fair, but I was rusty. Maybe my words had really come out more like "Have you seen my sister's wolverine?"

Whatever it was, the gorgeous women jumped up excitedly and converged on me. I'd never engaged in a group hug with four blond French supermodel look-alikes before. Somehow I managed to endure it, thinking about the dean of students at Regis, who'd urged me to take Spanish because it was more practical.

I showed them the photo of the shooter from the surveillance video. One of them, Gabrielle Monchecourt, stared at it with widening eyes, then started jabbering a mile a minute. After getting her to slow way down, I managed to piece together what she was saying.

She thought she'd seen the shooter before! She wasn't a hundred percent positive, but maybe at a British Airways party in Amsterdam a year ago—where there'd been a lot of pilots from a dozen different airlines.

Another big break! A pilot! And another connection to what I'd been guessing from the first—had never really doubted. Well, maybe for just a second. How about that? My diplomacy and ham-handed attempt at French had actually paid off. Go Regis!

We finally had a lead solid enough to pursue.

I took my cell phone out into the hall and communicated the breaks in the case to Chief McGinnis.

"Nice work, Mike" was the first thing he said, stunning me. The second was almost as surprising—that he was giving me office space at the Police Academy on 20th Street, along with ten detectives to work my leads.

I did some head scratching at the chief's change of attitude as I drove to my new digs.

Chapter 38

WITH HIS ARMS FULL OF GROCERY BAGS, the Teacher had to use his foot to shut the battered door of the Hell's Kitchen apartment behind him. He placed the bags on the kitchen counter, tossed his guns on top of the fridge, and, without pausing, tied on his apron with a snug bow. He was starving, same as he'd been after yesterday's work.

Past noon, the pickings were pretty slim at the farmers' market in the north end of Union Square Park, but he'd managed to find some fresh Belgium endive and porcini mushrooms. He was going to use the porcini as a crust for the finely marbled Kobe fillet he'd scored at Balducci's on Eighth Avenue.

For a foodie like him, seeing what looked fresh at the market was the *only* way to decide what to make for dinner.

After crusting the steak, he couldn't resist a quick peek at the news. He washed his hands, went into the living room, and turned on the television. The first image that appeared showed a hovering helicopter and a million cops. Reporters were running around, interviewing scared-looking people on the street.

He shook his head, inhaling deeply, as he relived the shoot-out with the cops. Even with his training and unerring instincts, he so easily could have died right there and then. It was another sign that what he was doing was the right thing, the only thing. His baptism by fire had actually made him feel even more committed and passionate.

Back in the kitchen, he banged a cast-iron pan onto the Viking range and set the power burner on high. When the pan began to smoke slightly, he added a swirl of olive oil and carefully laid down the crusted Kobe with a loud, satisfying sizzle.

The smoky scent reminded him of the first time he'd met his stepfather, at Peter Luger Steak House out in Brooklyn. It was after his mom and dad had split up, when he was ten years old. He'd gone to live with his mom, and now she'd wanted him to meet her new boyfriend.

His beautiful mother had been a secretary at the investment banking firm Goldman Sachs, and her boyfriend turned out to be her boss, Ronald Meyer, a ridiculously wealthy and ridiculously old LBO specialist. The short, frog-faced geriatric had tried very stiffly to be buddy-buddy with him. The Teacher remembered sitting there in

Peter Luger's, staring at the doddering financier who had caused his family to be ripped apart, and being stricken with the almost irresistible impulse to ram his steak knife into the man's hairy right nostril.

Not long after that, his mother had become Ronald Meyer's trophy wife, and the Teacher had moved with her into Meyer's Fifth Avenue apartment. Overnight, like a kid in a fairy tale, he was suddenly setting foot in the strange new worlds of art and opera, country clubs, servants, Europe.

How quickly his initial anger had faded. With what disgusting ease and completeness he'd been lulled into a sheeplike stupor by the luxury of his newly upgraded lifestyle.

But now he realized that the anger had never gone anywhere. It had only grown, festering day after day through all the years since then, waiting to be unleashed.

He flipped the Kobe in the pan and opened a bottle of '78 Daumas Gassac that he'd been saving for a special occasion. He poured himself a tall glass and swirled it toward the good light coming in through the west-facing window.

Thinking about his crotchety stepfather, Ronny, made him smile and cringe, both. There were all the things Meyer had bought for him—the clothes and cars, the vacations, the Ivy League education.

But then, the graduation at Princeton. The awkward embrace he'd had to endure. The wretched "I'm so proud of you, son" that had emanated from the ninety-year-old's liver-colored lips. To this day, his skin crawled at the mere thought of being the offspring of the horrifying, ginger-haired skeleton his mother had used for a meal ticket.

"Should have killed you when I had the chance, you old shit," he said with a sigh. "I should have killed you at hello."

Chapter 39

I DECIDED TO MAKE MY WAY over to Bellevue to see if there was any chance of talking to the wounded transit cop.

As I drove there, I was struck by something I'd never realized before. After 9/11, apparently it didn't take too much to make Gotham residents jumpy about their personal safety. Talk about once bitten, twice shy, I thought.

Tourists were grouped beneath the awnings of the Central Park South hotels, looking warily up and down the street. A near-frenzied mob was trying to get the latest news feed from the giant TV at the CBS studios across from the Plaza. The sidewalks along Lex were clustered with office workers standing out in front of the modern glass towers. Urgently jabbering into cell phones and thumbing BlackBerries, they seemed to be waiting for evacuation instructions. There even seemed to be an early-rush-hour exodus of people pouring into Grand Central Station.

Maybe that had something to do with this, I suddenly thought. Maybe the killer wanted to create as much fear as possible.

If so, he had to be pretty pleased right now, because his plan was coming along just fine.

I didn't want to add my department Chevy to the clot of police vehicles already blocking Bellevue's ER entrance, so I parked near a rear loading dock and went in through the back.

Ed Korzenik, the veteran cop who'd been shot, was still in surgery. Miraculously, the bullet to his head had just grazed his skull. It was the .45 hollow point in his bladder that they were trying to deal with.

Ed had a large family, and many of them were there in the waiting room—wife, mother, brothers, and sisters. Seeing them, with their grief and devastation, gave me a sudden urgent need to call home.

My eldest son, Brian, answered. Of course he didn't have a clue about what I was doing, or even what was happening on the streets, and I was glad of it. We talked sports, the Yankees play-off hopes, what was going on at Jets camp. He'd be turning thirteen soon, I realized with near disbelief. My God, I'd have a house full of teenagers soon, wouldn't I?

I hung up with a smile on my face. That conversation was by far the best twenty minutes of my day.

Chapter 40

NEXT, I DECIDED TO DO something I'd been planning on since this morning — take a spin by the *New York Times* to talk with Cathy Calvin. It was time for us to have a little sit-down. Or, I guess, smack-down would be more precise. I wanted to know a couple of things. Mainly, where the hell did she get off making up theories and implying that I was her source?

After fighting my way through the crosstown traffic to 42nd Street, I remembered that the *Times* wasn't there anymore. I had to think about it before I could place them in their brand-new corporate headquarters on 40th.

I informed the security guy in the shiny new lobby that I was there to see Calvin. He looked up her name and told me she was on the twenty-first floor.

"Wait a second," he said, as I headed for the elevators. "I need to give you your pass."

I flashed him my gold shield, clipped to my tie.

"Brought my own," I said.

The twenty-first floor was deeper than I'd ever been in enemy territory. Along its halls, my shield earned me looks that were divided among shocked, nervous, and dirty. I found Calvin at a cubicle, typing furiously on a keyboard.

"More lies for the late city final?" I said.

She swiveled around toward me, flustered. "Mike — hey, great to see you." She put on a friendly smile, but I shut her down cold.

"Don't," I said. "Don't even start about how GQ I look. Just tell me why you're trying to get me fired. Mad because I wouldn't spill my guts?"

Her smile disappeared. "I'm not trying...to get you fired," she stammered.

"I don't care if you want to make up an unrevealed source. That's a personal decision. But when you imply that the source is me, it becomes my business."

"How dare you accuse me of making up something!"

I had to hand it to Calvin on one count—she knew that the best defense was a good offense.

"So you're saying I *did* tell you about the killer?" I said. "When was that, exactly? Maybe you have a tape recording or notes to refresh my memory?"

"God, how conceited you are," she said witheringly.

"Did you ever consider just once that maybe there were other sources in the world besides you?"

"So who? Who else could have given you all that 'it's just one killer' and 'changing outfits to avoid capture' crap?"

Her face suddenly took on an uncertain expression. "Look, I don't know if I can talk about this," she said, standing. "I need to clear it with my—"

I put a hand on her shoulder and sat her back down again, not roughly but not too gently either. "I'm trying to catch a killer here," I said. "You better tell me what you know. Everything. Right now."

Calvin bit her lip, then closed her eyes. "It was him."

"*Him?* What the hell is that supposed to mean?" I gripped the arms of her chair and leaned my face close to hers. "Open up, Cathy. My patience has worn real thin these last couple of days."

She was shaken now, I saw with grim satisfaction.

"The killer," she whispered.

I stared at her in disbelief, feeling like I'd been punched in the face.

"He e-mailed me yesterday afternoon," Calvin said. "Said he wanted to set the record straight, so there wouldn't be any confusion. I thought he was just a kook, but then he started describing everything. The what, when, where, and even why."

I stifled my outrage long enough to get some information.

"Tell me the why," I said. I already knew the what, when, and where.

"He pushed the girl under the train and killed the Polo clerk and the Twenty-one maître d' because, quote, 'He's out to teach this goddamn hole some manners,' unquote. He also said that regular, decent people didn't have to worry, but if you were an asshole, your days were numbered."

"Who the hell do you people think you are, withholding this from the NYPD?" I said. "You can't possibly be this stupid,"

"Calm down, Mike. My editors have been meeting all day to decide whether we should bring it to you guys. Last I heard, they were leaning toward full disclosure. And here. This will sweeten the deal." She took a printed sheet of paper off her desk and held it out to me. "It's his 'mission statement,' as he called it. He wants us to publish it."

I ripped the paper out of her hand.

Chapter 41

THE PROBLEM

Some people say the problem today is materialism. I disagree. There is nothing inherently wrong with things, nothing wrong with having money, or with being beautiful or appreciating beauty.

What is wrong is flaunting your things, your wealth, your beauty.

That is the disease.

I love our society, our country. Never before in the history of man has a nation been dedicated to human freedom. But human freedom requires dignity: respect for oneself and for those around them.

In that sense, we have grossly veered off course. Most of us know deep down that the way we behave is wrong. Yet because there are rarely any consequences, we go through with committing our daily acts of disgrace and disrespect.

That's why I've decided to start providing the proper motivation.

The penalty for obnoxiousness is now death.

I can be anyone. That person next to you on the train as you turn up your iPod, the person behind you in the restaurant as you take out your cell phone.

Think twice before you try to pull something you know for a fact you shouldn't be doing.

I am watching.

Best wishes,
The Teacher

I reread it three times before I put it back down.

It took me only another second to decide my next course of action—to give Cathy Calvin a shake-up that she'd remember for the rest of her life. I unhooked my handcuffs from my belt and chicken-winged her arm behind her back.

"What are you doing?" she cried, now in panic mode.

"Just what you think," I said. "They'll read you your rights at the station."

Her squeals of protest continued, and as I pinched down the second cuff on her slender wrist, a bunch of middle-aged white guys in rolled-up shirt sleeves and bow ties came tromping down the hall.

"I'm the city desk editor," one of them said. "What in the name of hell is going on here?"

"I'm the city cop," I said, "and I'm arresting this person for obstruction of justice."

"You can't do that," one of the younger Ivy Leaguers said, stepping in front of me. "Ever hear of something called the First Amendment?"

"Unfortunately, I have," I said. "I hate that one. You ever hear of something called a paddy wagon? Because that's where you're going to be sitting if you don't get out of my way. Hey, why don't you all come and finish your editorial meeting at Central Booking?"

Shocked and angered though they were, the reality of the situation prevailed. They backed off, and I perp-walked Calvin past them.

"Shut up and don't struggle, or I'll add a resisting charge," I told her. At least she was smart enough to know she'd better not push me any further. She sniffled and watched me with big tearful eyes, but she didn't argue anymore.

When the security guy in the lobby saw us, he jumped to his feet, looking astounded.

"Found her. Thanks," I said.

Outside, I bent Calvin over the hood of my Chevy and left her there while I stepped out of earshot and made a couple of phone calls. They were just to check up on the status of the case, but I wanted her to think that I was arranging her booking.

Only after that, very reluctantly, did I unlock the cuffs.

"You think this is all some kind of game, but it's not," I told her. "Your career decision probably cost some people their lives. Hope you get a promotion. Oh, yeah—and that you can live with yourself."

As I drove away, I glanced in the rearview mirror and saw her still standing there on the curb, with her face in her hands.

Chapter 42

MY NEW OFFICE AT THE POLICE ACADEMY turned out to be a barely converted old locker room on the third floor, but who was complaining? Right off the top, I spotted two essential pieces of equipment, a folding table and a phone jack. There was even a touch of décor on the bulletin board—a hotel surveillance photo of the Teacher with sniper crosshairs drawn on his face.

We were in business.

After I called up McGinnis and apprised him of the latest developments, I rounded up my crew of detectives. I was pleased that Beth Peters was in the group. I asked her to make copies of the Teacher's mission statement and pass them around.

"We need to get the airlines involved, Beth," I told her. "Send them the surveillance photo and have them send us

ID photos of their pilots for Mademoiselle Monchecourt to look through. Concentrate on the international carriers. British Airways in particular. Call up Tom Lamb at 26 Fed if you think you need some federal juice. And let's try to track down the florist who sold that bouquet to our killer."

"*Oui, oui,* boss man," Beth said, batting her eyes teasingly.

I turned back to my group. "Now that it's just cops here, maybe we can actually get something done," I said, and started handing out specific tasks. I wasn't used to being in charge and it felt weird, but they all hopped to it and seemed eager to do so. What a concept—people were actually doing what I asked. I decided I should try it at home.

I sent Nineteenth Precinct detectives back up to the Polo store and the 21 Club, to recanvass the areas with the photo and to interview all the employees they could find, including those that hadn't been working on the day of the murder. Maybe the Teacher had been to those places before, and someone could match a name to his face.

But they called back in to say they'd come up empty at both places. Both institutions had plenty of disgruntled employees and nasty customers. Just none that fit the shooter's description.

In the meantime, I checked downtown with Ballistics to see if the medical examiner had sent them the rounds that killed Officer Tonya Griffith.

"We got them, all right," the senior tech, Terry Miller, said. "The twenty-two-caliber was mushroomed, but I could still make out the five lands, five grooves, and the left-hand twist to the barrel. It has the same markings as the bullet that killed the Twenty-one maître d'. I can pretty much ID it in my sleep by now."

That was a strong point in our favor. The second we nailed this guy, we'd have evidence lined up and ready to go.

During the lulls when I didn't have anything pressing to do, I sat and reread the manifesto that Cathy Calvin had given me. The penalty for obnoxiousness was now death? And I'd thought the nuns in grammar school were harsh. This guy might think of himself as the Teacher, but in truth, he was more like a vigilante.

What was it exactly that had set him off? The fact that some people had more money than he did? No, I realized. He hadn't just picked his victims out of a hat. He must have had some previous contact with them in order to be offended to such an enraged degree. He had to have money himself.

I spent a lot of time looking at his picture, too. He definitely didn't look like a mentally unbalanced, reclusive, on-the-fringe type like Berkowitz or the shooters at Columbine and Virginia Tech. He was smiling and seemed confident—was actually a strapping, handsome man.

I scratched at my developing five o'clock shadow.

What the hell was up with this guy?

Chapter 43

AROUND SIX P.M. I was alone in the office, with a newly installed computer. All the detectives were out on the bricks. I heard a tap at the door.

Damned if it wasn't Cathy Calvin standing there, practically wringing her hands with nervousness.

"Must have taken a lot of investigative skill to find me here," I said. "I'm impressed."

"Quit it, Mike. Please? I came to—I won't even say apologize, I know that's no good."

She was right, and I started to tell her so. But she actually seemed sincere. I noticed, too, that she'd changed out of her usual businesswoman combat uniform into a light, summery dress. It made her look softer, more feminine—really quite pretty.

"Just because I didn't run you in doesn't mean it's finished," I said. "The department's going to be all over your editors."

"They deserve it. I mean, I'm not just blaming *them*. I knew how wrong I was. It's just—" She stepped into the room, closing the door most of the way behind her. I could smell her perfume in the warm, still air. "This job makes you crazy," she said. "The competition's unbelievable. It's turned me into a monster. When I started thinking about what I'd done, I just came apart."

She drifted closer. It was clear that she wanted comforting, and I admit I was tempted to let her slip inside my arms and nestle her face against my chest.

But that temptation was easy to brush aside.

"My job hasn't made me a nicer guy, either, Cathy," I said. "But you've got to know where to draw the line— it goes with the turf. I figure when the day comes that I can't find that line anymore, that's the day I hand in my badge."

My tone was no more inviting than my words. She stopped her approach.

"I'm leaving you a peace offering," she said. She took an envelope out of her purse and dropped it on the table, then retreated to the door.

"Go ahead and hate me, Mike," she said. "I just want you to know I'm really not like that. I'm *not*."

Then she was gone.

Of course she wasn't really like that, I thought. Not until the next time she stood to gain by it.

Inside the envelope was a copy of the Teacher's original e-mail to her.

And on the bottom, he'd left her a Yahoo Instant Messaging ID where he could be contacted: TEECH1.

Through my clenched teeth, I called Calvin a bitch for not giving me this right away. Peace offering, my ass. Then I sat at my desk and tried to decide what to do with it.

Setting up a trace was difficult and complicated. In order to get the Internet company to assist, court orders would first have to be procured, and even then it could turn out that the message may have come from a public library or a college.

I made up my mind that we didn't have time for that, and took a stab in the dark. Quickly, I created a Yahoo Instant Messaging ID for myself.

Then I sent a message to the Teacher.

MIKE10: Got your mission statement.

What happened next blew me away. After only a brief pause, an answer came back.

TEECH1: What did U think?

It was him!

MIKE10: Very interesting. Could we meet?

TEECH1: U R a cop aren't U?

I debated lying, then decided against it. Treating the guy like he was stupid wouldn't get us anywhere.

MIKE10: Yes. I'm a Detective with the NYPD.

TEECH1: I didn't mean to kill those cops, Mike. I like cops. They R among the few left in this world who actually believe in good and evil. But I needed to escape. What I'm doing is bigger even than the lives of 2 good people.

MIKE10: Maybe I could help U get your message across.

TEECH1: I'm doing just fine, Mike. Death and murder get people's rapt attention. Their ears R perking up BIGTIME.

Chapter 44

HOVERING TENSELY over my keyboard, I tried a different tack.

MIKE10: Maybe if U talked to someone U could work out your problem in a different way.

TEECH1: Don't ever go there. I don't have problems. I solve them. People think they can keep on screwing others with impunity. Why? Because they have money. Money is scrap paper with a number written on it. It doesn't make U immune to your human responsibilities.

MIKE10: The clerk and the maitre d and the stewardess didn't have money. Something else about them must have bothered U. I really do want to understand U, so please tell me. Why did U murder them?

TEECH1: Murder?

MIKE10: U R the same person who shot those people?

TEECH1: Of course. I only object to the word. Murder implies that those animals I wiped out were human beings. Their families should say a prayer and thank me for emancipating those pathetic slugs from the ignoble slavery that was their existence.

Now we're getting somewhere, I thought.

MIKE10: R U doing God's work?

TEECH1: Sometimes I think so. I can't claim to know how God intercedes in the world. But it could be through me. Why not?

Teacher? The only class this guy could teach was how 2B nuts.

MIKE10: I can't believe that God would want U to kill people.

TEECH1: He works in mysterious ways.

MIKE10: What R U going to do next?

TEECH1: YR. IDTS. Wouldn't U like to know. Now I said it to those cops, and I'll say it to U. Stay out of my way. I know U think U need to catch me, but I'd take a real serious re-eval on that if I were U, Bennett. Because if U or NE1 else gets between me and what needs 2B done, I swear to Almighty God I'll kill U B4 U get a chance to blink.

Christ on a bike, he knew who I was! He must have figured it out from the *Times* article. Why hadn't Calvin just printed my home address while she was at it?

MIKE10: Guess I'll have to take my chances.
TEECH1: That's a dangerous way to think, Bennett. That's what those two in the train car thought. Right before I erased them from existence. When is my mission statement going out?

I passed my hands through my hair, forcing my distraught brain to think fast. Getting his message to the world was obviously very important to him. Maybe we could use that to gain some leverage or draw him out.

MIKE10: We can't let that happen. Not until we get something in return.
TEECH1: How about I'll let U live. That's my final offer.

I'd been holding back my anger pretty well, but at last it jumped ahead of me. I was sick of this smug, cop-killing piece of crap. Before I could stop myself, I engaged in a slight episode of IM rage.

MIKE10: In that case instead of going on the front page,

your manifesto of nonsense is going in my circular file. U catching my drift, U deluded freak?

TEECH1: U just cost another citizen his life, cop. I'll kill two people a day if that message doesn't go out. U don't have the slightest conception of who U R messing with. My message will reach the world if it has to be written in your blood. TTYL. YFA!

I sat there staring at the screen. TTYL stood for "talk to you later," I knew. I did have four preteens. But what was YFA? You something something.

Then I got it.

I turned and stared at the crosshairs over the Teacher's face up on the wall, imagining my finger squeezing the trigger.

Yeah. Right back at you, Teech.

DETECTIVE
MICHAEL BENNETT

Part Three

LIFE LESSONS

Chapter 45

SITTING IN THE QUIET of his apartment's shaded living room, the Teacher chucked his Treo across the couch, and knocked back the last of the Daumas.

He grinned as a ball of sweet fire softly exploded in his stomach. He flipped on the TV set and channel surfed. Not only NY1, but the national networks were all over the hotel and subway shootings.

The people on the street looked solemn, downright paranoid. God, this was fun, he thought. Fucking with their heads was so addictive. He started laughing when a very concerned-looking cop was interviewed. Was that MIKE10? The asshole who just so lamely tried to get him to stop?

He held his sides as the hilarity of it all suddenly overwhelmed him. Tears actually came out of his eyes.

"Better than Disney World on the Fourth of July," he said to the screen as he wiped at a joyful tear.

He clicked off the set with the remote and extended the recliner all the way back, thinking about the French-woman he'd killed. She'd been even more attractive than a fashion model—curvier, less plastic, with an air of real sophistication. She'd virtually lit up the room with her sexuality and femininity.

Now she was as dead as the guys in the Pyramids. As dead as the dark side of the moon. Dead and gone forever and ever, amen.

It served her perfectly goddamn right, her and all the rest who thought they could skate through this life on their looks and bank accounts. Pride goeth before the fall. Make that the trigger pull in this case.

Deluded freak? he thought, recalling the cop's text message as he closed his eyes. Now, now. Wasn't that a tad harsh?

After all, one man's deluded freak was another's aven-ging dispenser of justice—swift, final, and complete.

Chapter 46

THE ELEVEN P.M. NEWS carried wall-to-wall coverage of the shootings. Both reporters and anchors seemed quite critical of the way the NYPD was handling the case. ABC actually interviewed people on the street about whether they thought the cops were doing enough.

I watched a skinny taxpayer waiting for a bus answer with a sneer and a thumbs-down.

"They stink," he said. "My four-year-old daughter could catch this guy."

"So what are we waiting for?" I growled at the screen. "Somebody bring that kid in here." I balled up my sandwich wrapper, tossed it at the still-yammering jerk, and turned away, rubbing my eyes into the back of my skull.

I'd already sent the Teacher's mission statement and our IM exchange over to Agent Tom Lamb to see if the

FBI's document division could cull out some new insights, but I hadn't heard back. Gabrielle Monchecourt, Martine Broussard's stewardess friend, was ready to look at photos of airline personnel, in hopes that she could match the Teacher to the pilot she'd seen at a party. But we were still waiting for those photo ID books, and she was scheduled to get on a plane to Paris in the morning.

And if our shooter stayed true to his history, the new day was going to bring more than just a sunrise. Time was of the essence, as my seventh-grade teacher, Sister Dominic, had often reminded us.

I finally decided it was time to go from proactive to in-your-face active. I sent a couple of Midtown North guys to pick up Mlle. Monchecourt and take her to Kennedy Airport. Then I started calling airline corporate security people. I'd already talked to them umpteen times, but now I made it clear that if those photo books weren't available when she got there, the NYPD was going to assume that some insider was protecting the shooter, and those airlines would be shut down until the situation got straightened out. Probably it would take several days.

That got through to them. By midnight, my guys at Kennedy reported back that our witness was going through photos.

I decided to take a break before I collapsed. I announced to everyone within earshot that my cell phone would be on. Then I headed home to check on the sick.

I arrived at my apartment in the nick of time. As I

walked in, I found Seamus in the dining room, pouring a shot of Jameson's into a plastic Curious George cup.

"Shame on you, Monsignor," I said. "We have big-people glasses in the cabinet over the fridge. You can set me up one, too, while you're at it."

"Very funny," Seamus said. "As if it was for me! That poor lad Ricky's throat is so sore, I thought I'd give him a little Galway remedy, as they say. There's nothing a spot of Jameson's and some warm milk and sugar won't cure."

I couldn't believe my ears. "Did you fall down the altar steps?" I said, pulling the bottle away from him. "Your little Galway remedy will land us in family court. I can't believe I actually have to say this out loud: Don't give the children any whiskey!"

"Oh, well," Seamus said with wounded dignity, grabbing his coat. "Have it your own foolish way. Tell Ricky to bear up like a man. Seamus out."

I reluctantly decided I'd better not have a drink after all and put away the whiskey, then checked in again with my detectives out at Kennedy. The Air France stewardess had gone through both the Delta and Aer Lingus books, but didn't recognize anyone.

British Airways was still holding out. They had the pilot book ready to show, but were still waiting for final permission from their CEO, who was on holiday somewhere in the Italian Alps.

"Right, of course," I said. "Everyone prefers the Italian side nowadays. Saint Moritz is so over. Tell him when the next victim goes down, we'll have the crime-scene photos sent up to his suite with his morning espresso."

After I hung up, I made the command decision to stay and sleep under my own roof. I went into my bathroom to take a quick but glorious shower. But when I pulled back the curtain, I almost had a heart attack instead.

My five-year-old, Shawna, was sleeping in the tub.

"What are you doing in here, daisy flower?" I asked, lifting her out. "When did pillows become tub toys?"

"I just don't want to make any more messes for you to clean up, Daddy," she croaked.

She started shivering as I tucked her back into her bed. Gazing down at her, I asked myself the question that kept coming back to me time and time again over the last year. What would Maeve do? I grabbed a flashlight from the pantry, went back to Shawna's room, and whisper-read her one of her favorite Magic Tree House books until she fell back to sleep.

"How'm I doing, Maeve?" I asked after I stepped out into the hall. "And don't worry. It's okay to lie."

Chapter 47

AFTER SHOWERING, I found Mary Catherine in the kitchen, taking sheets out of the dryer.

"For God's sake, Mary, it's one o'clock in the morning," I said.

"Has to be done," she replied, striving valiantly for her usual crispness, but with her weariness showing underneath.

I stepped in to help her fold, and she went over the sick list.

"For the moment, everybody seems fairly stable," she said. "All the puking seems to have run its course, thank the Lord, but now the bug's rising into their lungs and nasal passages. We'll be out of tissues by noon tomorrow is my guess."

"On it," I said. In the morning, I'd send Seamus out to

our Costco in Jersey to fill up the van. Boy, did our doorman love it when he saw that coming.

When the laundry was done, I took the basket from Mary Catherine's hands and said, "Why don't you get some sleep now?"

But I couldn't persuade her to leave. She insisted on sleeping in a chair in the living room in case somebody needed her. Too tired to argue, I took off my suit jacket and plopped down in the chair opposite. What the heck, I was already dressed for the next day. I was going to be one wrinkled detective—Cathy Calvin wouldn't have approved—but I needed to be ready to go the second I heard any news.

Everything in my body ached. I was so exhausted that even with all the stress and adrenaline and anticipation of the case, my eyelids clunked shut like they were made of lead.

"I always knew coming to America would pay off big," Mary Catherine said after a minute. "All the sweet perks. Like, is it kiddy vomit I'm smelling, or has Yankee Candle come out with something new?"

"Neither, young lass," I said, smiling with my eyes still closed. "That's the refreshing aroma of my Yankee sweat socks that I forgot to toss in the laundry. I told you that you should have left when you had the chance. G'night."

Chapter 48

THE TEACHER AWOKE with a start—sat bolt upright, gasping for air, his heart thumping.

Sleeping peacefully had never been a problem for him, but now that was ruined. Every time he started to drift off, that cop's phrase, "manifesto of nonsense," rang continuously like a gong through his head.

Bennett was just messing with him, he assured himself fiercely. But doubt kept creeping into his thoughts, driving his anxiety and making it impossible to rest. What if his message hadn't been clear enough? With his head buzzing, he couldn't decide. He checked his alarm clock and gritted his teeth. One a.m. How could he perform tomorrow if he was up all night worrying?

He plumped his pillow and closed his eyes again, turning to one side and then the other, trying to get comfortable.

For five minutes, he tried concentrating on his breathing. But it was hopeless.

That goddamn cop had gotten to him.

He sat up again and finally got out of bed. Somehow, he needed to burn off this bad energy.

Through the south-facing window in the living room, he could see the Empire State Building, illuminated up with red lights. Across the street at the modeling agency, a party was going full tilt. There was plenty of action out there—plenty of ways to scratch an itch like his.

Maybe a walk, he thought. A little stroll around the block.

He dressed and was twisting the front doorknob open when he realized he'd forgotten something—his guns. He couldn't believe it! That was a measure of how rattled he was.

He stepped back into the office and reloaded both Colts, then threaded their baffled stainless-steel suppressors—Swiss-made, top-of-the-line Brügger and Thomets—to the barrels. He strapped the weapons around his waist and pulled on a coat.

Dangerous world out there, he thought as he quickly descended the tenement stairwell toward the street.

Never know who you might run into.

Chapter 49

PIERRE LAGUEUX, fashion photographer extraordinaire, felt like a joy-filled bubble as he walked down the back stairs of the West Side Models agency.

Not just any bubble, either. High as he was on some top-grade MDMA, the drug otherwise known as Ecstasy, he felt like a *très chic* bubble of Cristal champagne.

It was almost unfair how well life was working out for him, he mused. Only twenty-seven and already rich. Handsome, heterosexual, French, and very, very talented at taking pictures. The hardest part about being him was — the thought made him giggle — waking up.

He had a real eye, they said. They, meaning the people in the fashion world who actually counted. In spite of his youth, the word *icon* was being whispered. His name was dropped in company with Ritts, Newton, Mapplethorpe.

Sorry, fellas, move over. There's a new *enfant terrible* in town.

And best of all, the parties. Tonight, already a fabulous dream, was just beginning, and how many more would he have? He could practically see them in an endless array stretching out before him. As long, elegant, and dark as the row of designer suits in the gymnasium-sized closet of his loft down on Broome Street.

All around him, the world breathed, *Yes.*

He stepped out onto the street. The night was young—just the way he preferred his ladies. Like the barely legal, new Ford Nordic blonde he'd just "met" in the back stairwell. He could actually fall in love with her, if only he could remember her name.

"Pierre?" a woman's voice called.

He craned his neck, raising his stubbled face toward the sound. It was she—his new nameless lovely, as statuesque as the figurehead of a Viking ship, standing on the fire escape above him. Or was she an actual flying Valkyrie? As high as he was, it was hard to tell.

"Catch!" she said.

Something sailed down toward him, dark and diaphanous, and settled into his outstretched hands—a warm, wispy weight that was barely there. A feather from an angel wing? No, better. Thong panties. What a wonderfully American parting gift! How Girls Gone Wild!

He blew her a kiss, removed the silk handkerchief from the breast of his cashmere Yves Saint Laurent sport coat, and inserted the undergarment in its place. Then he continued on his way to Tenth Avenue to cab to his next soirée.

He was midway up the east side of the block when he spotted a man standing alone on the sidewalk, alongside the train overpass.

A fellow reveler, was Pierre's first thought. But then he saw the guy's serious face.

He stared unabashedly. He was always on the lookout for a striking photo image, always honing his eye. That was probably the reason he would be immortal. And this figure—there was something tragic in the way it stood against the dark, otherwise completely empty street. It was the essence of noir. So Hopperesque.

But more still, there was also something about the man's eyes. A startling, yearning intensity in them.

As mesmerized as he was, it took Pierre a good thirty seconds before he saw the two silenced pistols the man was holding beside his thighs.

What?

Pierre's drug-addled mind scrambled for comprehension. The girl in the stairwell, was the first thought it grasped. Was this an angry rival?

"Wait!" Pierre said, raising his hands placatingly. "She said she had no boyfriend. Please, monsieur, you must believe me. Or perhaps you are her father? She is young, yes, but very much a woman—"

The Teacher shot him twice in the crotch with the suppressed .22, and once in his throat with the .45.

"Not even close, French fry," he said, watching the worthless hedonist bounce face-first off the sidewalk.

He knelt beside the fallen man and pulled his hair back from his forehead. With his teeth, the Teacher uncapped a Sharpie and began to write.

Chapter 50

AS THE TEACHER HEADED BACK into his building, the last thing in the world he expected was the small, attractive blond woman who rose up furiously from the outside steps.

"I finally found you, you son of a bitch!" she screamed.

Holy crap! the Teacher thought, panicked. It was his publicist, from his former life — the life he'd abruptly abandoned when he'd started on his mission two days ago.

"Wendy," he said soothingly. "I've been meaning to get back to you."

"How gallant of you," she fumed. "Considering I called you thirty-six fucking times. *Nobody* no-shows the *Today* show! You've ruined yourself! Worse, you've ruined me!"

He glanced around nervously. Standing out here

arguing wasn't cool. If somebody hadn't already discovered the dead Frenchman, they would any second now.

But then he realized that she was falling-down drunk, with bloodshot eyes and a smell like a brewery. A plan snapped into his mind. Perfect.

"I can do better than explain, Wendy," he said, with his most charming smile. "I'll make it up to you, ten times over. Got an e-mail that's going to blow your doors off."

"Make it up to me? How are you going to un-demolish my business? You know how hard I worked to get you booked? At this level, you don't get a second chance. Now I'm over."

"I'm talking Hollywood, baby. I just heard from the *Tonight Show*," he lied. "Leno's hot to have me on. It's going to fix everything, Wendy. I promise. Hey, come on upstairs with me. I'll cook you breakfast. You loved it when I did that last time, right? How about some fresh Belgian waffles?"

She turned away from him, trying to remain angry. But she failed, and started slurring out words in drunken honesty.

"You don't know how much I missed you. After that night we had, and then you didn't call me, and—"

The Teacher put his finger to her lips. After a few more seconds of resistance, she nibbled his first knuckle.

"We'll have a better time tonight," he said. "If you're really good—or should I say, really bad?—I'll even warm the syrup," he said, deepening his killer smile.

Finally, she smiled back. She removed a compact from her purse and touched up her hair and makeup. Then she took his hand and walked upstairs with him to the apartment.

Inside, he locked the door behind them.

"What's it going to be first?" he said. "Food or e-mail?"

"I want to see that e-mail. Are you kidding?" she said, kicking off her high heels excitedly. "I can't wait!"

"It's in here. Follow me."

As they walked through the spare room door, her gaze flicked across the corpse on the bed. She took two more steps before she stiffened and spun back to stare at it, abruptly seeming sober.

"Oh, my God!" she breathed. "What is that? What's going on here? I don't understand."

Unceremoniously, the Teacher shot her in the back of the head with the silenced .22. Then he dragged her into the hall closet, dumped her Manolo Blahniks on top of her, and shut the door.

"Yeah, well," he said, wiping his hands. "It's a long story."

When he fell back into in his bed, his eyelids suddenly felt like manhole covers, and his breathing slowed to its usual peaceful rhythm.

Who needs warm milk? he thought as he softly faded into sleep.

Chapter 51

WHEN MY CELL PHONE WENT OFF, it took me a second to distinguish the sound above the constant hacking of the Bennett sick ward. I groped for it in a stupor, noting that the time was just after three a.m. For all my big hopes, I'd gotten maybe ten minutes of real sleep.

"Yeah, Mike, Beth Peters here. Sorry to wake you, but we just got word. A fashion photographer, shot dead on a sidewalk in Hell's Kitchen. Looks like you-know-who."

"I'm just waiting for my chance to send you-know-who to you-know-where in a handbasket," I said grimly. "Any witnesses?"

"I don't think so," she said. "But one of the uniforms said he actually wrote some kind of a message. I didn't quite catch that part. You want me over there, or—"

"No, you mind the store," I said. "I'm closer. Give me an address."

After talking to Beth, I called Chief McGinnis, hoping I'd get the chance to wake him up to deliver the latest happy news. Unfortunately I had to settle for his voice mail.

Unbelievable, I thought, putting away my phone. The shooter seemed to be speeding up, shortening the interval between kills—giving us less time to figure things out. That was the last thing we needed now.

"Don't tell me you have to go back in," Mary Catherine said, still camped out in the chair opposite mine.

"This city never sleeps and apparently neither does its latest psychopath." I heaved myself to my feet and rooted around the darkened room until I lucked onto my keys, then opened the lockbox in the closet to get my Glock.

"Are you going to be all right?" I asked her. It was a pretty stupid question. What was I going to do if she said no?

"We're fine," she said. "*You* be careful."

"Believe me, if I get near this guy, I won't give him a chance to hurt me."

"Driving, too," Mary Catherine said. "I'm concerned. You look like you just crawled out of a crypt."

"Gee, thanks for the compliment," I said. "If it's any consolation, I feel even worse."

I proved it immediately by walking smack into my front door, before I remembered I had to open if first.

But in the elevator down, I started looking on the bright side. At least this time, the guy had the decency to murder somebody on the West Side, so I didn't have far to drive.

Chapter 52

THE CRIME SCENE TECHS were still stringing yellow ribbon when I arrived at the murder site on 38th Street.

"Nice work," I said to one of them. "Tape's looking sharp. How'd you score a new roll?" A little hamming it up for the waiting cops and techs is pretty much expected from the arriving homicide detective, and, as loopy as I felt, I was more than happy to oblige.

"You gotta know the right people," a burly guy with a mustache growled back. "This way, detective." He lifted the waist-high plastic ribbon to make it easier for me to limbo underneath.

"I mean, this is what I call a crime scene," I said. "Garbage in the street? Check. Lifeless citizen? Check—"

"Wiseass detective? Check," Cathy Calvin called from behind the barricade.

"Backstabbing reporters, present and accounted for," I continued, without looking at her.

An Amtrak on its way to anywhere but Hell's Kitchen gave a tap of its horn as it rumbled beneath the sidewalk train bridge we were standing on. I had a sudden impulse to vault off the bridge onto its top. I'd always dreamt of riding the rails.

"Even moody, *cine noir* sound effects," I said, giving the techs a satisfied nod. "You know how much money a Hollywood studio would have to spend for this kind of authenticity? You guys have really outdone yourselves. I honestly couldn't have asked for better."

On the way over, I'd learned from Beth Peters that the victim was a heavy in the fashion industry. I'd started to wonder if this situation had parallels to the Gianni Versace murder—if the Teacher was some twerp on the outskirts of the rich and famous, who'd decided to reach out and grab his fifteen minutes of fame the hard way.

The hard way for other people.

I squatted down and looked at the corpse. Then I jumped up and stumbled backward, suddenly and totally wide awake.

"4U Mike, YFA!" was written across the victim's forehead in Magic Marker.

As I looked up and down the shadowed street, I realized that my hands were trembling. They wanted to draw my Glock and kill that son of a bitch. I clenched them into fists in order to still them. My gaze turned back to the young man lying on the sidewalk. I cringed at the sight of his blood-drenched crotch.

I cursed myself for provoking the Teacher, but then I stopped beating myself up. He would have killed again anyway. He was just using a cheap, ugly pretext to cast blame on me.

I'd wait until I came face-to-face with him. Then I'd turn loose my rage.

Chapter 53

WHEN I GOT BACK TO MY BUILDING, even my doorman Ralph knew better than to mess with me. It must have been the stark expression on my face.

Upstairs, I made sure all the locks on the doors and windows were secured before I found my bedroom.

It was going to require smelling salts to wake me come morning, but I did not care. I was not going to brush my teeth. I refused to even take off my shoes. I was going to fall into my bed and sleep until someone wrenched me out of it with great physical force.

I had just pulled my beloved body pillow to my chest when I heard the giggling. It was coming from the other side of the bed.

No, I prayed. *Please, Lord. No.*

The pillow was tugged out of my grip. A wide-awake Shawna lay there staring at me with a beaming smile.

"Sweetie, this isn't your bed," I pleaded softly. "This isn't even the bathtub. Do you want a pony, Shawna? Daddy will get you a whole herd of ponies if you let him have some rest."

She shook her head, immediately getting into the spirit of this new game. I felt like weeping. I was doomed, and I knew it. The problem with the youngest kids in a big family is that by the time you've gotten to them, you realize it's actually easier to do things for them than to sit around and agonizingly wait for them to do things for themselves. They instinctively know this. They sense the emptiness in threats the way an ATF dog can detect explosives. Resistance is futile. You are theirs.

As this was going through my mind, I heard more giggling, then felt the movement of something small climbing into the bottom of my bed. I didn't even have to look to know that Chrissy was getting into the act. She and Shawna were as thick as thieves.

Next, tiny hands separated the largest and second largest toes of my right foot.

"Toe pit sensitivity training," my daughters screamed in glee as they wriggled their fingers between my toes.

I couldn't take any more, and I sat up to tell them they had to go back to their own beds. But I stopped when I saw the undiluted delight radiating off them. What the heck. At least they weren't puking.

Besides, how could you argue with a light beam and an angel?

"All right, I'll show you some sensitivity training," I mock-threatened.

Their happy shrieks threatened to shatter the light fixture as I tried the Vulcan nerve pinch on both of them simultaneously.

A few minutes later, after an elaborate ritual of arranging stuffed animals and squish pillows, I managed to tuck in my daughters next to me.

"Tell us a story, Daddy," Chrissy said as I collapsed again.

"Okay, honey," I said with my eyes closed. "Once upon a time, there was a poor old detective who lived in a shoe."

Chapter 54

"BENNETT? YOU THERE?!"

I lunged up from the mattress, hand groping for my service weapon, as a shrill voice drilled a hole in my right eardrum. Then I realized with bewilderment that I was in my own bedroom filled with morning sunlight, not some murky, death-harboring alley of nightmare. My cell phone, folded open, was resting on my pillow beside where my head had been. One of my kids must have answered it and helpfully stuck it next to sleeping daddy's ear.

"Yeah?" I said, lifting it with an unsteady hand.

"Nine o'clock meeting at the Plaza, and I don't mean the Oak Room," Chief of Detectives McGinnis snapped, and hung up as sharply as he'd spoken.

Not only did I make it into my unmarked Chevy in ten minutes flat, I was even showered and dressed. I got the car rolling and dug for the Norelco I kept in the glove compartment, feeling like I'd died and gone to heaven. I must have gotten close to five hours of real, delicious sleep.

I strode through the doors of One Police Plaza with a full forty seconds to spare, and took the elevator up to twelve, to the same cramped conference room where the first task force meeting had been held. The same tired and wired-looking cops were sitting there. I poured myself a coffee, grabbed a chocolate glazed, and took my place among them.

Right on time, McGinnis came barreling in, holding a copy of the *Post* above his head. "HAVE YOU SEEN THIS MAN?" the headline read, below the surveillance video shot of the Teacher.

"The answer is yes," he announced, tossing the paper across the conference table. "We had an Air France flight attendant pick out our shooter an hour ago."

Spontaneous applause ripped through the room. Thank you, God, I thought, punching fists with Beth Peters beside me. I was so juiced, I decided to let slide the way that McGinnis had said *we,* with no mention of exactly who *we* were.

Our lead had paid off! Now we actually had a real shot at this animal.

"Suspect's name is Thomas Gladstone," McGinnis said, handing out printouts from a large sheaf. "He's a former British Airways pilot—lives in Locust Valley, out on the island. Was an air force pilot before that."

Locust Valley? I thought. Wasn't that the place where everyone's name sounded like Thurston J. Howell III? Pilots made decent money, but they weren't anywhere near that kind of food chain. I wondered if that explained some of the upscale targets. Maybe Gladstone had gotten snubbed at Polo and 21, or something along those lines, and decided that undertipping just wasn't going to cut it in terms of showing his dissatisfaction.

"We've got a triggering incident, too," McGinnis said. "Turns out Gladstone was scheduled to fly out of Heathrow to New York last week, but they caught him drunk and he got the ax. *And* we just found his car, littered with parking tickets in the Locust Valley commuter lot."

I nodded grimly. Now we were getting somewhere. Losing a job was high up there on the list of why people went on rampages.

"We have an arrest warrant yet?" I said.

"We will by the time we bag this skell's sorry ass," McGinnis said. "ESU's waiting downstairs. Who's up for a little trip to the Gold Coast?"

I shot up out of my chair with the rest of the surrounding cops, grinning. I'd never even touched my coffee, but for some reason I felt completely refreshed.

Chapter 55

LOCUST VALLEY'S TOWN SQUARE seemed to consist solely of slate-roofed antiques shops, boutiques, and salons. Our designated staging area was a parking lot on Forest Avenue behind something called a "coach and motor works." Call me a philistine, but it looked suspiciously like a gas station to me.

Nassau County Bureau of Special Operations and even some Suffolk County Emergency Service police were already there waiting for us. When a cop killer is involved, interdepartmental cooperation is more than a given.

"Morning, guys," I said, and gathered everybody over by my car for a briefing.

The Nassau crew already had surveillance set up around Gladstone's four-acre property. There were no signs of activity there, and no one had gone in or out. Calls to the inside of his house were picked up by the answering machine. Gladstone had a wife named Erica and two co-ed daughters, I learned, but they hadn't yet been located.

Tom Riley, the Nassau Special Ops lieutenant, tossed digital photos of the front and back of Gladstone's house onto the hood of my Chevy. The place was a gorgeous sprawling Tudor with a covered patio and a swimming pool in back. The landscaping was immaculate—Japanese maples, chrysanthemums, ornamental grasses. Definitely not the kind of house one usually associated with homicidal maniacs.

Studying the layout, we talked strategy about how to enter. There would be no attempt to negotiate. We'd gotten the arrest warrant, and we were going in. But considering the firepower Gladstone had, plus the fact that he'd already iced one cop and put another into a coma, no precaution was overlooked.

We decided that a breach team would storm the front door while snipers covered the narrow facing windows. If Gladstone showed his face in one, he'd be going down.

Since this was my case, I claimed the honor of following right behind the breach team to search the second floor.

"That door looks pretty solid," I said. "What are you going to use? A battering ram?"

A young, muscular NYPD ESU sergeant held up a sawed-off shotgun and racked its slide.

"Brought my skeleton key," he said, smiling around a chaw of tobacco. He actually seemed to be enjoying himself. I was glad he was on my side.

As the team geared up to start moving, I reached into my jacket and dropped another photograph onto the hood of the car. It was a picture of Tonya Griffith, the young woman transit cop Gladstone had murdered.

"Just a little reminder of why we all got out of bed this morning, gentlemen," I said. "Let's ring this scumbag's bell."

Gladstone's house was three blocks away, on a wooded street called Lattingtown Ridge Court. Our vehicles pulled out of the parking lot and cruised there, lights and sirens off.

As we arrived, I gave the green light over the radio. Two Emergency Service diesel trucks suddenly swerved into the driveway and across the lawn. A half-dozen tactical cops spilled out from behind them. Within seconds, I heard two crisp explosions—the front door hinges being shotgunned off.

As the cops shouldered the door aside and piled through it, yelling and tossing flashbangs, I flung open my car door and rushed in with them. I took the stairs two by two, with my Glock drawn and my heart pulsing like a strobe light.

"Police!" I screamed, kicking open the first closed door I encountered. It was a bathroom. There was nothing inside. Nobody. Curtain rings jingled as I ripped down the shower curtain. Just a shower caddy filled with shampoo bottles.

Damn! I thought, rushing back out into the hall, swinging my pistol from side to side.

Where was Gladstone?

Chapter 56

THE FRAMED PHOTOGRAPHS of well-dressed, smiling people that lined the hallway rattled as I stormed along it.

"Police!" I yelled again. "We're all over you, Gladstone. This is the police!"

At the far end was another door, this one slightly ajar. I tightened my grip on the Glock's trigger and rammed the door with my shoulder.

It opened into a large, tray-ceilinged master bedroom suite. I cleared the corners first, scanned the bed, and ...

My face jerked away in shock, as if I'd been punched. My gun almost slipped from my fingers before I managed to shove it back into its holster. Then I covered my nose and mouth with a hand as the vile coppery scent of blood and death washed over me.

We were too late.

This guy, I thought.

"Oh, my God," a woman breathed from the hall behind me. It was Beth Peters, frozen with shock.

This guy.

I stepped out into the hall and got out my radio.

"Up here," I said weakly. "Second floor."

"Do you have him?" McGinnis yelled.

"No," I said. "Not him."

What we had was a bound, half-naked woman on the bed, drenched in a bloody sheet. Through the open door-way of the bathroom beyond I could see a woman's foot hanging over the tub rim. Another young woman, a girl really, lay facedown in blood beside the toilet, hog-tied with lamp cord.

Shaking my head, I approached the bodies for a closer inspection. The two women in the bathroom were barely in their twenties. Both of them were completely naked. The woman in the bedroom was older—maybe their mother, Erica Gladstone. My gaze caught a wedding photo lying in a corner, its glass cracked from being knocked to the floor. I picked it up and held it beside her lifeless face. She was so battered, it took me a full minute to confirm it was a match.

I couldn't believe it. Gladstone had shot and killed his wife and their two daughters. His own flesh and blood.

Other cops were coming into the room now. I could

hear their exclamations of horror and disbelief behind me. I stayed where I was, staring at the blood-soaked carpet and sheets.

This was the worst crime of all, an atrocity, an outrage against humanity. God, I wanted to get my hands on this sick prick. Better yet, get him in the sights of my Glock.

Chapter 57

IT WAS ELEVEN THIRTY A.M. when the Teacher stopped in front of an electronics store at 51st and Seventh. All the TVs that he could see through the big plate-glass windows were tuned to the Fox News Channel.

"Spree Killer Update," scrolled across the top and, "Live from Locust Valley, Long Island" across the bottom.

Hey, I know that place, he thought, smiling, as he watched the cops swarming on the lawn in front of the mansion.

Well, how about that? Score one for the gumshoes. They'd actually caught his scent. He'd started to wonder if they ever would.

But it didn't really matter. He'd have to be a little more careful now, but he'd still be able to get all his work done. They were playing checkers while he was playing grand-master chess.

"Mommy, Mommy! Look, look!" a small Indian kid said as he pressed his face up against the store window in front of an Xbox 360. "Pokémon, Pikachu, Squirtle!" he cried.

His sari-clad mother slapped him on the backside before yanking him away down 51st.

Watching them go, the Teacher remembered the day, long ago, when he'd gone with his mother to get the last of their belongings from the lousy row house he'd grown up in. His dad had stood in the doorway, drinking a bottle of Miller beer and holding back the Teacher's little brother, who was crying and straining to go with Mommy.

"No, buddy," his dad kept saying. "You're Daddy's boy now, remember? You're going to stay with me. It's Okay."

But it wasn't okay, was it? the Teacher thought.

He shook his head in disbelief, remembering how he'd just sat there in the cab of the moving truck. At first, he'd been embarrassed that the neighbors would see, until he realized they weren't his neighbors anymore. After that, he'd actually been happy. He'd had to share a room with his stupid little brother, but now he was going to go with his mom, and he'd have his own room. His brother was a baby, he'd decided.

The Teacher's cheeks bulged as he let out a long breath.

No, it wasn't okay, he thought, shaking off the memory. But it was getting there. It would all be as okay as it was ever going to be, very soon.

He looked at himself in the plate-glass reflection. He was clean-shaven this morning, wearing a skintight Armani blazer over his tall, tapered frame, with a white silk shirt open at the throat and crotch-biting Dolce and Gabbana jeans—over-the-top, go-f-yourself, moneyed sex and style. Real Tom Ford.

Screw that stubbly-faced, Unabomber-look-alike picture of him on the covers of the *Daily News* and the *Post*, he thought. The only people who'd glanced twice at him on the sidewalks this morning were horny-looking forty-year-old ladies and hornier-looking gay men.

Nothing had changed. He would go over like Rover.

He took out his Treo, double-checked his next target, and adjusted his pistol at the small of his back before stepping out into the sidewalk crush.

This was a real good one coming up—somebody who'd been in dire need of his comeuppance for quite some time.

The Teacher put a little pep in his step as he flowed east with the sheltering crowd.

Chapter 58

WITHIN HALF AN HOUR of our storming the Gladstone mansion, news vans had outnumbered Range Rovers on Lattington Ridge Court. Alongside the barricades, I counted at least four newsies, pointing their surface-to-air-missile-like shoulder cams at the house. I felt like calling in air support. We were under siege.

I gladly handed over the master bedroom to the arriving Nassau County Crime Scene guys.

"So, is it true? A trifecta on the Gold Coast?" one of them said with a shake of his head. "I knew that was Dominick Dunne out by the mailbox."

Downstairs, the law enforcement were standing in clusters, smoking, drinking coffee, and wisecracking like bad guests at the world's worst cocktail party.

I waded through them and scanned the photographs

on the walls in the family room. I took down three that I thought we could use in tracking Gladstone. He looked like a pilot, handsome, flat-bellied, and steely-eyed. Even his grin seemed muscular, that of a man who always got what he wanted.

"Hey there, you sick son of a bitch," I said to him.

I couldn't help looking at the rest of the pictures. Little girls at picnics, preteens at the beach, young ladies graduating from high school. The Gladstone daughters had been beautiful, but nothing compared to their mother, Erica. Black-haired and pale-eyed with high cheekbones, she looked like a queen from a fairy tale.

But the grille of her Lincoln Navigator was sticking into the room, thrust through the shattered wall beside her studio-photographed portrait.

Too bad Sophocles had come in at the last minute and written the fairy tale's ending.

I located the home's office past some French doors near the front of the house. I used the fax machine to send the pictures to the deputy commissioner of public information so he could get them out to the press, then I sat down at the antique desk and started opening file drawers.

Right off the top, the Amex bills were staggering. Four-hundred-dollar hair appointments here, three-thousand-dollar charges to Bergdorf Goodman there. Mrs. Gladstone paid more for skin care than I had for college tuition. Apparently, being rich was extremely expensive.

After a few minutes more of searching, I finally found

what I was looking for—charges to both the 21 Club and the Polo store.

I also found something in the bottom file drawer that, at first, I thought was some kind of contract. Actually, it was. A contract of divorce.

Bingo, I thought. That helped to explain things more. Two factors commonly made people go berserk—divorce and getting fired. Gladstone had experienced both within a short time period.

But what I really needed was something that would tell me where Gladstone might be hiding, and where he might strike next. I kept looking.

It was twenty minutes later when I found a book of press clippings on one of the built-in shelves. It contained mostly local newspaper society clippings. Erica at charity functions, sometimes with, but mostly without, her prince of a husband. The most recent one showed a picture of Erica draped in satin, tulle, and diamonds at a Wall Street AIDS benefit, at Manhattan's Customs House.

A silver-haired man was holding her near-naked waist. His name, I read in the caption, was Gary Cargill.

It took me less than a second to make the connection that Cargill was the name at the top of the divorce papers.

Yet another crushing blow to Gladstone's ego. His wife had started seeing her divorce attorney.

Suddenly my eyes opened wide. If I was as crazy as Gladstone and I'd been raked over the coals like him, who would I want to take out?

I dropped the book as I spun around and grabbed for the phone.

"What city and listing, please?" asked the phone company information computer in a gratingly calm voice.

Mine was much more frantic.

"Manhattan!" I yelled. "A lawyer named Cargill!"

Chapter 59

"SO YOU'VE DECIDED it's time for you and your wife to part company," celebrity divorce attorney Gary Cargill said with all the grave emotion that the statement and his five-hundred-dollar consultation fee deserved.

"But for me and my hedge fund to *keep* company," said Mr. Savage, Cargill's latest client. In his casual, devil-may-care designer outfit, Savage looked loaded, like a real winner. Gary thought he recognized the face from somewhere, but he couldn't quite place it. *Fortune* magazine?

Ah, hedge fund, Gary thought. *The two sweetest words in modern English.*

"That's why I came to you," Savage went on. "I've heard you're the best. I don't care how much it costs, either, so long as that whore doesn't get one red cent."

Slowly, ruminatively, Gary leaned back in his cashmere-upholstered office chair. His meticulously designed, oak-paneled office resembled the library of an English country manor, but with extra features. Country manors usually didn't command floor-to-ceiling forty-story views of the MetLife, Chrysler, and Empire State buildings.

"I can assure you that you've come to the right place," he said.

Then he frowned as the light on his Merlin interoffice phone began to blink. He had explained emphatically to the temp his one cardinal rule — never, ever, ever interrupt him when he was meeting with a client for the first time. With the amount of money these fish spent, you couldn't even imply you had other clients. Didn't she understand that he was about to hook a whale here?

The BlackBerry on his belt suddenly vibrated, startling him again. What the hell was going on? He glanced down at it in annoyance.

There was a message from the temp, entitled 911.

"I'm terribly sorry, Mr. Savage," he said. "I left instructions not to be interrupted." He rolled his eyes, one wealthy, important man to another, bemoaning the quality of help these days. "If you'll excuse me for just a second."

He opened the phone and scanned the message.

NYPD called. Your client could be the Killer! Get out of there!

He heard a strange coughing bark, and the BlackBerry suddenly leaped out of his hand.

Wiping particles of plastic and glass out of his eyes,

Gary tried to focus on the client. Mr. Savage was standing now. He tucked a long pistol into his belt, then turned and lifted the travertine coffee table behind him. It must have weighed well over a hundred pounds, but Savage reared back and threw it effortlessly through one of the floor-to-ceiling windows. A deafening explosion of shards of flying glass sent Gary to his knees, scrambling to hide behind his desk.

"C'mon, Gary. Don't tell me you didn't think it would all come back to haunt you?" the man yelled over the wind that suddenly roared through the office. Paralyzed, Gary watched legal papers fly off his desk in an eddy over Park Avenue.

"Noooo!" he suddenly yelled, making a desperate try to run. He got as far as the edge of his desk before the Teacher shot out both his kneecaps with the silenced .22.

The pain was more incredible than Gary had ever believed possible. He tottered to the edge of the glassless window and almost fell through, just managing to wrap an arm around the metal frame. He clung there for dear life, staring four hundred feet down to the concrete and crowds on Park Avenue.

"Here, let me give you a hand," the Teacher said, stepping over. "No, hold that thought. Make it a foot." Viciously, he stomped the heel of his Prada wingtip into the trembling lawyer's chin.

"Noooooo!" Gary screamed, as his grip tore loose and he plunged downward.

"You said that already, fucker," the Teacher said with a laugh, watching the body twist and tumble through the last few seconds of its life.

When Cargill finally smacked into the plaza out in front of the building, the impact sounded more like a TV set than a person exploding.

The Teacher strode to the office door and swung it open. In the corridor outside, some people were running in panic, while others sat frozen, shivering like trapped rabbits behind their desks.

He trotted to the rear stairs with the gun held by the side of his leg, wondering if there was anyone stupid enough to get in his way.

Chapter 60

EVEN AFTER A NINETY-MILE-AN-HOUR RIDE back into the city, I still couldn't believe it. Gladstone had actually been in Cargill's office when I'd called! I'd missed stopping him by seconds.

I screeched up in front of the Park Avenue office building. Behind the crime scene tape lay a lot of glass and one very, very dead lawyer.

"Shot him in the kneecaps first, then must have thrown him," Terry Lavery said as I walked up. "I'm not the biggest fan of lawyers either, but sheesh." I followed his gaze up the sheer glass face of the building to the gaping empty rectangle near the top.

"Any idea how he got away?" I said.

"Came down the service stairs. We found some clothes in the stairwell. He had his choice of exits. There's seven from the basement and four from the lobby. Must have changed and got out before the first radio cars got here. This is worse than the Yankees losing streak. How long can this guy stay so lucky?"

Beth Peters came over to join us. "You hear the latest?" she said. "Dozens of sightings of Gladstone in the last hour. From Queens to Staten Island. Some woman even claimed he was in front of her on line at the Statue of Liberty."

"I heard on 1010 WINS that a bunch of those clubs over on Twenty-seventh in Chelsea were closed last night because everyone's too afraid to go out," Lavery said. "Not to mention the Union Square Cafe waiter who actually stabbed a suspicious customer at lunch because he thought he was the killer."

Beth Peters shook her head. "This town hasn't been this jumpy since the Dinkins administration."

My phone rang again. The readout told me it was McGinnis. I took a deep breath as I flipped it open, guessing I wasn't going to like what he told me.

I was right.

Chapter 61

RUSH HOUR WAS IN FULL SWING by the time the Teacher got to Hell's Kitchen. A kind of pity had overtaken him as he'd gazed sympathetically at the clogged, screaming traffic before the Lincoln Tunnel.

The sight was almost too painful to behold. The bovine faces behind the windshields. The glossy billboards that dangled above the congestion like carrots beckoning trapped, witless donkeys. The Honda and Volkswagen horns feebly bleating in the polluted air like sheep being led to slaughter.

Something out of Dante, he thought sadly. Or worse, a Cormac McCarthy novel.

"Don't you know that you are made for greatness?" he'd wanted to shout at them as he skirted the plastic bumpers and overheating SUV grilles. "Don't you know you were put here for something more than this?"

He climbed the stairs to his apartment, now wearing the blue Dickies work clothes that he'd changed into before he'd escaped. He knew it was a pretty lame disguise, but the fact of the matter was, it didn't have to be that great. With its millions of people and exits and entrances and subways and buses and taxis, the city was virtually impossible for the police to cover.

The cops had been actually screeching into the plaza in front of the building entrance as he'd left the stairwell. He had simply walked through the bank attached to the lobby and used *its* exit to the side street.

He sighed. Even the ease with which he'd gotten away was somehow making him feel blue.

Safely inside his apartment, he pulled his recliner over to the window and sat. He was tired after his walk, but it was the good kind—the manly, righteous exhaustion that came from true work.

The sun was starting to set over the Hudson, its light washing the faded tenements and warehouses with gold. Snatches of memory came to him as he gazed at it.

Scaling chain-link fences. The heat of the concrete through his sneakers. Stickball and basketball. His brother and he playing in one of the rusted playgrounds alongside Rockaway Beach.

Those were from his old life, his real life, the one he'd

been ripped out of when his mother kidnapped him and took him to rot on Fifth Avenue.

The irrevocable nature of what had happened to him pierced him like a heated needle. There was no going back, no do-over. His life, so crammed full of all the crap that was supposed to make him happy, had been ultimately and completely worthless.

He cried.

After a while, he wiped his eyes and stood. There was still work to do. In the bathroom, he turned on the tap in the tub. Then he stepped into the spare room and lifted the corpse off the guest bed.

"One more," he whispered to it lovingly. "We're almost done." With a tender, caring smile, he carried it to the bathtub.

Chapter 62

HALF AN HOUR LATER, the Teacher went to the kitchen and took a pint bottle of Canadian Club whiskey out of the cabinet above the sink. Carrying it in both hands almost ceremoniously, he stepped into the dining room.

The corpse was now respectfully arrayed on top of the table. He'd washed it in the tub, even shampooed and combed the blood and brain matter out of its hair before carefully dressing it in a navy suit and tie.

The Teacher had also changed into a suit, tasteful black, appropriate funeral attire. He tucked the bottle of whiskey into the inside pocket of the dead man's jacket.

"I'm so sorry," he whispered, leaning down to kiss the pale, lifeless forehead.

Back in the kitchen, he took his Colt pistols off the counter and quickly loaded and holstered them. The cops would be here any time now.

He removed a full red plastic fuel can from beneath the kitchen sink and carried it into the dining room. The strong, faintly sweet smell of gasoline filled the entire apartment as he soaked the body, making the sign of the cross—starting at the forehead, spilling fuel down to the crotch, then shoulder to shoulder across the chest.

"In the name of the Father, the Son, and the Holy Ghost," he said solemnly.

He looked at the face one last time, the sad blue eyes, the half frown on the rigid mouth. Sobbing quietly, he backed to the apartment's front door, sloshing a generous gasoline trail across the hardwood floor behind him.

The Zippo he took from his pocket had a marine insignia on it. He wiped his cheeks with a deep breath and placed the cool brass of the lighter to his forehead for a moment. Had he forgotten something?

He booted the empty gas can back toward the dining room, thumbed back the lighter's starter, and tossed it with a deft casualness, a winning card onto a gigantic pot.

Not a thing, he thought.

The loud basslike *whump* blew his hair back as a ball of flame shot back into the apartment like a meteor. The dining room went up like a pack of matches.

For another few seconds, he stared, mesmerized, at the ink-black smoke freight-training from the doorway.

Then he closed the door, took out his keys, and locked up tight.

Chapter 63

THE DOORMAN OF 1117 FIFTH AVENUE wore a suit and hat that were the same exact hunter green as the awning.

"Can I help you, sir?" he asked as I walked into the lobby.

"Detective Bennett," I said, showing him my badge. "I need to see Mr. or Mrs. Blanchette."

Erica Gladstone, the murdered wife in the Locust Valley mansion, had turned out to be one of *the* Blanchettes. Her father, Henry, ran Blanchette Holdings, the private equity and takeover firm that made companies, and even hedge funds, tremble.

I was there to notify them of Erica's death, and maybe pick up a lead on their berserk son-in-law.

The elevator up to their penthouse apartment had fine wood paneling and a crystal chandelier. An actual butler in a morning coat opened the front door. Behind a wall of French doors to his right, steam rose from a rooftop *swimming pool*—an Olympic-sized, infinite-horizon number that seemed to meld into the unspoiled, twenty-story vista of Central Park trees that lay beyond.

"Mr. and Mrs. Blanchette will be downstairs in a moment, Detective," the sleek butler said with an English accent. "If you would follow me to the living room."

I stepped into a silk-wallpapered chamber the size of an airplane hangar. A gallery's worth of professionally lit paintings hung from the double-height walls above designer furniture and sculptures. I gaped at a Pollock the size of a putting green, then exchanged eye contact with a massive stone Chinese dragon that could not, no way, have fit into the elevator.

The duplex would have been the slickest, most opulent, luxury apartment I'd ever laid eyes on *without* the pool. And I read *Architectural Digest*. Well, at least every time I went to Barnes and Noble.

"Yes? Detective Bennett, is it? Henry Blanchette. How can I help you?" The speaker was a short, amiable man in running shorts and a sweat-soaked New York Road Runners T, coming through a door. I was happily surprised that he seemed more like a kindly accountant than the Gordon Gekko type I'd been prepared for.

"What's this about?" an attractive, fiftyish platinum blond woman demanded sharply, stalking into the room behind him. She wore a makeup bib over a melon-colored silk dressing robe. Both Mrs. Blanchette's appearance and her attitude were more like what I was expecting.

I inhaled deeply, bracing myself. There's no easy way to tell someone that their child is dead.

"There was a shooting," I said. "Your daughter, Erica, was killed. She died instantly. I'm terribly sorry."

Henry's mouth and eyes seemed to triple in size. He stared at me, confused, as he stumbled back against the edge of a mod-looking mohair club chair. His wife sank, dumbfounded, onto an antique chaise.

"What about the girls?" Henry said softly. "I haven't seen them in years. They must be grown now. Do they know?"

"Jessica and Rebecca were murdered, too," I had to tell him. "I'm very sorry for your loss."

His wife gasped, her eyes filling with tears. Henry brought his hand up as if to say something, then lowered it.

"I'm afraid it gets worse still," I said, dropping the third and final bomb in my arsenal of grief—getting it over with as quickly as I could. "We believe they were shot by your son-in-law, Thomas Gladstone. And that he's also responsible for the string of killings that have been going on around the city."

Mrs. Blanchette's tears stopped like a faucet, and now I could see nothing in her face except rage.

"I told you so!" she screamed at her husband. "I told you marrying that trash would be . . ." She collapsed again, unable to continue.

The billionaire hung his head, staring into the oriental carpet between his sneakers as if trying to read something in the pattern.

"We had a falling-out," he said.

He seemed to be talking to himself.

Chapter 64

"IT'S NOT FAIR, Henry," Mrs. Blanchette wailed. "After all my. . . . What did we do to deserve this?"

I had a hard time believing what I heard. But people handle grief in strange ways.

"Is there someplace where your son-in-law could be hiding out?" I said. "Another apartment in the city? A vacation house, perhaps?"

"Another apartment! Do you have any idea how much we paid for the Locust Valley house we bought Erica?"

In her mind, clearly, somebody like me wouldn't have an inkling about that sort of thing. I turned to her husband.

"What was the nature of the falling-out?" I asked.

Mrs. Blanchette rose from her chair like a boxer after the bell. "What possible business is that of yours?" she said, glaring at me.

"As you can see, my wife's quite upset, Detective," Mr. Blanchette said, without lifting his eyes from the carpet. "We both are. Could you question us later? Maybe after we've had a little while to..."

"Of course," I said, leaving my card on the sideboard. "If you think of something that might help, or you want more information—anything I can do—please call, okay?"

As I stepped out of the elevator downstairs, I spotted the green-uniformed doorman talking Spanish with one of the maids, laughing and probably flirting.

They got quiet as I walked over to them and showed him my shield again.

"Detective Bennett, remember?" I said. "Can I ask you a few questions? Won't take a minute."

The maid edged away, and the doorman shrugged. "Sure. I'm Petie. What can I do for you?"

"You know Erica Gladstone?" I said.

"Ever since she was a little girl."

"What happened between her and her parents?"

Petie suddenly looked as green as his jacket. "Ah, I never heard nothin' about that, *amigo*," he said. "You'd have to ask them, you know? I just work here."

I put a friendly hand on his shoulder. "Look, I understand the secret code—don't talk about the tenants. Relax. I don't need you to testify in open court. I need you to help me nail this nut job who's going around shooting everybody. We think it's Erica's husband, Thomas Gladstone."

"Chingao!" the doorman said, his eyes widening in shock. "Oh, my God! For real?"

"For real. Come on, Petie. Let's get this guy."

"Yeah, yeah, you bet," he said. "Erica, okay, let's see. She was a wild kid. Real wild. Drugs. A couple of rehabs. We're talking before her sweet sixteen. When she'd come home from Sarah Lawrence, we had standing orders not to let her in if nobody else was home.

"Then she seemed to straighten out. She married some blue-blood kid from her daddy's firm, had a couple of daughters. But all of a sudden, she got divorced and took up with the second husband, the Gladstone guy. He was the pilot on the father's corporate jet, was what I heard. The parents went ballistic, especially the Lady of the Manor, as we call her. She got Gladstone fired, and cut Erica off at the root." The doorman shook his head knowingly. "Shooting smack when you're thirteen is one thing, but, by God, you sleep with the help, you're dead meat."

"Did Gladstone and Erica ever come here?" I said.

I could tell from his face that he wasn't happy about answering this one, but he looked down at the gleaming marble chessboard lobby tile and nodded.

"One Thanksgiving. I don't know, maybe three years ago. Them and the daughters showed up, dressed to kill—bottles of champagne, big smiles. I figured they'd been invited and I sent them on up. But five minutes later, they came back down again, and the girls were crying like babies. Then that old witch actually tried to get me written up because I didn't call first. Yeah, sorry. My bad for thinking you'd maybe want to see your only daughter and grandchildren on Thanksgiving."

I nodded. "Thanks, Petie," I said. "You just told me what I wanted to know."

This was the next place that Gladstone would hit, I could feel it. He'd been saving the Blanchettes, especially the mother. He was going to pay her back, make damn sure she realized he existed.

I was nervous about even having the thought, for fear of a jinx, but I was pretty sure I'd finally done it—finally gotten one step ahead of our shooter.

Outside, I called Beth Peters on my cell.

"Good news," I said. "Get hold of the ESU, and everybody haul ass over here to Eleven-seventeen Fifth. It's stakeout time."

Chapter 65

AS THE TEACHER WALKED along Tenth Avenue looking for a taxi, he passed a bar that had a fake wagon wheel out front and a row of Harleys parked beside it. The sad old Irish song "The Streets of New York" was spilling out from its doorway into the street. Still feeling his own grief after the "funeral," he decided to step inside.

Maybe that was just what he needed—a drink.

The young woman behind the scarred pinewood bar had the arms of a football player and metal rings piercing various parts of her face.

The Teacher ordered a Bud with a shot of Canadian Club, and nodded to a group of ironworkers having a retirement party in the shadowed backroom.

When his whiskey came, he knocked it back. Here's to you, buddy, he thought, fighting another round of tears.

He was on his second shot and Bud when news of the spree killer came on the TV. He thought about asking the bartender to turn it up, but then decided no. Attracting unneeded attention was a bad idea.

"Fucking cops," a gruff voice suddenly said beside him. The Teacher turned to see a monstrous ironworker, with eyes as red as his long, Viking hair. "Here's an idea, flatfoots. How 'bout taking your heads out of your fat, doughnut-padded asses and just catch the sick son of a bitch already."

"Sick?" the Teacher said. "Ballsy, is what I say. He's only offing rich, yuppie assholes. He's like a vigilante. Doing this city a favor. What's the big deal?"

"Vigilante? What are you? His PR guy?" the tattooed welder said, glaring malevolently. "Friggin' goddamned freak. I'll rearrange your face. I swear to God, I will. You must be as sick as he is."

"Jesus, what the hell am I saying?" the Teacher said, clapping his hands to his face in chagrin. "I just came from a funeral. I guess I'm still all fucked up about it. You're right. I'm really sorry. It's wrong to even joke about the tragedy that's going on. Let me buy you a beer."

"A funeral, huh? That's tough," the big guy said, softening.

The Teacher motioned to the Lordess of the Rings for two more. When the drinks arrived and he set one in front of the welder, he seemed to trip clumsily and sent a bar-stool crashing to the floor.

"Oh, no," the Teacher moaned. "Sorry. I guess I've had a couple too many."

"Yeah, you better start taking it easy, pal," the welder said, and bent down to pick up the fallen stool.

The Teacher broke one bottle over the back of his head, driving him to the floor, and the second across his stunned face. The bleeding man hardly had time to groan as the Teacher stretched his forearm across the tarnished brass footrail and broke it with a ferocious stomp. It sounded like two pool balls knocking together.

So much for not attracting attention, he thought as he backed for the exit.

"Repeat after me, carrottop," he called from the doorway. "Not sick, just ballsy."

Chapter 66

IT TOOK FIVE MINUTES for the Emergency Service Unit guys to get to the Blanchettes' building. After Steve Reno and I walked through the exits and entrances, we decided to suit up a cop as a doorman, put another in the lobby's coatroom, and station a team of commandos in an unmarked surveillance van across the street beside the park.

After triple-checking that our trap was set, I put Reno in charge and decided to quickly do something I'd been needing to do for a long time.

The sun was going down over Jersey when I pulled up my unmarked car beside Riverside Park, behind my building. I walked along a path, crossed a desolate ball field, and crouched down beside an oak sapling in a clearing that faced the Hudson. I cleaned up some cigarette butts and an Aquafina bottle at the base of the tree, tossed them into the bag I'd brought, and then sat down.

The fledgling tree was the one my kids and I had planted after my wife, Maeve, had died. She was actually buried in the Gates of Heaven Cemetery up in Westchester, but whenever I needed to speak to her, which was pretty often, I usually ended up here. Most of the time, I'd just sit, and after a while it would almost be like she was there with me—just out of sight behind me, the way she'd been on the countless picnics we'd had here with our incredibly motley crew.

When I glanced back over my shoulder at my apartment house, I could see two of my kids in the kitchen window. Fiona and Bridget, was my guess. Maybe they were missing their mom as much as I was. Wishing she was still around to take care of them, cheer them up, make things right again.

I waved up at them. They waved back.

"We're hanging in there, babe," I said to the wind. "By a toenail, maybe, but what can we do? I love you, though, if that's any consolation."

When I went up to my apartment, Mary Catherine met me at the door. Something was wrong. I could see a troubled look wavering there in her usually stoic blue eyes.

"What is it, MC?" I said.

"Seamus," she said gravely.

I followed her into my bedroom. Seamus was beached on top of the covers. His eyes were closed and he looked even paler than usual. For a second, I honest-to-God thought he was dead. Then he let out a string of gasping coughs, his thin chest shaking beneath his Roman collar.

Oh, Lord, I thought. Really not good. He'd finally caught our flu. Which, for an eighty-plus-year-old like him, was extremely dangerous. It suddenly hit me how stupid I'd been to even let him come around. I panicked for a second. What would I do if I lost him, too?

But I would lose him anyway, one of these days, an evil little voice whispered in my ear. Wouldn't I?

I shook off the thought, went to the kitchen, and got the bottle of Jameson's from the cupboard. I poured a couple of fingers into a Waterford crystal tumbler and added some heated milk and sugar.

"God love ya, boy," Seamus said to me, after taking a couple of sips. "Now give me a hand out of bed, and I'll be on my way back to the rectory."

"Just try to get out of here, old man," I said. "I dare you. Lay there and finish your medicine before I call an ambulance on you."

Chapter 67

I WAS STILL STANDING over Seamus when my oldest boy, Brian, ran in.

What now?

"Dad! Mary Catherine! In the kitchen! Quick!"

I raced after him into the hall. The kitchen had gone dark. That was all we needed right now—some kind of blackout. Damn prewar building's wiring was falling apart just like everything else. It would probably start a fire. I sniffed for smoke in the walls and tried to remember where I'd put the fuses.

"Psych!" yelled all my kids as the light flicked on.

On the kitchen island, two plates were set up with Tombstone pizzas on them. They'd even made a salad. Trent was pouring Diet Cokes with the dish towel draped over his arm, like a three-and-a-half-foot-tall sommelier.

"Now, hold on a second. You guys are supposed to be in bed," I said as Mary Catherine and I were ordered to sit. "And what did you do with all the dirty dishes?"

"Chill, Pops. It's all being taken care of," Jane said, pushing in my chair for me. "We're feeling better now. We decided you and MC need to take a load off already. You work too hard. You guys should learn to relax a little."

After we were done, coffee was prepared, and we were led into the living room.

What happened next was incredible. The vacuum came on. Assembly lines formed. Toys and art supplies miraculously rose from the floors and furniture and returned to their proper places. One of my little jokers started to sing "It's the Hard-Knock Life" from *Annie* as he scrubbed at a puke spot with a wet paper towel, and the rest of them joined in.

As I sat there on my beat-up sectional, sipping my too-sweet coffee, something brightened in my chest. Though Maeve was gone, she had accomplished a miracle. She'd taken the best of herself—her sense of humor, her love of life, her ability to do for others—and somehow injected it into my silly kids. That part of her would never die, I realized. That could never be taken away.

"Dad, stop! This is supposed to be making you happy," Julia said.

"What are you talking about? I'm thrilled," I said, wiping my wet face. "It's just the Pine-Sol. It always irritates my eyes."

Chapter 68

IT WAS COMING ON EIGHT P.M. when I got back to the Blanchettes' building on Fifth. I parked at a hydrant on the Central Park side, and before crossing the street I rapped a hello on the party rental van where the Emergency Service Unit guys were staked out.

My buddy Petie, the doorman, waved to me as I stepped under the awning. He had a new partner with him now. I grinned when I saw the face underneath the ridiculous green hat. It was ESU Lieutenant Steve Reno.

"Good evening, sir. May I get you a psycho?" he said, touching the hat brim with a white glove.

"I wish somebody could," I said. "No sign, huh?"

"Not yet, but I did make ten bucks in tips. Mike, did you know these Blanchette people are holding a charity fund-raiser tonight? How does that make sense when our guy's only joy in life is offing filthy rich New York types?"

I was stunned. "Are you kidding? A fund-raiser? Is that right, Petie?"

He nodded. "It's been scheduled for months. Too late to cancel."

I shook my head. I still couldn't believe it.

"Which part of 'your psychopathic son-in-law is coming to gun you down' aren't they getting, do you think?" I said as I headed for the elevator. Not to mention that they just learned that their daughter and granddaughters had been brutally murdered.

When the butler opened the penthouse door, I spotted Mrs. Blanchette out by the pool. A maid was standing beside her, and an elderly Latino man in maintenance clothes was sitting at the pool's edge, apparently about to slide into the water.

"What's going on out there?" I said.

"Mrs. Blanchette dropped an earring in the deep end," the butler explained as the maintenance guy submerged himself.

"Why don't they just drain it?" I said.

"It wouldn't be refilled by the time the first guests arrive at nine, sir. Mrs. Blanchette insists on tea lights during the cocktail hour."

"Of course," I said. "The tea lights. What was I thinking?"

The butler's face had a peculiar, pained expression.

"Detective, perhaps you should have a word with Mr. B.," he said. "I'll fetch him, shall I?"

I nodded, wondering what that was about. As he hurried off, I walked out to the pool to try to talk sense to Mrs. Blanchette.

"Ma'am?" I said.

She whirled around like a sequined cobra. The contents of the big martini glass she was holding sloshed onto the maid's dress. I could tell from her eyes and her breath that she'd already downed several of them. Maybe drinking and staying busy were her ways of working through her grief.

"Get me another one," Mrs. Blanchette said impatiently, thrusting the glass at the cowed maid. Then she turned her attention to me.

"You again. What is it now?" she said.

"I must not have been clear about the danger you and your husband are in," I said. "Your son-in—I mean, Thomas Gladstone—is targeting you, without question, as we speak. It's not a good time to have people over. I'm going to have to ask you to postpone."

"Postpone?" she said furiously. "This is the Friends of the Congo AIDS Benefit—in planning for the last year. Steven is flying in from the coast just for tonight. Sumner actually cut his vacation short. Do I have to supply last names? There'll be no postponing anything."

"Mrs. Blanchette, people's lives are at stake here," I said.

Instead of responding to me, she ripped a cell phone from her bag and flipped it open.

"Diandra? Hi, it's Cynthia," she said. "Could you put Morty on?"

Morty? Oh, Lord, I hoped it wasn't the Morty I thought it was. I didn't need that name dropped on me. Not even an ounce of it.

She stalked away, talking. The maintenance guy, up for a breath of air, stared at her back and muttered a Spanish word that was not used in polite company.

"You said it, *amigo,*" I told him.

When she came back a moment later, she shoved the phone at me, with a look of triumph on her face.

"Who is this?" came a harsh male voice.

"Detective Michael Bennett."

"Listen up, Bennett. This is Mayor Carlson. There'll be no more crazy talk of canceling this event. We can't cave in to terrorism."

"It's not exactly caving in to terrorism, sir."

"That's how it will look. Besides, my wife and I are attending, so that's an end to it. You call the commissioner and tell him to beef up security. Do I make myself clear?"

Right, I felt like telling him. A highly visible police presence will really be great for our trap. What did another bunch of dead citizens matter, compared to twisting by the pool with the A-list?

But those were the kinds of thoughts I grudgingly had to keep to myself.

"Whatever you say, *your honor,*" I said.

Chapter 69

AS I WALKED BACK INSIDE, I met the butler returning with Henry Blanchette. I'd never seen a more unhappy-looking man.

"I'm sure you're finding my wife's behavior somewhat odd, Detective," he said.

"That's not my job to judge."

"She has a very hard time dealing with stress," he said with a sigh. "There've been times in the past when much slighter things than this have pushed her over the edge. She goes into denial, drinks, and takes pills, and she's impossible to deal with. But soon she'll break down, and then I'll take her to a discreet clinic, where they know her well. So if you'll just bear with us for a little while longer."

"I'll do my best," I said, actually feeling sorry for Henry.

On top of his own grief and the danger of the situation, he had a crazy woman on his hands.

For the next half hour, I followed the mayor's orders. I called Chief McGinnis, and within minutes a dozen plain-clothes cops and detectives arrived on the back elevator along with the caterer.

I finagled the guest list from the butler and stationed two cops at the penthouse door with it, although it wasn't like they'd really need to match names to faces, what with all the Hollywood, Washington, and Wall Street celebs due to arrive. I got several more men to pose as waiters, and even posted a couple of detectives outside by the roof pool. With this maniac, who knew? He might try to scale the building like Spider-Man, or maybe paraglide onto the roof.

Then I made a security check, going upstairs and wandering through the cavernous duplex apartment. This place could have fit even my family comfortably, and would still have a few rooms left over. I passed by his-and-her master bedrooms, marble bathrooms that ancient Roman emperors would have found plush, a white-on-white French château–inspired library with an ornate, coffered ceiling. Any minute, I expected to turn a corner and find gold and gems just dumped out onto the oriental rugs like pirate treasure.

I was passing by yet another bedroom when I heard human sounds. It was probably just one of the platoon of maids, but better safe than sorry. I drew my Glock and held it down beside my thigh.

But instead of a maid, it was Mrs. Blanchette that I glimpsed through the doorway. She was sitting on a small canopy bed, crying. Her husband arrived at her back and embraced her, his cheeks wet. She rocked back and forth, keening, her fists squeezing and pulling at the bedspread as he whispered in her ear.

This was their daughter's room, I realized as I reholstered. I regretted all the negative thoughts I'd had about her. Despite appearances and her bristly personality, the woman was going through hell. A place I knew all too well.

I retreated as quietly as I could. At the top of the stairs, I spotted a photo of Erica, with a man I assumed was her first husband. They were walking with their daughters on a glowing white-sand beach beside deep blue water, laughing, the wind whipping their hair back.

As I stared, I thought of all the pictures I had of Maeve and the kids. All the happy moments, frozen and captured forever. That was it, wasn't it? What life was all about. What could never be taken away. The moments shared with family and the people you loved.

Chapter 70

I COORDINATED SECURITY from the Blanchettes' grand-hotel-sized kitchen — the farthest, most out-of-the-way corner of it that I could find. The last thing I needed was to be standing by the penthouse's front door when the mayor arrived, so hizzoner could give me another earful.

Despite the short amount of time we'd had to beef up security, we'd managed to do an excellent job. Fortunately, the employees of the Blanchettes' upscale catering firm had worked UN events and presidential fund-raisers, so we were able to get background checks from the Feds without too much fuss.

It was the guests and hosts who turned out to be the pain in the butt. When we insisted on bag checks at the door, I thought some of them would have to be sedated.

We reached a compromise only when a borrowed metal detector was shuttled up from the Manhattan criminal courthouse, on the order of Mrs. Blanchette's good friend the mayor.

About the only high note came when the Cajun head chef, Maw-Maw Josephine, heard that one of the Midtown North detectives had volunteered down in the Big Easy after Hurricane Katrina. Next thing we knew, all us cops were getting hooked up with as much gumbo, shrimp, and corn bread as we could stuff ourselves with.

It was ominously quiet during the first hour, as the most favored guests arrived for the pre-event private dinner. Of course I was relieved that everyone stayed safe, but on the other hand, I was hoping Gladstone would make a move so we could nail him to the floorboards. His unpredictability was burning a slow hole through the lining of my stomach. Or was that Maw-Maw's Tabasco jambalaya?

I'd just done my hundredth radio check with the bored-stiff ESU gang across the street at Central Park, when Beth Peters rang my cell phone.

"You're not going to believe this," she said excitedly.

"What? We got him?"

"Get over here to West Thirty-eighth near Eleventh Avenue, and maybe you can tell me," she said.

What the heck did that mean? And West 38th? That where the French photographer had gotten whacked.

"Come on, Beth, no games," I said. "What's going on?"

"I'm honestly not sure, Mike," she said. "I just really need you over here. The scene'll be easy to spot. It's the building with all the fire trucks out front. Oh, yeah, and the horses."

Horses?

Chapter 71

THE TOP OF THE HELL'S KITCHEN tenement was still smoldering when I pulled my Chevy up on the sidewalk behind a FDNY rescue truck.

Beth Peters came over to meet me as I climbed out, blinking in astonishment at what I saw.

"I told you, you wouldn't believe it," she said.

She'd been true to her word. A herd of spooked-looking horses was milling around on the sidewalk beyond the fire lines. As she and I followed a smoke eater into the building, he told us that a stable of Central Park buggy horses was right next door to the blaze.

Well, why not horses at this point? I thought. We already had an outlaw and gun fighting. All I needed was a white hat. Maybe I could borrow one from that Naked Cowboy lunatic in Times Square.

The walls of the top-floor apartment were even more blackened than the Cajun shrimp I'd just eaten. Beth talked to some CSU techs in the wasteland of one of the torched rooms, then handed me a dust mask before guiding me to a scorched lump of ash in the center.

My stomach clenched like a fist as I stared down at a badly burnt body. The fire had charred and melted its features into a horror movie rictus.

"I had the techs take some dental shots. And we got Thomas Gladstone's dentist, out in Locust Valley, to e-mail us his X-rays," Beth said. "The ME's pretty sure it's a match."

The surprise of seeing the horses was nothing by comparison to that. My jaw just about went unhinged.

"You're telling me this is Gladstone?" I said.

"One and the same."

I know it's not right to disrespect the dead, but I couldn't deny that I was pleased. This ulcer-inducing case was finally over. In fact, I couldn't help smiling, and I let out a long sigh of relief as what felt like a piano was lifted from my back.

"What do you know?" I said. "He offed himself, huh? Literally went down in a blaze of glory. Thank God it's over."

But Beth was shaking her head. I'd spoken too soon.

She crouched beside the corpse and moved her gloved finger to a small circular hole in the temple. Then she showed me the bigger hole on the other side of the head, a jagged exit wound.

"Shooting yourself is pretty easy, but shooting yourself and then setting yourself on fire, well, that's a notch trickier," she said.

"Maybe he did it the other way around," I tried desperately. "Torched the place first, then *boom*."

"So what happened to the gun? Even if it melted, there'd be traces left, but the techs haven't found any. Plus Cleary says there's fly larva embedded in the left upper arm. That means he's been dead for two, maybe three days. And *that* means—"

"Gladstone couldn't have killed all those people," I finished for her. I dug the heels of my hands into my eyes.

"Sorry, Mike, but he's not our shooter."

I cursed under my breath. *If it wasn't Thomas Gladstone, then who the hell was it?*

"That's not all," Beth said, standing. She led me to a closet with a barbecued door and walls.

I winced at the slight young blond woman crumpled up inside it. The fire hadn't gotten to her too badly, but she was still very dead—shot in the back of the head.

"We found her purse. Name's Wendy Stub. Twenty-six. Her business card says she's a publicist at Stoa Holdings, a hotshot Park Avenue South PR firm."

A publicist? What was her connection to this?

As I listened to firemen ripping open the walls in the

other rooms, I wondered if FDNY was still hiring. A midlife career change seemed like just the ticket. Or maybe the stable next door could use a horse whisperer, to help the poor creatures get over their trauma.

Beth was watching me inquiringly. "What now?"

"You're asking me?" I said.

Chapter 72

RUSH HOUR WAS STILL in full swing when the Teacher's cab stopped behind a police car that was parked in front of the Pierre Hotel. It made him a little nervous, but Vinny, the doorman, came bustling over to open the taxi's door like nothing was out of the ordinary. Cops didn't come to places like this to pick up people—they came to protect people. Still, the Teacher kept his face averted and his hand on the butt of his .45 as he got out.

"Welcome home, Mr. Meyer!" Vinny said. "How was your trip? Paris, wasn't it?"

That's where he'd told everyone at the Pierre he was going. In fact, he'd gone infinitely farther. To other dimensions. But now he was home, the place where he'd actually lived for the past three years.

"It was great, Vinny. Especially the food," the Teacher

said, smiling despite himself. He'd liked Vinny since the moment he decided to move into the world-famous hotel. That was right after his mother had passed away, and he'd become the sole beneficiary of the twenty-four-million-dollar Ronald Meyer fortune. He'd decided that he owed it to his asshole stepdaddy to blow every last red penny of the old man's dough. And he'd kept his Hell's Kitchen apartment as a command center.

"What's up with the cop car?" the Teacher asked casually.

"Oh, Jeez. You probably didn't hear. There's this fucking—pardon me—freaking maniac going around shooting people the last couple of days. Killed a stewardess at a hotel on Sixth and a maître d' at Twenty-one. It's in all the papers. They think it's some rich guy who flipped his lid. So they got cops everywhere they got rich people. Which is everywhere around here, I guess. My cousin, Mario, he's a sergeant down in the Village, he says the rank and file are psyched they're making a fortune in OT. Isn't this world nuts?"

"I'm with you there, Vin," the Teacher said, letting go of his gun.

"Hey, any more word on that Food Network thing? I'm sick of that Emeril already, with that 'bam' shtick."

"Patience, Vinny. Good things come to those who wait."

"If you say so, Mr. Meyer. What's up? No bags?"

"Some kind of mix-up out at Kennedy. What else is

new? Be along later, they said. Right now, I just need a drink."

"You and me both, Mr. M. Have a good one."

Inside the Pierre, the concierge, Michael, echoed Vinny's greeting. "Mr. Meyer. Welcome back, sir." The Teacher liked the concierge almost as much as he liked Vinny. Michael was a small, blond, circumspect man with a soft, discreet voice, who managed to be incredibly helpful without kissing your ass—a true quality person.

Without any fuss, Michael went into the mailroom behind the check-in desk and retrieved the Teacher's mail.

"Oh, before I forget, sir. Barneys called an hour ago and said that your final fitting is ready whenever you are."

The Teacher literally felt a sudden cold shiver race like an icy snake down his spine. His suit was ready.

The one he would die in.

That was what he would call a true final fitting.

"Excellent. Thank you, Michael," he said, flipping through his mail.

He stopped when he got to the oversized envelope with the embossed invitation. "Mr. and Mrs. Blanchette," the return address read. He nodded with satisfaction. Someone he knew from his former life had gotten him on the guest list. The Blanchettes had no idea who Mr. Meyer was.

"Michael?" he said, tapping the envelope against his chin as he walked toward the elevator.

"Yes, sir?"

"I need an emergency appointment at the in-house salon."

"Done, Mr. Meyer," Michael said.

"And would you please send up a bottle of champagne? I think a rosé should do it."

"Dom Pérignon? Veuve Clicquot?" Michael said, immediately remembering his favorites.

"How about both?" the Teacher said with his winningest smile, what he called his Tom Cruise special. "You only live once, Michael. You only live just once."

Chapter 73

AN HOUR AND FORTY-FIVE MINUTES LATER, the Teacher stood in front of a floor-length triple mirror in Barneys.

"Does the gentleman like what he sees?" the salesman asked.

The navy cashmere suit the Teacher now wore was a Gianluca Isaia, the bootlicker had told him in the loving, reverent tones of a saint uttering the name of God. The silk shirt was a Battistoni, the cap-toed lace-ups from Bettanin and Venturi.

He had to admit, he looked pretty darn good. James Bond–suave. Like the latest actor, including new blond hair, thanks to the cut and dye job.

"The gentleman loves what he sees," the Teacher finally said with a grin. "What's the bill again?"

The fitter toted up numbers on a cash register. "Eighty-eight twenty-six," he said after a minute. "That includes the socks."

Oh, *including* the three-hundred-dollar socks. What a bargain.

"If the accessories are too pricey, I could show you something else," the salesman said, with a clear trace of condescension in his voice.

Out of his peripheral vision, the Teacher could see that the immaculately dressed little suckass actually had the nerve to roll his eyes.

These luxury store salespeople just didn't learn, did they? Exactly when was the last time *you* dropped four figures on a suit? he wanted to ask the jaded piece of crap. Like so many other people, this guy was practically begging for a bullet in the empty space between his ears.

The Teacher took a steadying breath. Gear it down, he told himself. That's it. Good boy. This was no time for a silly temper blowup. This close to the goal line, this close to making things right.

"I'll take it," the Teacher said, reaching into his Vuitton beside the mirror. His fingers played across the checkered steel grip of one of the two 50-round Intratec Tec-9 machine pistols waiting there under the butter-soft napa leather like loyal friends.

He reluctantly passed them by, instead retrieving his billfold and his American Express Black card.

"Even the socks," he said.

Chapter 74

"YOUR CUTE DOGGY is what his name?" the turbaned taxi driver asked in a heavy accent, as he pulled up in front of the Metropolitan Museum of Art.

"Finishing Touch," the Teacher said. He paid the man and tugged the platinum blond Maltese out of the cab.

He'd bought the dog at a boutique pet store on his way over here. It was going to be his prop for doing recon around the Blanchettes' building. An extremely well-dressed metrosexual walking a lapdog in that part of the Upper East Side would seem like wallpaper.

The Teacher headed up the park side of Fifth, with the nervous little dog straining at its leash. A full block south of the Blanchettes, he stopped and scanned the busy activity out in front of their apartment building. There was a double-parked line of Bentleys and limos, with doormen hustling back and forth as well-heeled ladies and gentlemen exited town cars and stepped under the awning.

One thing struck him as odd. He'd expected extra security, but he didn't see any besides the doormen. Well, so much the better. His lips curved in a smile. His destiny was holding strong. He was at the finishing line, about to enter the winner's circle.

The plan was to gain access with the invitation he'd finagled. If he was stopped or searched, he would simply draw the Tec-9s, now hanging in their custom holsters under his arms, and start firing. Kill his way into the elevator. Go upstairs and blast everyone dumb enough to get between him and the Blanchettes.

In a way, he actually hoped there would be some resistance. The Blanchettes would hear, and it would give them something to think about as he made his way closer.

He was gearing himself up for action when he walked past a van on the park side of the street and heard the sound—a strange kind of squelch. A radio, he realized. Inside the catering van! The cops had the place staked out after all.

That cold, snaky shiver ran down his spine again, and his breathing became labored. By sheer willpower, he kept walking casually along, pulling the dog as if he did this every day.

What was the right move if they challenged him? Shoot? Run? Maybe this was his final chance, and he should go for the Blanchettes right now. Rush across the street into the lobby, guns blazing.

He palmed the cold grip of the Tec under his left arm and thumbed off its safety. Whatever happened next, he wasn't going to die alone. Goddamn cops. Why couldn't they have stayed useless for just another five minutes!

He chanced a quick look over his shoulder. Nobody! They weren't coming. He started breathing more easily. Christ, he'd been lucky.

Two blocks north, the Teacher made a hard left and bolted into Central Park. The mutt started yapping grating on his fried nerves, as he dragged it along the darkened path.

Calm down, he told himself. He was safe. He put the Tec's safety back on. Now he had to think. This wasn't like the Pierre, with a cop car sitting out front in plain sight. The obvious lack of security, with a major event going on, should have tipped him off. Those sons of bitches had set some kind of trap! That asshole, Mike Bennett, no doubt. He'd somehow guessed what the Teacher had planned.

But the Teacher had read a lot of strategy and war books in his day. *The Art of War, The Book of Five Rings, The Prince.* They all essentially advised the same simple, yet not so simple thing. Figure out what your opponent *thinks* you're going to do next, then do something else. Deception is the art of war.

He was halfway around the reservoir jogging track when the answer came to him. An inspired plan to get around Bennett's trap—a little end run. Yes, that was it. Yes, yes, yes. He pressed a shaking hand to his grinning mouth. Bingo. It was perfect, better than his original plan. He'd pulled out a game winner right at the buzzer.

His grin widened as the dumbass face of Detective Bennett appeared in his mind.

"You had your shot, Bennett," he whispered to himself.

He let go of the leash and drop-kicked the squealing Maltese into the darkness.

"Now, it's my turn."

DETECTIVE
MICHAEL BENNETT

Part Four

THE POOR BOX THIEF

Chapter 75

SITTING IN THE DARKENED HOLY NAME confessional booth, Father Seamus Bennett silently blew his running nose and lifted his Sony minirecorder.

"Poor box stakeout," he whispered into the microphone. "Day two."

Sick, my ankle, he thought, sniffling. He'd never been sick a day in his life. Stay in bed? Didn't Mike know that at his age, lying down was a hazard to be avoided at all costs? Who knew if he'd ever be able to get back up again? Stay on his feet and stay busy, that was the thing.

Besides, he had a parish to run. Not to mention a dastardly poor box thief to collar. It was clear by now that nobody else was going to do it. The overrated NYPD was no help, that was for sure.

Twenty minutes later, he was starting to doze off when

he heard a sound — very faint, tentative, a creak that was barely there. Stifling a sneeze, Seamus slowly drew open the confessional's velvet curtain with his foot.

The noise was coming from the middle aisle's front door! It was opening an inch at a time. Seamus's heart rate kicked into overdrive as a human figure, shadowed in the dim glow of the votives, emerged from behind it. He watched, mesmerized, as the thief stopped beside the last pew, stuck his arm up to the shoulder down into the poor box opening, and removed something.

The object was a folder of some kind. So that's how it had been done, Seamus thought, watching the felon slide coins and a few bills out of the folder into his hand. He'd used a type of retrievable trap that would catch any money dropped in the box. Ingenious. For a poor box robber, he was a true mastermind.

Except for getting caught red-handed, Seamus thought as he removed his shoes and stood quietly. Now for the arrest.

In just his socks, he crept out into the side aisle. He was less than ten feet away from the culprit, approaching silently from behind, when he felt a nasty tingling sensation in his sinuses. It was so fast and powerful that he was helpless to hold it back.

The sneeze that ripped from him sounded like a shotgun blast in the dead silence of the church. The startled figure whirled around violently before bolting for the door. Seamus managed to take two quick steps before his socks slipped out beneath him and he half dove, half fell forward with outstretched arms.

"Gotcha," he cried, tackling the thief around the waist.

Coins pinged off marble as the two of them struggled. Then suddenly his opponent stopped fighting and started... *crying?*

Seamus got a firm grip on the back of his shirt, hauled him over to a wall switch, and flipped it on.

He stared in disbelief at what his eyes told him. It was a kid. And not just any kid.

The poor box bandit was Eddie, Mike's nine-year-old son.

"For the love of God, Eddie. How could you?" Seamus said, heartbroken. "That money goes to buy groceries for the food bank, for poor people who have nothing. But you—you live in a nice apartment with everything you want, and you get an allowance besides. Don't tell me you're not old enough to know stealing is wrong."

"I know," Eddie said, wiping his teary eyes, with his gaze on the floor. "I just can't seem to help it. Maybe my real parents were criminals. I think I got bad blood. Thieves' blood."

Seamus snorted in outrage. "Thieves' blood? What a crock." He shifted his grip to the young man's ear and marched him toward the door. "Poor Mary Catherine must be worried sick about you. You're supposed to be home. You're going to have a thief's black-and-blue behind once your father hears about this."

Chapter 76

BY THE TIME I GOT BACK to the Blanchettes' on Fifth Avenue, the party had amped up considerably. I heard dance music blaring as I got off the elevator. In the wood-paneled foyer, I was nearly blinded by flashbulbs as spit-shined executive types and their exotic-looking wives got their social register pics taken.

Was being a cop in this town unbelievable, or what? I thought. From an actual bowels-of-hell tenement fire to *The Bonfire of the Vanities* in ten minutes flat.

The butler had announced that Mr. and Mrs. Blanchette were unable to be present owing to a family emergency but wanted the guests to enjoy themselves. They took him at his word. Glamorously and barely dressed teenage socialites were bumping and grinding in the now dark and strobing party room. I passed a living statue, a transvestite Bettie Page impersonator, a woman in a Vegas showgirl costume, a guy dressed like a bird. I shook my head as he flapped past. Was he the endangered species they were trying to save? No, this event was for a different charity, but I couldn't remember what.

"*Who* is your dermatologist?" someone yelled near my ear as I pushed my way through the crush. "These white truffles are so complex yet so simple," somebody else announced.

I turned as someone clapped me on the shoulder. It was a middle-aged man in a black suit with traces of a suspicious white powder under his nose.

"Hey, I haven't seen you since the open," he said. "How was Majorca?"

"Great," I said, backing away toward the kitchen.

I even spotted one of the *New York Times* editors who I'd almost arrested, talking with some men in suits out by the pool. Probably deciding what tomorrow's news would be.

When I finally made it back to my kitchen command corner, I sat for a moment with my forehead pressed against the cool, soothing granite of the counter.

The newest revelation, still ringing through my aching skull, didn't make sense. How could Thomas Gladstone *not* be the man we were looking for?

No matter how I put it together, I couldn't get it to add up. Gladstone gets divorced and loses his job, and then someone *else* kills his family? And what about the little fact that our eyewitness, the Air France stewardess, ID'd him from a photo lineup? Was she lying? If so, why? Did we need to reinterview her?

I took a break from being baffled to call in to the security detail. Everything seemed normal. No activity on the street. All of the building's ground-level doors and windows had been checked and rechecked.

"We've got it all wired tight," Steve Reno radioed up from the lobby.

"Like my nerves," I radioed back.

"Go ahead and have a glass of Cristal, Mikey," the SWAT lieutenant said. "Or maybe krunk with some of those debutantes. We won't tell. You gotta do something to relax."

"Busting a move is tempting," I called in to my radio. "But fortunately, Steve, all I gotta do is retire."

Chapter 77

AT A DIFFERENT luxury apartment building, the Teacher knelt over the sidewalk grate and started working on it with a crowbar. There were no cops staking out this place, he'd made good and sure of that.

Within five minutes, he was able to swing the grate open. He hopped down inside and silently closed it back over his head. This was a filthy, squalid way of doing things, but if you wanted to get into one of Manhattan's Fort Knox–like, prewar buildings, you had to make some sacrifices.

The beam of his penlight, held in his mouth, played over the concrete where he squatted. The filth came up to the ankles of his three-hundred-dollar socks — mounds of cigarette butts and gum wrappers; sodden, unrecognizable garbage; an empty crack vial.

He shrugged off his jacket, wadded it up, and held it against the dust-caked basement window beneath the grate. He hit the window with a single sharp punch, breaking out the glass. He stilled, listening for an alarm or outcry. There was nothing. He reached in, found the window latch, and squirmed his way into the darkened basement.

He walked quickly down a corridor lined with dusty storage bins piled with beat-up luggage, old wooden skis, stationary bikes, eight-track tapes. High society kept the same crapola as most other idiots, he thought. He slowed as he approached a doorway with the sound of Spanish music behind it—no doubt the super's apartment. But the door stayed closed as he silently moved along.

Past it, on the right, he came to an old-fashioned manual elevator. Inside that, he let the outer door slide quietly closed before easing shut the brass lattice of its inner gate.

That was when he noticed that his hand was bleeding. Crimson drops were rolling off his thumb, splashing on the worn linoleum.

Wincing, he pulled up his sleeve. Christ, he'd sliced the back of his arm wide open when he'd punched the window. How did you like that? He was so jacked up, he hadn't even noticed.

Well, what was a little blood? he thought, clicking off the safeties of the Tec-9s. He pulled back the elevator switch and started to ascend.

There'd be a lot more of that soon.

Chapter 78

WHEN THE TEACHER LET GO of the freight elevator lever, the car did a funny little bounce. He held his breath, listening, as its humming motor silenced with a clack and it stopped dead in the shaft. Still nothing.

The floating feeling of elation in the pit of his stomach was insane now, like he'd swallowed a Macy's Thanksgiving Day parade balloon. How many years of his life he had wasted running away from it, denying it? He loved being at war with anyone and everyone. The thrill of it was better than sex, drugs, and rock and roll put together.

Quick now, he thought, sliding the brass inner gate back silently.

It opened onto a narrow back landing, a service entrance with two doors and some garbage cans. He put his ear to the closer of the doors. Inside, he heard water running, the bang of a pot being put on a stove, loud voices that sounded like children.

He pressed the thumb of his injured hand to the doorbell. Footsteps approached. He was prepared with a ruse about delivering a package to the Bennett residence. Or, if the door opened a few inches on a chain, to just ram it with his shoulder.

But the lock tumblers clicked and it started swinging freely inward.

You've got to be kidding me, he thought. Not even a "Who's there?" Hadn't they heard about the crime wave?

His heart double-dribbled against his chest as the door opened all the way.

Chapter 79

WHEN I DUCKED MY HEAD OUT of the kitchen about ten minutes later, I could see that the Blanchettes' party had kicked into full tilt. The mayor was dancing techno with somebody's trophy wife, and she was laughing her head off like a hyena. All around them, others were behaving more like raucous teenagers than the dignified adults they no doubt were during their day jobs.

I exchanged perplexed looks with one of the Midtown North undercovers who was posing as a waiter.

"I guess it just ain't a party until the guy in the bird costume is deejaying in front of your Pollock," he said.

Then a voice spoke through my earpiece.

"Mike? Uh, Mike? Um, could you get in here?" It sounded like Jacobs, one of the Midtown North detectives.

"Where's here?"

"The kitchen."

"What's up?"

"You, uh, just need to come, okay? I'll show you when you get here. Over."

What now? I thought, heading back to the Blanchettes' kitchen. Jacobs had sounded weird, even upset. Well, things had been going so smoothly, maybe something had to give.

I hurried into the kitchen.

And stopped still.

Jacobs was beside the back door, standing over a young guy who was lying on the kitchen floor. I recognized him as another detective, Genelli, from the Nineteenth Precinct.

"Oh, my God," I said, striding toward them. "What the hell happened to him?" Had somebody bashed him? Was our shooter here after all?

Genelli briefly tried to lift his lolling head, but it thunked back to the floor.

"He's okay," Jacobs said. "Dumbass rookie, he got bored out by the pool, started drinking beer and playing quarters with a couple of the college girl guests. Next thing, one of them comes to tell me he passed out. Sorry to be coy, Mike, but I didn't know what else to do. We don't get him out of here before the mayor sees him, he's going to get fired."

"Him and me both," I said, grabbing Genelli's arm. "Open that back door and ring the freight elevator before anybody sees us."

Chapter 80

MARY CATHERINE WAS DRYING HER HANDS with a dish towel when the back doorbell rang. She assumed it was a delivery that the doorman downstairs had okayed, which happened fairly often. Nobody could get up here without going past him.

But her towel fluttered to the floor as she stared at the man standing there. Her gaze went first to his bloody hand, then flicked to the two evil-looking guns he was holding, then to the wide grin on his face.

"Bennett residence, I presume," he said, pressing the snub-nosed black barrel of one of the machine pistols to the tip of her nose. Blood streamed down his wrist, within inches of her staring eyes.

Oh, my good Lord, she thought, struggling to stay calm. What to do? Scream? But it might enrage him, and who would hear her, anyway? Sweet Jesus—this man here, and the worst of it was that all the kids were home!

Still smiling, he tucked the threatening gun into his jacket.

"Aren't you going to invite me in?" he said. She stepped back reluctantly. There was nothing else she could do.

"Thank you," he said with mocking politeness.

When he spotted Shawna and Chrissy at the kitchen island, he lowered the other gun and hid it behind his leg. Thank God for that, at least. They watched him with mild curiosity. At their age, the sudden appearance of a stranger was just one of thousands of other mysterious things. The flu that had kept so many of the Bennett kids home from school had also wreaked havoc with their bed times.

"Hey, who are you?" Chrissy said, sliding off her stool and starting toward him to make friends.

Mary Catherine swallowed, fighting the urge to dive across the kitchen and scoop the child up. Instead, she stepped forward to intercept Chrissy and caught her hand.

"I'm one of your daddy's friends," the man said.

"I'm Chrissy. Are you a police officer, too? Why is your hand bleeding? And what's that behind your leg?"

"Put a sock in the brat," the Teacher said quietly to Mary Catherine. "This 'why is the sky blue' crap is really pissing me off."

"Go watch the movie now, girls," she said.

"But I thought you said *Harry Potter* was too scary," Shawna said, giving her a distressed look.

"It'll be okay this once, Shawna. Just do it. *Now*."

The little girls scurried away, finally frightened by their nanny's harsh tone rather than by the man who might kill them.

He lifted a carrot stick off the cutting board and bit into it.

"Get on the phone and tell Mike he needs to get home fast," he said to Mary Catherine as he chewed. "You won't be lying if you say it's a family emergency."

Chapter 81

"ALL RIGHT, YOUNG MAN, it's Judgment Day," Seamus said as he guided Eddie through the Bennetts' front door.

Then someone on the other side of the door yanked it open, jerking the knob out of his hand.

Indignant, he started to say, "Well, that's a fine way to welcome—"

His sentence died at the amplified click in his ear. He peered to his left and saw a gun, a big one. A tall blond man in a suit pressed it to his temple.

"Another kid?" the man said, looking at Eddie. "What is this, a day care center? And a priest, too? Wow, that's normal. Now I see why Bennett puts in so much overtime. I'd work twenty-four/seven if I had to live in this psych ward."

Seamus's stomach clenched as he instantly put it

together. This was the serial shooter Mike was trying to catch. He must have fixated on Mike. Talk about nuts.

Maybe he could calm the man down, Seamus thought. Be the fatherly counselor. It was his job, after all.

"I can see you're troubled, my son," he said as the gunman guided him into the living room. "There's ways to make this right, and I can help you. Unburden yourself, confess your sins. It's never too late."

"Just one little problem, you doddering imbecile — there is no God. So I'm going to take a rain check on the sin thing."

Doddering? Seamus thought angrily. Time to switch to plan B.

"Well and good, then," he said, ignoring the gun and turning to stare defiantly into the killer's eyes. "I'm happy to know you'll be going straight to hell where you belong."

The kids gasped.

"Watch it, padre. Shooting kids isn't against my religion. Priests, either, for that matter."

"It's Monsignor to you, asswipe," Seamus said, still glaring at him like they were about to go fifteen rounds.

Seamus heard another, even louder gasp. Then he realized with shame that the killer was right. He was acting like an old fool. He had to tone down the temper and look out for these kids.

The psychopath grinned.

"I like your guts, old man, but mouth me like that

again, and you'll be saying midnight mass at the pearly gates with Saint Peter."

Suddenly Fiona, the closest of the huddled group of children, let out a troubled grunt and doubled over. When the gunman realized what was happening he jumped back. But not fast enough to avoid her upchucking a stream of vomit onto his shoes.

Good girl, Seamus thought.

The man made a face of pure disgust as he flicked puke off his fancy footwear. Then his look turned confused when he noticed that Jane was furiously scribbling the whole scene in a notebook.

"You people are something else," he muttered. "Bennett's going to thank me when I put him out of his misery."

Chapter 82

AFTER THE GENELLI "INCIDENT" was safely taken care of, I got a call from Mary Catherine. She said that Jane had become really, seriously ill—temperature of a hundred and two, and she couldn't stop vomiting. Mary didn't know whether or not to take her to the emergency room. Could I come home right away?

I didn't see any choice. Luckily, things were still quiet here. I put Steve Reno in charge and headed for the door. The mayor, having a photo op in the foyer, gave me a nasty look as I walked by him. Was he pissed that the killer hadn't shown?

Outside, the cold air and lack of headache-inducing dance music hit me like a refreshing tonic. I crossed the street to my Impala, taking deep breaths and rolling my stiff neck. I turned the engine over and squealed a right onto Eighty-fifth.

As I cut through pitch-black Central Park toward the West Side, I went back to brainstorming. Why did somebody kill Thomas Gladstone, his family, and a bunch of other seemingly random, hoity-toity New Yorkers?

Insanity? The guy was a psycho, sure, but he was organized, smart, very much in control. I didn't believe that the killings were random, on impulse. He had a reason for what he was doing. Revenge? Maybe, but revenge for what? There was no way even to guess. Maybe both those things figured in, along with God-knew-what-else.

About all I was sure of was that he had to be somebody connected to Gladstone.

I turned down the Chevy's police radio and turned up the real one to soothe my aching skull. Fat chance: 1010 WINS was going on about the serial shooter. So was CBS 880, so I twirled the dial over to ESPN sports talk.

But there was no escape there, either.

"Our next caller on the Giants Report is Mario from Staten Island," the announcer said. "What's shaking, Mario?"

"My mom, mostly," the caller answered, in a Rocky Balboa voice. "She lives in Little Italy and she's afraid to open her door. When are the cops going to catch dis friggin' guy? Jeez!"

"I'm working on it, Mario," I said, shutting off the damn noise box as Beth Peters rang my cell.

"Mike, I hope you're sitting down. We just got word. The apartment is rented to a guy named William Meyer. Turns out this guy is a military contractor from Cobalt Partners. You know, the company that provides security to Americans in Iraq? The one that's in super-deep shit from that recent shooting incident."

I'd been busier making news more than listening to it, but I vaguely remembered something about it. Shots had been fired at a convoy of State Department officials, and the Cobalt security people had returned fire into a large crowd. Eleven people had died, four of them children. An indictment was expected.

"This William Meyer is the main suspect. He was supposed to be on the *Today* show this morning to defend himself but bailed. Before Cobalt, he was in the marines, Special Ops. That would definitely jibe with our guy's military tactics and shooting skills."

"Any idea why Gladstone was in Meyer's apartment?" I asked.

"Absolutely none, Mike, but at least now we have a name. We're trying to put together his picture. We'll get him. It's only a matter of time."

Chapter 83

WILLIAM MEYER, I thought as I went up my elevator to my apartment. The way this guy had been taking people out, he seemed more like Michael Myers, the psycho from the movie *Halloween*.

There were still so many unanswered questions. I remembered that Gladstone had been in the air force. Had he and Meyer been old service buddies? I would have asked one of Gladstone's friends or relatives, but they were all dead. Shot by Meyer, if our newest theory was right. Had Gladstone pissed Meyer off or something? And what about the fact that Meyer had been ID'd as Gladstone? They even looked the same?

The scent of apples permeated the foyer outside my apartment. On the antique mail table we shared with our neighbors, a silver bowl was brimming with apples, gourds, and cute baby pumpkins. A gold-and-crimson-colored dried-leaf wreath hung on their door.

While I'd been out chasing a psychopath and staring at charred bodies, Camille Underhill, the Martha Stewart clone next door, had done up our alcove in autumnal splendor. I'd have to remember to thank her when this was all over.

Then I glimpsed my own reflection in the mirror above the table, and it stopped me cold. I was as pale as death. I had garment bags under my eyes and a thumb-sized smudge of tenement-fire soot on my chin. Worst, my face was creased by a scowl that was taking on a permanency.

It was time to start getting serious about finding a different line of work, I decided. The sooner, the better.

Inside my apartment, I started down the hall toward Jane's room, but then spotted flickering blue TV light coming from the living room. It was late for the kids to be up, but maybe Mary Catherine had stuck the others in front of the tube so she could take care of Jane. I didn't hear any coughing or retching sounds. Was the epidemic over?

When I first stepped into the darkened living room, my guess seemed right. On the TV screen, Harry and Ron were running down a corridor of Hogwarts, and kids were sitting all over the sectional and various beanbag chairs.

Then I realized that all ten kids were there, including deathly sick Jane. Stranger yet, both Mary Catherine and Seamus were with them, staring at me urgently.

"Why the heck is everybody up this late?" I said. "Did

J. K. Rowling come out with another book or something? Come on, gang, it's time to hit the sack."

"No, it's time to unholster your gun and kick it over to me," said a voice behind me. The living room light flicked on.

That's when I spotted the lamp cord that bound Seamus and Mary Catherine to the dining room chairs they were sitting on.

What!? No, not here! Oh, my God. Son of a bitch!

"I'll say it once more. Your gun, unholster it and kick it over here," the voice said. "I suggest you be very careful. You know exactly how well I shoot."

I turned around to finally come face-to-face with my nightmare.

The witnesses had done a good job, I thought. Tall, athletic, with a handsome boyish face. His hair was blond, but obviously dyed. And he did look like Thomas Gladstone. I could see why the stewardess had ID'd him. This guy looked like an older, slimmer version of the deceased pilot.

Was he Gladstone? Or Meyer? Could the dental records on the body in the tenement be wrong?

I also couldn't help noticing how his finger was very tight on the trigger of the machine pistol he pointed steadily at my heart.

Keeping my hands visible, I drew my Glock from my belt holster, set it on the hardwood floor, and booted it over to him. He picked it up and shoved it inside his belt, revealing the butt of yet *another* gun. Talk about armed to the teeth. Christ, this guy was scary.

"Time for a little man talk in here, Mick," he said, gesturing toward the kitchen with his chin. "Me and you got a lot of catching up to do."

Chapter 84

"NOW, DON'T DO ANYTHING SILLY, kiddies. Just sit still," the gunman said to my family in a peppy, condescending tone. "I'll be listening, and if I hear something I don't like, you'll make me put a bullet in your daddy's head. That'll ruin his whole day."

I could see the kids cringe, and little Shawna, sitting in Juliana's lap, was crying while Juliana tried to comfort her. Christ, that was just the kind of thing they needed to hear after losing their mother less than a year ago. I'd gladly have killed the son of a bitch for it—just for being in my house.

With a gun at my back, I walked into the kitchen and sat at the island, choosing the stool closest to the block of knives by the stove. If I could get him to let down his guard, I'd grab one and go for him, I decided. I wouldn't mind getting shot, but I needed to be sure. If I failed, we'd all be dead.

But the shooter stayed on the other side of the island, on his feet and very watchful.

"I heard you've been looking for me," he said with smug sarcasm. "Well, here I am. What can I do for you?"

I said a quick silent prayer of thanks for my years as a hostage negotiator. I was able to stay calm despite the adrenaline bulging my veins. Let all that training and experience take over, I told myself. Maybe I could talk my family to safety.

Maybe? What was I thinking? *Maybe* wasn't an option. I *had* to. That was all there was to it.

"This is between me and you," I said calmly. "As long as we keep it like that, I'm fine with whatever you want. Just take me out of here or let my kids go. I'll tell them not to talk to anybody, and they won't. Like you said, they don't want to see me get hurt."

"Actually," he said, "this thing is between me and whoever I say it's between. The Bennett Bunch is staying right here."

"Okay," I said. "Then let's you and me leave. I'll do whatever you say and I won't try anything."

"I'll think about it," he said.

"Why don't you tell me what I can do for you?" I said. "You want to get away? I can arrange it."

He shook his head, still with his sardonic smirk, then opened my fridge and came out with a couple of cans of

Bud. He popped the top off one and handed it to me before crunching one for himself.

"Budweiser? In a can? Jeez, Mike," he said rolling his eyes. "Where do you keep the potatoes that complete your Irish seven-course meals?"

He took a sip of his and pointed to mine.

"Go on. Tilt your elbow, Mikey. Loosen up a little. Looking around for me must have been thirsty work. Not to mention dealing with that crew of curtain climbers in the living room."

"If you insist," I said, and took a long hit of the cold beer. It tasted damn good.

"See? There you go. A little levity goes a long way. I knew we could be friends, that you were the guy I could explain myself to."

I took another drink. The way my nerves were jangling, I could have gone through a twelve-pack. I set the Bud on the counter and stared at him with as much concern and understanding as I could muster. Oprah would have been proud.

"Explain away," I said. "I'm more than happy to hear what you have to say, William? That's your name. William Meyer, right?

"Sort of," he said. "My name used to be Gladstone. But my parents got divorced and our family split up. I went with my mom, and my stepfather adopted me and changed my name to Meyer."

So that's why we didn't get a hit on any relatives for Gladstone, I thought, shaking my head.

"That's what this was all about in a way," the killer said. "My turning my back on my name and on my brother."

Much as I wanted to see this psychopathic, cop-killing, walking infection on an autopsy table, the hostage negotiator in me won the day. Meyer wanted to tell his story, and if I could keep him talking, the more time I bought and the more likely he was to relax.

"Can I call you Billy?" I said, in a voice that would make any therapist proud. "I've worked a million cases, but I've never heard anything like this. Will you tell me about it?"

Yeah. Tell me all about how much smarter you are than the rest of the world, you evil prick.

Chapter 85

JUST AS I'D FIGURED, Billy Meyer didn't need any prodding.

"Like I said, when I was ten, my parents got divorced, and my mom got remarried to a very rich financier. I went with her, but my little brother, Tommy, stayed with my dad. Pop was a nice guy, but a drunk. He worked cleaning trains for the Transit Authority, and that was the height of his ambition. As long as it kept him in booze."

He took a slug of his beer. Good, keep drinking, I thought. Maybe I could get him to let me bust out the Jameson's, and we could do shots. He'd get drunk and pass out. Or better yet, I could brain him with the bottle. I was all for that.

"My life completely changed," he went on. "I went to snobby Collegiate and on to even more elitist Princeton.

But after I graduated, instead of heading off to Wall Street like my stepdad wanted, I rebelled and joined the marines instead. I started out as a grunt and ended up in Special Ops. I trained as a pilot, like my brother."

At the top of his class, no doubt, I thought remembering his efficiency with a pistol.

"When I got out of the service, I joined up with the multinational corporate security firm Cobalt. It was great. Iraq was just starting up. It was just like Special Ops only better. All the action I wanted. It was great while it lasted. Cobalt's the firm that's been catching some heat lately. You follow current events, Mike?"

"I do what I can," I said.

"Well, the FBI is actually going to try to charge me with murder. Of course I killed those people. You let off shots in the direction of my men, crowd or no crowd, you're getting them back and then some. The Feds want to indict us for staying the fuck alive? Screw that. I came back to fight that nonsense. Point out the little fact that we were in a war zone. Cobalt hired a PR group to rep us. We were going to go on the morning shows and talk circuit. It was all set up."

He paused to take another sip.

"Didn't work out?" I tried.

"Well, that was before I came home to my apartment here in the city to drop off my bags and found my brother."

The psychopath suddenly looked down at the floor. A pinched, sad expression clouded his face. I wouldn't have believed he had that kind of feeling in him.

"My brother blew his brains out, Mike. They were on the coffee table all over my rug. There was a three-page suicide note on the table. Turns out things had totally turned to shit for him while I was away. He'd had an affair with a stewardess, and his wife, Erica, found out and filed for divorce. The big money, the fancy house—all that stuff was hers, so he was out in the cold. Then came the final blow. He got busted for tossing back a few before a London–to–New York run, and bingo, he lost his job."

This time, I took a sip of my Bud, trying to mask my confusion.

"At the very end of my brother's note was a list. It was a list of people who had wronged him, the ones who 'made him do it,' as he said."

Billy Meyer let out a deep breath and made a "there you have it" gesture with his gun-free hand, looking at me as if he'd just explained everything.

I nodded back slowly, trying my best to look as if it all made sense now.

"Standing over my poor brother's body, I had an epiphany. I'd abandoned him when we were little. I never called him, never wrote, always blew him off. I was a self-centered prick. The more and more I thought about it, I realized I'd fucking killed him as sure as if I'd pulled the trigger myself. My first reaction actually was lifting the gun. I wanted to kill myself, too. That's how messed up I was."

If only you'd gone with that immediate instinct, I wanted to say. *Think long, think wrong.*

"That's when I decided it. Screw defending myself in the indictment. Screw my career, my life, everything. All I ever wanted in life was a mission, and I decided that righting the wrong that had been done to my brother would be my last and final one. I decided to give Tommy a going-away present. Maybe he didn't have the balls to get back at the people who fucked up his life, but I did. I decided to send out the Gladstone brothers with a bang."

So we'd been right, I thought. The victims were people who had wronged Thomas Gladstone. Only Gladstone wasn't the one killing his enemies. It was his brother. We'd gotten the sequence wrong, I realized. It wasn't a murder spree that ended in a suicide, but a suicide that had inspired a murder spree.

"So all that stuff you wrote about society was bull?"

"I believe most of it, I suppose. But it was mainly just smoke to cover my tracks. There were a lot of people on the list. I needed time. I needed you to think my targets were random. Screw with the enemy's head: Tactics 101. It was working, too, until you came along and stumbled between me and the last two people left on my brother's note."

He gestured with the gun for me to stand.

"Which brings us to why I'm here, Mikey. You got in the way of my taking out Erica's parents. You're going to have to make that up to me. Fortunately, I've come up with an alternate plan, and you're going to help. So drink up that beer of kings, pal. Last call. We're going for a little ride."

Chapter 86

THANK GOD, was my first thought. If we got out of here, my family would be safe. That was all I wanted.

At gunpoint, he walked me out of the kitchen, back into the living room. But then with his free arm he scooped up Chrissy, still in her Barbie pajamas, off the couch.

"No!" I yelled. I managed to restrain myself from lunging for him, afraid he'd start shooting.

But Eddie screamed, "Get off her!" and jumped from the couch, trying to tackle Meyer. He went flying backward even faster as Meyer kneed him in the chest.

"Get your rug rats under control, Bennett, or I will," Meyer snarled at me.

"Guys, stay where you are," I ordered the kids, then turned back to the killer. "Billy, relax. I already said I'd help you. We don't need to bring her. Besides, she's sick."

"Her condition's going to get a lot worse if you don't do what I say. That goes for all of you. I see a cop car, this family is going to be short two place settings at breakfast tomorrow." Holding my squirming little girl under his arm, Meyer gestured me back toward the kitchen with his pistol. "Come on now, Mikey. We're going down the freight elevator."

I hesitated for the briefest second as we passed the knives, but then kept walking.

"Wise decision, buddy," Meyer said, jamming the gun barrel against my ear. "I knew we'd start to grow on each other, me and you."

We went down the back elevator and came out the side entrance of my building on 95th Street. Not a soul was in sight as I led him to my unmarked Impala. He put me behind the wheel and took Chrissy into the back seat with him.

"She's not wearing a seat belt, Mikey, so I'd drive carefully if I were you. Go to Broadway and head uptown, and do me a favor. Turn that police band up."

We rolled uptown to Washington Heights.

"Make a left up here," he said when we got to 168th.

Over the building tops, I saw the steel lattice tower of the George Washington Bridge.

"Find an on-ramp for the outbound side," Meyer said in my ear. "We're going across."

Why were we heading to Jersey? Not to load up on cheap gas, that was for sure. Was this his escape plan? It was impossible to guess what was going on in that crazy mind.

I managed to make eye contact with Chrissy in the rearview mirror. She looked scared, but she'd settled down, and was holding up more incredibly than I could have imagined. I love you, Daddy, she mouthed. I love you, too, I mouthed back. Don't worry.

I didn't know much, but I was certain of one thing as I piloted us carefully onto the bridge. This sick bastard wasn't going to harm my daughter. No matter what.

Chapter 87

WHEN MAEVE AND I had first brought home our oldest daughter, Juliana, I used to have this terrible recurring nightmare. In it, I'd be feeding Juliana in her high chair, and all of a sudden, she'd start to choke. I'd put my finger in her mouth, give her the Heimlich, but absolutely nothing would work. I'd wake up sweating and gasping, and I'd have to go to her room and hold a mirror to her tiny cheek and see it fog with her breath before I could let myself go back to sleep.

Because that, without question, is a parent's greatest fear. To be helpless, not able to do anything, when his child is facing harm.

I glanced in my rearview mirror at Meyer, sitting next to my daughter. At the heavy, oiled automatic pistol he held loosely in his lap.

My dry throat felt like it was caked with dust as I

swallowed. My whole body was covered in a cold sweat. The steering wheel was slick with it, practically slipping out of my hands.

You live long enough, I thought as misery shook through me like a low-voltage shock, even your worst nightmares may come true.

I glanced in the mirror again, and this time I saw a pain-filled light in Chrissy's eyes. It was the same look she'd gotten when I'd read her *The Velveteen Rabbit* for the first time. She was starting to really understand how wrong this ride was.

The last thing we needed was for her to start crying, and irritate the human time bomb sitting next to her. When I'd attended the FBI Academy in Quantico, I'd learned that when you're kidnapped, you want to be as unobtrusive and cooperative as possible.

"Chrissy?" I said, struggling to keep the fear out of my voice. "Tell us a joke, honey. I didn't hear today's joke."

The sad light in her eyes diminished, and she cleared her throat theatrically. As the baby of the family, she knew how to perform.

"What do you call a monkey after you take away his bananas?" she said.

"I don't know, honey. What?" I said, playing straight man.

"*Furious* George!" she yelled, and started giggling.

I laughed along with her, watching Meyer's eyes for his reaction.

But they had nothing in them. They were the glazed eyes of a man buying a newspaper, or riding an elevator, or waiting for a train.

I glanced back at the road just in time to see that the tractor trailer in front of me had come to a dead stop. My heart locked as the huge truck's blood-red brake lights and sheer steel wall seemed to rush at us, filling the windshield. I mashed the brakes, with rubber squealing and smoking.

That the car came to a stop inches before decapitating me under the tailgate was a miracle. Add hysterical cops to the list of people God looks out for, I thought, wiping my sweating forehead.

"Get it together, Bennett," Meyer warned me harshly. "You get us in trouble, I'll have to shoot my way out of it. Starting right here."

Yeah, sure, my bad, I wanted to snap back. It's a tad hard to focus when your nerves are stretched past the snapping point.

"Take the next exit west off the interstate," he ordered. "Time to get off this road, anyway, the way you drive."

We pulled onto Route 46, a run-down industrial strip. I stared out at the old motels and warehouses, with patches of deserted desolate Jersey swampland in the spaces between them, trying to assess whether the slower speed and lack of traffic might work in my favor. If I jammed the car into a fishtailing spin, would that throw Meyer off balance long enough for me to grab Chrissy and run? It's hard to hit a target, especially a moving one, with a handgun.

But this guy was incredible with a pistol, there was no doubt about that. Just my luck.

Run or fight—both bad choices, but the only ones I had. Oh, God, help me save my daughter, I prayed. What the hell do I do?

"Look, Daddy," Chrissy said, and an instant later, a violent roar shook through the car. Stunned, I thought maybe I'd actually hit something this time. For an insane instant, the thought of a roadside bomb even flitted through my mind.

It took me a couple more seconds to realize that the noise was from a plane coming in low over our car. As it dropped into sight ahead, I saw that it was a small, sleek corporate jet, landing on a runway behind the high chain-link fence on my left.

What the hell was an airport doing here? Newark was miles farther south down 95. Then I realized that this was Teterboro, a small private airport that a lot of corporations and jet-setters used when coming into New York. It cost a fortune, but it was only twenty or so minutes into the city, and there were no strip searches or waiting in line.

"Slow down and turn in here," Meyer said as we approached a stoplight.

I made the turn carefully, swiping again at the cold sweat now stinging my eyes. Whatever this son of a bitch had in mind, the addition of an airport somehow made it a thousand times worse.

Chapter 88

THE AIRPORT ENTRANCE ROAD called Industrial Avenue was lined with private jet management firms—small two-story buildings with hangars behind them and fenced, guarded parking lots in front. The guard booths were manned with uniformed Port Authority cops, I noticed.

Was this the time to make my move? Would they figure out what was happening before Chrissy, me, and maybe they, too, ended up dead?

I hung on once again, figuring I'd be better off if I knew what Meyer had in mind.

"Stop here," he said, when the road dead-ended. "Listen good, Bennett, because you're going to get only one chance. Turn around, then pull into the first hangar on the way back. They've got only one guard, and that's why

I brought you. You're going to use some of that on-the-job cop juice. Flash your badge and get us in."

"What am I supposed to tell him?" I said, wheeling the Chevy around in a U-turn.

"Get creative, cop, and make it good. Your daughter's life depends on it."

The Port Authority cop in the guard booth was a young Asian guy, who leaned out his window when we drove up.

"NYPD," I said, flashing my shield. "We're in pursuit of a homicide suspect that we believe might have climbed the fence off Forty-six, and be inside this area."

"What?!" the young officer said, squinting in at me. "I haven't heard anything about that. Homeland Security had us put sensors on the wire after 9/11. They should have picked the guy up." His gaze moved toward Meyer and Chrissy in the back seat.

I tensed, silently praying that he would deny my bizarre request, or even drop all pretense and go for his gun. My Chevy looked like what it was, an unmarked cop car. A passenger riding in the back seat would have looked extremely suspicious even by himself, let alone with my four-year-old daughter beside him.

Meyer would be distracted, and I could fling myself over the backseat on top of Chrissy. At least shield her with my body, and maybe get her out of there. Run like hell, somewhere, anywhere. It wasn't much of a plan, but it was looking like the only shot we'd get.

Instead, the cop's face turned even more perplexed.

"Who's the little girl?" he said.

"Her daddy was the one who got killed," Meyer piped in over my shoulder. "Give us a break already with the twenty questions, cuz. This is a homicide we're talking about. Time's a-wasting."

"I can't believe I wasn't notified about this," the Port Authority cop said almost to himself, with a shake of his head. "Okay, come on in. Park over by the hangar while I radio my sarge."

"Nice work there, Mikey boy," Meyer whispered as the stick gate rose. "I appreciate it so much, I'm going to give you and your brat five more minutes of life."

As we drove the twenty yards to the hangar, Meyer sneezed violently, then wiped snot off his face with his wounded hand.

"Your goddamned kids got me sick," he said.

As if on cue, something in my stomach heaved, and I doubled over and vomited all over the passenger footwell. So my dry throat and cold sweat weren't only from my bone-numbing terror, I realized, wiping my chin on my sleeve. The flu had finally caught up with me, too.

"That makes two of us," I said.

"Yeah, well, sick or not, the show must go on. C'mon now. Me, you, and the girl are going out. You listen to me, you two might just make it out of here."

I sat up, found Meyer's eyes in the rearview, and shook my head.

"Never happen," I said. "You want me to go with you, fine. But she stays here."

"Don't leave me, Daddy," Chrissy pleaded.

"What kind of mean father are you, Bennett?" Meyer said. "See, she wants to come." That ugly mockery was back in his voice again. He must have been feeling confident, now that he'd gotten this far. "Or would you rather I finish you both right here and now?"

"You're talking like that cop's the only one at this airport," I said. "Pull that trigger, and he'll call in the cavalry before the sound fades. You know damn well they've got a SWAT team here. M16s, sniper rifles, flashbangs, lots of drill practice. You're good, Billy, but you'll never get past them."

Meyer was quiet for several seconds. "I hate to admit it, Bennett, but you make a good point," he finally said. "That's another favor you've done me, so I'll do you another one back. We'll leave her here. It's just you and me now."

Chapter 89

OUTSIDE THE CAR, my sweat felt even colder, maybe because of the fresh air or maybe because I seemed to be running a fever now. On top of that, my stomach told me it wasn't completely done heaving up its inventory.

The roar of another plane screaming skyward drowned out everything else for a few seconds. As its echo faded, my heart was cut by the sound of Chrissy, crying in the backseat.

The Port Authority cop stepped out of his booth and came walking toward us. His hand was on the butt of his pistol and his face looked wary.

"Just got off the phone with the sarge," he said. "He's on his way over here."

I was opening my mouth, trying to come up with another quick lie, when Meyer shot him. No indication, no warning—just boom. The bullet hit the officer in the cheek, blood sprayed out the back of his head, and he dropped like a soup tureen that had been pushed off a table.

"No shit," Meyer said, crouching to take handcuffs off the downed cop's belt. "What did the sarge say?"

"You son of a bitch," I yelled, and I leaped on Meyer, swinging. It was an incredibly stupid thing to do, but I didn't think, I just reacted. I hit him as hard as I ever hit anyone in my entire life, a right hook to his ear that knocked him off his feet and sent him rolling over the cop's body onto the asphalt.

But goddammit, he got up with his gun clenched in his hand. I was shaking as he placed the still warm barrel in the soft spot under my chin, but he seemed amused instead of angry. He was actually grinning.

"Not bad, copper, but that's the only one you get," he said. "You gonna behave now? Or do I have to go back and see how your little girl's doing?"

"Sorry," I muttered, lowering my eyes.

"No, you're not," he said, then gave me a vicious kick in the rear, aiming me toward the private airport's main building. "But you will be."

The reception area inside looked like the lobby of a four-star hotel. Walls paneled with gleaming wood, leather furniture, marble coffee tables fanned with *Fortune, BusinessWeek, Vanity Fair.* The tarmac was visible beyond the windows.

A pretty, obviously pregnant receptionist was talking into a phone, but when she saw us she froze in place, gaping. The phone dropped from her hand, clattering on her desktop.

"Sorry to barge in unannounced," Meyer said airily, pointing the gun at her swollen belly. "We're just going to head out to the tarmac, okay? Don't bother us, and we won't bother you."

There was an empty executive waiting room through a door on the left. More leather chairs and a hundred-inch wide-screen TV blaring ESPN's top ten.

I jumped about five feet in the air as Meyer suddenly swung his gun around and blew a hole through the screen.

"Why should Elvis have all the fun?" he yelled, shoving me into another corridor. "Fifty-seven high-def channels now, and there's *still* nothing on."

He kicked open a door marked PILOTS' LOUNGE. We passed workout equipment, showers, a small kitchen.

Then the cold hit us again as we went through another door into a brightly lit hangar. Wind whipped through the building, across a steel walkway and stairs. There were tool carts, a portable crane, a mobile scaffold, but no people, thank God. Was he looking for a plane? There were none of those, either. Thank God again.

"Move it, Bennett," he said, yanking me out the huge double doors toward the string of blazing runway lights.

"We're going out there?" I said. "Looks kind of dangerous."

Meyer sneered. "Come on, cop, show some balls."

Striding toward the runway, we saw a plane approaching slowly down the taxiway from one of the other private hangars—a small orange-and-white Cessna, with a loudly buzzing propeller engine on each wing.

"Give me your badge, quick," Meyer ordered me. "And stay here. You move one step, your daughter's dead."

He tore the badge out of my hand and jogged toward the runway, shoving his gun into his belt. Standing in front of the plane, he held up the badge and waved his other hand frantically, like an enraged traffic cop. I could see the pilot behind the windshield, a young man with shaggy blond hair. He looked baffled, but he stopped the plane, and Meyer came around the wing.

A few seconds later, the pilot opened the door and Meyer stepped up into the plane. I couldn't hear what they said over the noise of the propellers, but I saw Meyer snake something out of his pocket and flick his wrist. A telescoping steel baton shot from his hand like a huge switchblade knife. He must have taken it off the dead Port Authority cop along with the handcuffs.

He blasted the kid across the side of his head twice, with a force I could almost feel. Then he reached in, unclipped the pilot's seat belt, and dumped him, unconscious, out onto the tarmac, with blood streaking his blond head.

"He says we can borrow his plane, Bennett!" he yelled at me. "How's that for luck? Get your ass over here."

I stood in the icy wake of the roaring propeller blades,

wondering if there was any chance I could run back to the car and make a getaway with Chrissy. But Meyer had his pistol in his hand again. I saw the muzzle flash and felt the snap of a round whip past my left ear. Before I could blink, another round ricocheted off the tarmac between my legs.

"Come on, Mikey, I want some company. Pretty please?"

I sucked in my breath and headed toward the plane.

Chapter 90

THE INSIDE OF THE CESSNA was as tight as a coffin. And less comfortable, I thought, trying to squeeze my long legs underneath the sharp console on the front passenger side. It didn't help that Meyer cuffed my wrists before strapping me tightly into my seat with a lap belt and shoulder harness.

I stared at the bewildering array of complicated-looking gauges and buttons on the huge dashboard. But Meyer's fingers moved across them with assurance. The propellers seemed to scream more loudly as he pushed forward one of six floor-mounted levers. Then he brought the one next to it up as well, and we started slowly moving.

We were making the turn onto the runway when we saw the fire truck—humongous, bright yellow, lights and siren blazing as it barreled down the middle of the runway to block our path. I recognized it as the Port Authority's Aircraft Rescue and Firefighting Unit. What was their nickname again? Something and Hoses?

A blistering spray of automatic rifle fire suddenly bloomed from one of the truck's side windows, and the tarmac in front of us exploded with puffs from the warning shots.

Holy crap! *Guns* and Hoses, that was it. Those guys were a crazy hybrid of firemen and cops who dealt with both plane crashes and hijackings.

Aim for the pilot! I mentally messaged them, scrunching down in my seat as far as I could.

Although at this point, I was willing to get shot if it meant finally stopping Meyer.

He did something with the foot pedals, and we made a quick U-turn back onto the taxiway. Then he jammed the throttle level up as far as it would go, and we were suddenly rocketing down the lane, dangerously close to the row of hangars.

My breath stopped when I saw the deicing truck that was parked squarely in our way. There was no chance we could miss it. At that speed, trying to turn the plane would have sent it into a violent, out-of-control spin.

Silently I said my last prayer as we raced forward to ram it broadside.

At the last second, Meyer pulled the yoke back. With our wheels practically scraping the deicing truck's top, we were airborne.

Chapter 91

EVEN NUMB WITH FEAR, I could feel my heart beating wildly through every square inch of my body as Meyer rocketed us up. I'd been to several plane crash sights in my time with the CRU. I knew all too well what happened to the human body when it struck something at several hundred miles an hour.

The plane seemed to be standing on its tail end, climbing straight up. I stared out at the ground lights that whirled below, feeling paralyzed with fever and fear.

My mind whirled, too, wondering what Meyer had planned. Where was he heading? Out of the country?

Not that it made much difference to me.

But mostly I thought about Chrissy. I hoped to God she

hadn't seen Meyer shoot the cop—hoped somebody had found her and called home by now.

"You know how crappy it was to lose my brother—not just once, but twice?" he said, raising his voice over the roar of the engines.

I shook myself out of my stupor. All of a sudden, I felt free. I had nothing left to lose if I was going to die, anyway. And I was damned if I'd be listening to his garbage when it happened.

"I'd have some sympathy for you, asshole," I snapped back. "Except lots of people have it tough and don't feel the need to go around shooting innocent, defenseless people and kidnapping little girls."

"Screw that bullshit. When I was in aviation training, they told me, 'Kid, you see those people down there on the desert floor, looking like little ants? Well, we want you to fire these bullets the size of butter knives down on them one thousand times a minute. Don't worry that after you're done, there'll be piles of bloody rags where human beings were standing. Just ignore it.'

"But I'm also supposed to ignore the *real* assholes back here in the States. The ones who make people miserable, who don't give a fuck if they treat somebody so bad it drives them to suicide—the selfish pricks who really make this world a mess. Leave them alone? I think not." Meyer shook his head. "They can't have it both ways. They taught me to kill for our country, and that's exactly what I'm doing. But this time, I'm doing it by my own rules."

And I thought my fever was making me sick. Now this guy was using a war vet trauma to excuse his evil.

"That was a tragedy, all right," I said.

"Killing for this country?"

"No," I yelled into his ear. "That you didn't die for it."

Chapter 92

I SWUNG AWAY FROM HIM and stared out the window, trying to figure out where we were. It was hard to tell, but I knew that we'd taken off in an easterly direction.

The plane ride wasn't helping my stomach any. It was obvious that Meyer's piloting skills were a little rusty. Every few seconds, we'd pitch to the right or left, swoop down a couple of hundred feet and then back up again.

But after we'd been up there a few minutes, he managed to smooth it out.

"Okay, Bennett, I'm ready for the final act," he growled at me. "Time to finish what I started. Pay the Blanchettes a little visit. Plow into their bedroom at three hundred miles an hour, and you're going with me. I told you not to get in my way, you goddamned idiot."

Something in me had known all along that he intended

to kill us both, but I'd refused to really wrap my mind around it. But now it was for sure.

Then I thought, *Oh, no, it's not.*

Although my wrists were cuffed, my fingers were free. I furtively started working to undo my lap belt.

Within another few minutes, flying dangerously low and dangerously fast, we were approaching the giant lit-up towers of Manhattan. I recognized the vast, darker rectangle of Central Park, with its tree-lined pathways and glimmering reservoir.

And I shuddered when I spotted our target—the Blanchettes' Fifth Avenue building. It was directly ahead, looking like it was racing toward us with dizzying speed. In no time, we were so close I could see the tea lights floating moodily on the surface of the rooftop pool.

I gave the seat belt a final yank, and it came loose. Then I lurched as hard as I could to the left and head-butted Meyer.

Seeing stars, I thought I got about as much as I gave, until I saw Meyer's blood-spurting nose mashed flat against his face. He was making a low animal noise as he went for the gun in his lap. I leaned all the way over against my door. Then I ripped my legs out from beneath the console and slammed my feet up against his chin.

The kick landed hard with both heels. His head snapped back and the gun went flying somewhere behind us. The plane was going crazy, careening into a wild arc and plunging downward. I didn't care. I kept on kicking him again and again—his head, his face, his neck, his chest—literally trying to drive him through his door, out of the airplane. With each blow, I screamed like a madman.

I might have succeeded, except he somehow extended the steel baton and whipped it down flush between my legs. I screamed again, this time from pain, and curled up with my eyes rolling back into my head.

Meyer paused to wrestle with the airplane, managing to pull it out of its dive and aim it through the building corridors and toward Central Park. Then he hit me on the forehead. It felt like he'd cracked the whole front of my skull. The world went gray as he shoved me back down into my seat.

His last measured blow with the baton whiplashed my head so hard into the door beside me that the window broke. I saw wheeling lights and blood streaming down the interior of the plane like a dark curtain, before my body went limp and my eyes closed.

I was just about gone, but somewhere deep in my head, a tiny spark of consciousness fought to stay lit.

Chapter 93

MAYOR CARLSON WAS ON THE THIRD MILE of his before-bed elliptical machine trek when Patrick Kipfer, one of his deputy chiefs, stuck his head in the doorway of Gracie Mansion's basement gym.

"The Commissioner," he said. "I forwarded it to your cell."

The mayor hit the elliptical's Pause button and lowered the volume of the hanging TV before he lifted his phone.

"Commissioner?" he said.

"Sorry to bother you, Mort," Commissioner Daly said. "We got a hostage situation. One of our homicide detectives, Mike Bennett. His family said a man came into their apartment and abducted him and his four-year-old daughter."

Bennett? the mayor thought. Wasn't he the cop who

was at the Blanchettes, the one who'd wanted to shut down the party?

"Tell me it isn't the spree killer."

"We have to go on that assumption."

Carlson wiped his sweating face on his NYU T-shirt.

"Goddammit. Do we have any idea where they went? Any ransom demand? Any contact?"

"Nothing so far," Daly said. "This happened less than an hour ago. His unmarked vehicle is missing, so we've notified state troopers and our guys."

"I know you're doing everything you can, Commissioner," the mayor said. "You think of any way I can help, let me know immediately."

"Will do."

The mayor stared at the Pause button on the elliptical after he placed his cell back down. Should he call it a night? No, he decided, reaching for the button. No excuses. His cholesterol was through the roof. Not to mention how tight his suits were getting these days, with all the fundraiser food. Just do it, and all that garbage. Besides, what good would he be to the city if he had a heart attack?

He was just getting back up to pace when Patrick returned and stuck his head in the doorway.

This time, the mayor hit the Stop button as he lifted his cell phone.

"The commissioner again?"

"The other commissioner," his aide said. "Frank Peterson, from Port Authority Police."

The mayor gave him a puzzled look. Christ, when it rained, it poured. What did the *Port Authority* commissioner want?

"Frank? Hi. What can I do for you?" the mayor said.

"One of our cops, a young guy named Tommy Wi, was just shot dead out at Teterboro," Peterson said somberly.

The mayor shook his head in disbelief as he stepped off the machine. First a kidnapping, then a murder?

"That's . . . ," he started to say, but couldn't find a word. "What happened?"

"Just before Officer Wi was shot, he called in and said an NYPD detective had asked for access to the tarmac. Two minutes later, a twin-engine Cessna was hijacked by a pair of men. Nearby, we found an NYPD unmarked radio car with a little girl inside, saying her daddy is Detective Mike Bennett."

"Mr. Mayor" his aide Patrick said, coming in again with another cell phone in his hand. "It's important."

Christ, another call? He had only two ears.

"Sorry, Frank, can you hold a minute?" he said to the Port Authority commissioner. What now? he thought as Patrick traded phones with him.

"Hello, Mayor Carlson," said a crisp male voice. "Tad Billings, assistant director of Homeland Security. You've heard about the hijacking at Teterboro?"

"I'm starting to," Carlson said curtly.

"FAA radar is tracking the Cessna over the Hudson, heading east, inbound toward the city. An F-15 has been scrambled and is en route from McGuire Air Force Base in south Jersey."

"What?! An F-15?!"

"Part of the new Federal Homeland Security statute," Billings said. "Teterboro spoke to the FAA. FAA spoke to North American Air Defense. NORAD scrambled a jet. I just got off the phone with General Hotchkiss. The jet pilot has been authorized to shoot the Cessna down."

"You can't be serious. We think there's a cop on that plane, an NYPD homicide detective. He's being held hostage!"

"The air force has been made aware of that. They'll try to establish radio contact, but time constraints and the hijacker's unpredictability are important factors. This is a major threat to your entire city, sir. As harsh as it is, as reluctant as we are to put the life of an innocent on the line, we unfortunately have to prepare for the worst."

And he'd worried about having a heart attack? A heart attack would have been a breeze, compared to this impossible-to-keep-up-with insanity.

"Is our conversation being recorded?" the mayor finally said.

"As a matter of fact, yes, it is."

"Then let me state for the record that you are all a bunch of heartless bastards."

"Duly noted, Your Honor," Billings said without hesitation. "I'll make sure to keep you up to date."

Chapter 94

THE F-15E STRIKE EAGLE was less than a mile out from McGuire Air Force Base when the pilot, Major James Vickers, fired the afterburners. Sapphire-blue flame shot from the jet pipes of the aircraft's Pratt and Whitney F100 engines, and the state of New Jersey was suddenly rolling beneath him like the belt of a treadmill turned to sprint.

Located eighteen miles south of Trenton, McGuire for the most part was a C-17 cargo plane and KC-10 tanker refueling plane base. But in the aftermath of 9/11, in order to cover all future threats to New York City, a contingent of the 336th Fighter Squadron had been discreetly re-deployed sixty-four miles to the north. At the aircraft's top speed of nine hundred miles an hour, that distance evaporated in an eyeblink.

Which was what happened a moment later as the F-15 double-boomed, breaking the sound barrier.

Like opening a can of biscuits, Vickers thought with a shake of his flight helmet. You know the pop is coming, but damn if it don't always surprise you.

"Okay, we've got him," said Captain Duane Burkhart, the weapons systems officer, or wizzo, as they were called, sitting in the cockpit seat behind Vickers. "The Cessna's transponder is still on. It's lighting up the LANTIRN screen like a Christmas tree."

LANTIRN was the plane's Low Altitude Navigation and Targeting Infrared for Night system. Since the small plane's transponder was still operational, they could actually fire a missile now if they wanted.

"You heard the CO," Vickers said. "We need to try radio contact first, and at the very least we need a visual."

"Yes, sir," Burkhart said with uncharacteristic nervousness in his voice. "Just letting you know."

No wonder Duane had the jitters, thought Major Vickers. He'd envisioned many combat missions upon graduating from the Air Force Academy six years before. But never one that took place over the Jersey Turnpike.

"This is wild, isn't it?" Burkhart said as the New York City skyline, unmistakable from seven thousand feet, approached rapidly on their right. "Those bastards hitting the towers was the reason I joined up."

"You're a true patriot," Vickers said sarcastically, dropping altitude and buzzing by the Statue of Liberty. "I hitched up for the subsidized on-base bowling."

"You should be able to get that visual now," Burkhart said.

"Roger that." Vickers spotted the blip that appeared on the canopy's electronic air-to-air combat heads-up targeting display. The Cessna was moving south down the Hudson three, maybe four miles ahead, and closing fast.

Vickers flicked a button at the top of his joystick with his thumb and the pairs of AIM Sparrow and AIM Sidewinder missiles, nestled under the wings, hummed as they powered on, high-explosive attack dogs tugging the chain.

He had already been given the firing order by the time he'd finished strapping in. He didn't need to know who or what was on the Cessna—only to knock it out of the sky.

"Cessna Bravo Lima Seven Seven Two," Burkhart said into the radio. "This is the United States Air Force. Turn around and land back at Teterboro or you will be brought down. This is your only warning."

The Cessna pilot's voice crackled back. "Don't bullshit me, ace. I used to fly one of those things. You can't risk it. You could wipe out half of Manhattan."

"That's a risk we're prepared to take," Burkhart said. "I repeat. This is your final warning."

This time there was no answer.

Had the guy really been a fighter pilot? Vickers wondered. If it was true, that added a wrinkle.

He rolled his neck as the targeting radar lock alarm suddenly sounded.

"Well, you can't say we didn't warn 'em," he said.

The siren quit as the Cessna suddenly swung a hard left west in between the stone and glass towers. It was in Manhattan airspace now, somewhere around 80th Street.

"No!" Burkhart cried. "Shit on a stick! We're too late!"

"Keep your shirt on," Vickers said, jogging the joystick between his knees to the right, screaming the dull silver-colored jet in over the West Side. He was coming over Central Park a split second later when the Cessna reappeared ahead above Columbus Circle, then immediately vanished again, weaving through the city's high-rises, using them for cover.

Though the missile lock siren came back on, he knew he couldn't chance a missile now. That bastard in the Cessna was right. If he missed, a big chunk of midtown Manhattan would be history.

Vickers squinted beneath his flight visor as his gloved finger reached for the trigger of the twenty-millimeter Gatling gun. He kept it there, waiting for his chance.

Chapter 95

I WAS WIDE AWAKE when I heard Meyer's radio exchange with the fighter pilot, although I was wishing I wasn't. I didn't know which hurt worse, my head or my groin.

"The hell with the Blanchettes," Meyer said, talking to himself now. He was ignoring me, assuming I was unconscious or dead. "Why waste this stellar opportunity on those old fools? Let's hit this fucked-up country where it'll hurt the most — the Big Apple's pride and joy. *Then* they'll read my Manifesto of Nonsense."

I stayed slumped in my seat, but opened my eyes just enough to see that we were rocketing southward down Fifth Avenue.

Straight toward the glittering, spire-topped, man-made mountain face of the Empire State Building.

One more try, I thought, gritting my teeth against the

pain. I was going to die in a fiery explosion anyway. Maybe I could keep us from taking anybody else along—except for the psycho beside me.

Meyer hadn't bothered to strap me back into my seat. Quietly, I took a long, deep breath.

Then, with every ounce of strength I could muster, I threw my left elbow up into his Adam's apple.

He reared backward, clutching his throat with one hand and clawing at my face with the other. I lunged into him, pinning him against his door and grabbing the wheel.

"We're going out over the bay," I screamed into his headset microphone. "Shoot us down!"

For the next few seconds I had the edge of surprise, and I managed to wrestle the plane into a sharp westward arc. Banking perilously, we skirted the northwest corner of the Empire State by no more than a couple hundred yards.

But Meyer was strong and he came back, pounding at my face and trying to regain control. As the plane yawed wildly from side to side, we battled like caged panthers, snarling, punching, butting heads—both of us injured, both desperate. Once again, we were losing altitude fast.

But this time we were heading out over the bay. I clung to the wheel with everything I had to keep us on that course, my shoulders tensed for the fireball from the fighter jet that was going to blow us into cinders any second.

"Our Father who art—" I started mumbling through my teeth, as the expansive emptiness of the last sight I would ever see raced up to meet me.

Then I heard a high-pitched sort of whining sound.

Sweet Jesus, this is it, I thought.

An instant later came one long, continuous, eardrum-rupturing string of explosions that tore the roof and entire back of the plane away like wet tissue paper.

But I was still there, still alive. I could see streaking fire behind us, but it was a trail of burning fuel, not the entire plane exploding.

My mind was scrambling to rectify that when I realized that our gliding dive was turning into a plummeting headlong fall. The bolts of my seat groaned as we shook and rattled, and my shoulder harness bullwhipped my chest.

Strangely, it brought me a window of peace. Not the kind of light at the end of the tunnel that people who thought they were dying sometimes describe, but just calm.

An instant later, we hit with a tremendous splash, like a returning NASA shuttle.

Chapter 96

THE IMPACT WAS CRUSHING, slamming me around the cockpit, but we still had enough forward momentum to skid across the water's surface for a few more seconds. Otherwise, it would have been like smashing into concrete. That, and the fact that I'd been wedged in tight with Meyer's harnessed body when we hit, was probably what saved me.

As I tried to believe that I was still alive, I felt something wrong with my neck. I wiggled my fingers to see if I was paralyzed. They would barely move, but I realized that was because my wrist was broken. Half the dashboard gauges were now sitting in my bleeding lap. But apparently, my neck was only wrenched, and the rest of me was more or less intact. I was able to get my arms going, then my legs.

Burning debris was scattered all around on the dark

surface of the bay, and water was pouring inside, already covering my ankles, as what was left of the plane sank fast.

Then came a massive flash of orange and a blast of intense heat from the pilot-side wing. Pitch-black smoke that smelled horribly of burning plastic seared my face. Another fuel compartment must have gone up. The flames surged ferociously, eating into the plane's interior. Within half a minute, they would engulf it — and me.

Meyer was still strapped into his seat, unmoving — knocked out by the impact, or dead.

I wasn't about to find out which.

With my unbroken hand and my last bit of strength, I pulled myself out of the now doorless passenger-side threshold and dropped into the frigid water. Gasping, I eggbeater-kicked backward as fast as I could.

Then, through the smoke, I saw movement inside the plane — something struggling in the flames. No! It was Meyer.

Clothes on fire, he rolled out the same doorway I'd just departed. Both he and the flames disappeared as he hit the water with a sizzling splash.

He surfaced right next to me! I lurched away, kicking at him, as he clawed at my eyes with a burnt hand, making a sound that was like an animal screech.

That was when the weirdest thing of all happened. A euphoric, druglike rush swept over me, and my face split into a huge smile. I swung my arm around his neck in a headlock, threw my weight on top of him, and took us both under.

The sound of the world ceased as I dragged him down through the cold, dark water. With newfound strength, I turned up the pressure, throttling him to crush his throat against his spine.

It was glorious.

In my entire life, I had never been as confident or as single-minded as I was at that moment. If there was one outcome that I was sure of in all of my existence, it was that this evil thing I held in an unbreakable headlock, this murderous bastard who had threatened my family and very nearly murdered me, wasn't ever going to make it up into the land of living again. I was going with him, but it was the best possible way I could go.

Time disappeared from my mind. I had no idea how much of it passed before he stopped struggling. But finally, as the air in my lungs gave out, so did my strength. I held onto him until the last possible instant before he slipped out of my fading grip.

Alone, I kept on twisting through the water—up, down, I didn't know which, and it didn't matter. I was done for, numb, too weak to move. My aching, burning lungs screamed for air. In a few more seconds, my body would be forced to inhale cold salt water.

But even as I paid the ultimate price, that peace was still with me.

Suddenly, ahead in the water, I saw a pale luminous

form floating toward me. It had to be a hallucination. I had just been through about as much trauma as a human being could endure.

I stared at it in terror as it came closer. Then, with certainty, I knew everything was okay.

Because it was my wife, Maeve.

Everything fell into place. She was the reason I'd survived the crash—my guardian angel, watching over me just like I'd prayed for her to do.

But as I reached out to touch her glowing hand, she shook her head sadly and vanished.

The next thing I knew, there were other human shapes around me—big dark ones, with nothing ethereal about them. Rough hands gripped me and something rubbery was shoved between my teeth.

With my mouth forced open, I couldn't hold my breath any longer. The dam burst, and my starving lungs sucked in desperately.

But instead of the bilgy water I'd been braced for, it was pure, sweet air—from the Aqua-Lung of a Coast Guard diver, I learned soon afterward, one of a team who'd helicoptered in to intercept the crashing Cessna, and plunged into the chilly bay to find me.

When those heroes got me back to the surface, other choppers and craft from the Coast Guard and city authorities were converging on the site, to contain the fire and search for survivors.

Thank God, I was the only one of those.

Run for Your Life

The crazy events weren't quite over yet. After the Coast Guard guys dragged me onto the deck of a cutter, I stood up and actually tried to dive back in. It took two paramedics to strap me, kicking and screaming, into a stretcher.

"Take it easy, Detective," one of them said, trying to calm me. "The pilot's gone. It's over."

"To hell with him!" The muscles in my face and throat felt like they were tearing as I yelled out at the flame-filled dark water.

"Maeve!" I screamed. "Maeve!"

DETECTIVE
MICHAEL BENNETT

Epilogue

HOCKEY STYX

Chapter 97

IN ADDITION TO MY WRIST, I'd broken an ankle and three ribs, which put me in the hospital for the next week. NYPD cops don't get paid all that much, but our health insurance is hard to beat, thank God.

The pilot of the F-15 that shot us down, Major Vickers, actually came to my room the night before I got out, in order to apologize.

"Are you kidding me?" I'd said, clapping the baby-faced twenty-eight-year-old on the back. "With that freak, I should have called in an air strike sooner."

A month later almost to the day, I hobbled into Holy Name Church, still on crutches. The altar looked like a formal garden. When the organ started, it played Handel's *Water Music*—Maeve's favorite.

We'd decided that her memorial would be entirely life-affirming, and all that sort of thing. We were even holding it on her birthday instead of the anniversary of her death.

So why, then, as the sad sweet chords swelled through me, did every cell in my body want to start sobbing?

I heard someone clear his throat in the vestibule behind me. It was my son, Brian. He was wearing a white robe, holding a brass crucifix. His fellow altar boys, Eddie and Ricky, stood just behind him with glowing white candles.

Father Seamus was approaching, checking his watch. "If you would be so kind," he said, glaring at me.

"I'll start when you do," I said.

"Mike, a moment," Seamus said in a serious tone as he led me over to the alcove where they did baptisms.

I thought I knew the sermon he was going to deliver. How much of a wretch I'd been in the last year. How I'd been too sarcastic, too spiteful, too pissed off. How I had to try to lose my anger or it would eat me up. He would have been right, too. I needed to stop. Stop being so hateful. Life was too short. If the Teacher taught me anything, it was that.

"Mike, listen," Seamus whispered as he put a warm arm over my back. "It's been almost a year now, and I just wanted to say how proud I am of you the way you've been holding your family together. Maeve's proud of you, too. I know she is."

What? I thought.

"To your seat now, boy. I have a mass to start."

I hurried past pews packed with friends and family to the front row.

Chrissy smiled, as she did what she called "nuggling" in next to my waist and held my hand. She was fine now. In the first days after the incident, I'd noticed every so often a heart-sickening look of sadness pass across her cherub's face, especially when the gang came to see me at the hospital. But recently, she'd started doing what kids do — moving on.

Something I could probably take a lesson from.

After the Gospel, Jane stood up and read — a poem by Anne Bradstreet, "In Reference to Her Children," which she'd found folded in the back of one of Maeve's cookbooks.

"My mom taught us exactly what Anne Bradstreet wanted to teach her kids," Jane said, clearing her throat. "*What was good, and what was ill, What would save life, and what would kill. Thus gone, amongst you I may live, And dead, yet speak and counsel give. Farewell, my birds, farewell, adieu, I happy am, if well with you.*"

That was it. I couldn't hold it back. I started crying. And believe me, I wasn't the only one. I hugged Jane tight as she returned to the pew.

After the ceremony, the girls surprised me with a picnic lunch in Riverside Park. I looked out over the Hudson, remembering seeing Maeve as a glowing angel in the water. If that was just a hallucination, so be it. Bring them on.

But a part of me, the best part, didn't think so.

I would see her again one day. Before, I had only hoped it was true, but now I *knew* it was.

I watched Eddie and Brian tossing a football. The doctor had told me my ankle wouldn't be ready to walk on for another couple of weeks, but what did doctors know? I dropped my crutches, hobbled out to join them, and intercepted a pass. Chrissy and Shawna leaped up immediately, and I let them tackle me. That's when the rest of my crew piled on. Even Seamus, who actually stripped the ball from my hands before merrily landing on my chest.

I closed my eyes as Meyer's ugly words filled my ears.

Is this all life is worth? This is what gets you out of bed in the morning?

You better believe it, you son of a bitch, I thought. And wherever you are, I hope you're *still* burning.

Chapter 98

WHEN WE GOT BACK to our building, there was a commotion at the entrance—protesters of some sort, circling in front of a News 4 camera, and other media people with microphones.

One of the picketers was holding up a sign that said KILLER COP.

What? There couldn't actually be a group of people who were angry that Meyer was dead!

But wait a second. This was New York City we were talking about. Of course, there could be.

Then, on another of the signs, I saw a picture of a young black man. Beneath it, big bold letters read: KENNETH ROBINSON WAS MURDERED. DOWN WITH THE NYPD!

I was stunned. These people were protesting the drug

gang hit man's death up in Harlem, from what seemed like ten years ago.

Before I could shut my unhinged jaw, my kids went running into the crowd. My God, what were the little maniacs doing? I watched helplessly as they squirreled through the line of picketers to the guy holding the shoulder cam. Then, taking turns, they just let loose.

"My dad's a hero!"

"He's the best person in the world!"

"My dad's great. You sure ain't!"

Eddie stayed frozen for a few seconds.

Then he shouted, "Ah, up yours with a hockey stick!"

The reporters thronged around me, hollering questions. I kept my cool and just shook my head. With the heroic assistance of my doorman, Ralph, I managed to wrangle my nutty gang inside the building.

"Guys, you can't do or say things like that," I told them, but Seamus, ignoring me, whooped and delivered high fives to everyone.

Ralph hurried over as we got to the elevator. "Mr. Bennett, please," he said anxiously. "The press say they want one statement from you. Then they go." It was clear that he really wanted them away from his building.

"Okay, Ralph, I'll take care of it," I said.

When I got back to the front door, the media people thrust an aluminum bouquet of microphones under my chin. I cleared my throat loudly.

"I do have a statement to make after all," I said. "I agree with my kids one hundred and fifty percent. Good-bye, everyone. And before I forget, up yours—each and every one of you—with a hockey stick."

Read on as James Patterson tells us more about
Run for Your Life and the Detective Michael Bennett series

Michael Bennett is one of my favourite heroes so far. He's got ten kids, which definitely brings a certain amount of craziness into his life. His wife was really the one responsible for adopting all these kids, who are all sorts of ages and hues and whatever. Then she dies, so Michael's a single father with all of these kids and he gets into these terrible police dramas.

Run for Your Life involves a spree killer on the loose in New York. He's a really interesting bad guy: he has a grudge, he's quite bright, he's a really good chef – he's got these things that shouldn't go together. Also, Michael's got a nanny from Ireland who's starting to like him, and he's starting to like her, so that's getting complicated. It's a good story.

We have a TV series which will be out next year. We got together with the show-runner from *CSI* originally and then *Bones*, and he's real, real smart. So I think it's going to be a great show. It's called '*The CRU*', with Michael Bennett as the star.

Do you have hopes to make this another long-running series?
I always have hopes to make them all long-running series, although God knows how many series I'm going to have out there after a while! I have written three Michael Bennett novels so far. I think two and three, *Run for Your Life* and *Worst Case*, are even better than *Step on a Crack*. When I start these books I always hope that they're going to be everything I want them to be, but it doesn't always work out that way. *Run for Your Life* turned out as well, or better, than I hoped it would.

Where did you get your idea for the series?
I think that it had to do with this notion of a single father of ten kids in a very tense job, which seemed to me to be the acid test

for what most of us go through: we have a family or we have responsibilities and we have this job which wants us 24/7. How do you somehow manage to make sense of that and balance it? That's what Michael Bennett does every day. I think most of us can really identify with that and say, 'Jesus, how does this guy get through his day?'

How do you name your characters?
I don't remember how this name came about. I like the name Michael, it's a nice name. I would choose Michael Bennett over James Patterson as a name. So if you happen to see books from Michael Bennett, you know that I changed my name.

In the book a killer called 'the Teacher' terrorises New York City. Did you have any teacher terrors growing up?
This is a weird story: I had Christian Brothers in High School, and we actually invited this Brother back for our reunion one year, which is kind of amazing when you think about it. We had this guy for Math and Science; every class he would come in and he would say, 'Who doesn't have their homework?' Whoever didn't would stand up and he'd walk up and say:

    'Mr Patterson, do you know what's going to happen now?'

    'Yes Brother'

    'Do you know why?'

    'Yes Brother'

    BOOM! He'd whack you. Then go to the next kid, same thing – every class, all year. We had Math in the morning so that's when people would get whacked. By the afternoon, for Science, everybody would have their homework done because they'd do it during lunch. So I suppose that Brother would qualify as a terror, although we kind of liked it, which is bizarre.

Worst Case

James Patterson
& Michael Ledwidge

**Detective Michael Bennett already has ten kids – and now
he must protect the children of Manhattan's wealthiest
citizens from a cold-blooded killer.**

Children of New York's elite are being abducted and held hostage.
But the criminal doesn't crave money – he only wants to test these
privileged kids to see if they know the price others pay for their
luxurious lifestyles. A wrong answer has fatal consequences.

To Detective Michael Bennett, it is clear that these murders are
only the beginning. Their killer has insanely grand ambitions – and
the entire city is about to be brought to its knees. With all of New
York in chaos, Bennett teams up with FBI agent Emily Parker and
the two set out to capture the mastermind before he sets in motion
his ultimate plan – a deadly lesson for the entire world.

Century · London

Turn the page for a sneak preview of

WORST CASE

DETECTIVE
MICHAEL BENNETT

Chapter 1

BOUND IN THE dark, Jacob Dunning thought about all the things he would give for a shower.

All his possessions? Done. One of his toes? In a heartbeat. One of his fingers? Hmmm, he thought. Did he really need his left pinkie?

Unidentified mudlike filth stuck to his cheek, his hair. Wearing only his NYU T-shirt and boxers, the handsome brown-haired college freshman lay on a soiled concrete floor in a very tight space.

An angry industrial hum raged in the vague distance. He was blindfolded, and his hands were cuffed to a pipe behind him. A gag around his mouth was knotted tight against the hollow indentation at the base of his skull.

The indentation was called the *foramen magnum*, he knew. It was where your spinal cord passed into your skull. Jacob had learned about it in anatomy class a month or so ago. NYU was step one in his lifelong dream to become a doctor. His father had an 1862 edition of *Gray's Anatomy* in his study, and ever since he was a little kid, Jacob had loved going through it. Kneeling in his father's great padded office chair with his chin in his hands, he'd spend hours poring over the elegant, fascinating sketches, the topography of the human body shaded and named like distant lands, like treasure maps.

Jacob sobbed at the safe, happy memory. A drop of luke-warm water landed on the back of his neck and dripped down his spine. The itch of it was unbearable. He would get sores soon if he wasn't able to stand. Bedsores, staph infection, disease.

The last thing he remembered was leaving Conrad's, an Alphabet City bar that didn't care about fake IDs. After a monstrously long chem lab, he'd been trying to chat up Heli, a stunning Finnish girl from his class. But after his fifth mojito, his tongue was losing speed. He'd called it a night when he noticed she was talking more to the male model of a bartender than to him.

His memory seemed to stop at the point when he stepped outside. How he got from there to here he couldn't recall.

For the billionth time, he tried to come up with a scenario in which everything turned out all right. His favorite was that it was a fraternity thing. A bunch of jocks had mistaken him for some other freshman, and this was a really messed-up hazing incident.

He started weeping. Where were his clothes? Why

would somebody take his jeans, his socks and shoes? The scenarios in his head were too black to allow light to enter. He couldn't fool himself. He was in the deepest shit of his young life.

He banged his head on the pipe he was chained to as he heard a sound. It was the distant boom of a door. He felt his heart boom with it. His breath didn't seem to know if it wanted to come in or go out.

He was pretty much convulsing when he made out a jangle interspersed with the steady approach of footsteps. He suddenly thought of the handyman at his parents' building, the merry jingle of keys that bounced off his thigh. Skinny Mr. Durkin, who always had a tool in his hand. Hope gave him courage. It was a friend, he decided. Somebody who would save him.

"Hppp!" Jacob screamed from behind the gag.

The footsteps stopped. A lock clacked open, and cool air passed over the skin of his face. The gag was pulled off.

"Thank you! Oh, thank you! I don't know what happened. I—"

Jacob's breath blasted out of him as he was hit in the stomach with something tremendously hard. It was a steel-toed boot, and it seemed to knock his stomach clear through his spine.

Oh, God, Jacob thought, his head scraping the stone floor as he dry-heaved in filth. Dear God, please help me.

Chapter 2

JACOB WAS UNCUFFED and pulled roughly for twenty or so steps and slammed into a hard-backed seat. Light spiked his eyes as his blindfold was sliced away, and his hands were cuffed again behind his back.

He was in a child's school desk in a vast, windowless space. In front of him was an old-fashioned wooden rolling blackboard with nothing written on it. Behind him was a cold presence that lifted the hairs from his neck.

Jacob sobbed silently as a lighter hissed. The faintly spicy scent of tobacco smoke filled the air.

"Good morning, Master Dunning," said a voice behind him.

It was a man's voice. The man sounded perfectly sane, highly educated, in fact. He reminded him of a popular English teacher he'd had at Horace Mann, Mr. Manducci.

Hey, wait. Maybe it *was* Mr. Manducci. He always did seem a little too, er, friendly with some of the male students. Could this be a kidnapping or something? Jacob's CEO father was extremely wealthy.

Jacob could actually feel the relief emit from his pores. He decided he'd take a kidnapping at this point. Ransom, being released. He was down with that. Please be a kidnapping, he found himself thinking.

"My family has money, sir," Jacob said, carefully trying to keep the terror out of his voice and failing.

"Yes, they do," the man said pleasantly. He could have been the DJ for a classical music station. "That's precisely the problem. They have too much money and too little sense. They own a Mercedes McLaren, a Bentley — oh, and a Prius. How green of them. You can thank their hypocrisy for bringing you here. Unfortunately for you, your father seems to have forgotten his Exodus twenty, verse five: 'For I, the Lord your God, am a jealous God, visiting the iniquity of the fathers upon the sons.'"

Jacob twitched violently in the hard chair as a stainless-steel pistol barrel softly caressed his right cheek.

"Now I'm going to ask you some questions," his captor said. "Your answers are very, very important. You've heard of pass-fail, haven't you?"

The pistol jabbed hard into Jacob's face, its hammer cocking with a sharp click.

"This test you're about to take is pass-die. Now, question one: What was your nanny's name?"

Who? My nanny? Jacob thought. What the hell was this?

"R-R-Rosa?" Jacob said.

"That's right. Rosa. So far, so good, Master Dunning. Now, what was her *last* name?"

Oh, shit, Jacob thought. Abando? Abrado? Something. He didn't know. The sweet, silly woman that he had played hide-and-seek with. Who'd fed him after school. Rosa, pressing her warm cheek against his as she helped him blow out the candles on his birthday cake. How could he not know her last name?

"Time's up," the man sang.

"Abrado?" Jacob said.

"Not even close," the man said in disgust. "Her name was Rosalita Chavarria. She was a person, you see. She actually had a first *and* a last name. Just like you. She was flesh and blood. Just like you. She died last year, you know. A year after your parents fired her because she was becoming forgetful, she went back to her home country. Which leads us to our third question: What was Rosa's home country?"

How the hell had this guy known about Rosa's termination? Who was this? A friend of hers? He didn't sound Hispanic. Again, *what* was this?

"Nicaragua?" Jacob tried.

"Incorrect again. She was from Honduras. A month after she returned to a one-room shack owned by her sister, she had to go for a hysterectomy. In a substandard hospital outside of Tegucigalpa, she was given a tainted transfusion of blood and contracted HIV. Honduras has the highest concentration of AIDS in the Western Hemisphere. Did you know that? Sure you did.

"Now, question four: What is the average life span in Honduras for an HIV-positive person? I'll give you a hint. It's a hell of a lot less than the fifteen years it is in this country."

Jacob Dunning began to cry.

"I don't know. How would I know? Please."

"That won't do, Jacob," the man said, jamming and twisting the barrel of the gun painfully against his teeth. "Perhaps I'm not making myself clear enough. There'll be no Ivy League A in this class. No tutors. No helpful strategies to maximize your score. You can't cheat, and the results are ultimate. This is a test that you've had your whole life to study for, but I have the feeling you were slacking off. So I'd try to think a little bit harder. HIV-positive life span in Honduras! Answer now!"

Cross Country

James Patterson

**Alex Cross tracks the scariest killer of them all –
to Africa and back.**

When Detective Alex Cross is called to investigate a massacre-style murder scene, he is shocked to find that one of the victims is an old friend. Angry, grieving, and more determined than ever, Cross begins the hunt for the perpetrators of this vicious crime. He is drawn into a dangerous underworld right in the heart of Washington DC that leads him on a life-threatening journey to the Niger Delta, where heroin dealing, slave trading and corruption are rife.

At the centre of this terrifying world, Cross finds the Tiger – the psychopathic leader of a fearsome gang of killers who are not what they seem. As Cross tracks the elusive Tiger through Africa, he must battle against conspiracy and untold violence.

Alex Cross is in a heart-stopping chase that takes him across a vast and uncompromising landscape and finds him not only hunting for a horrific killer, but also fighting for his own survival.

'[*Cross Country*] opens with one of the most chilling murder scenes I've read in a long time . . . High-octane stuff'
Daily Express

'You're just completely engrossed in it from start to finish. Absolutely incredible . . . The story is unrelentingly exciting.'
BBC Radio 5 Live

arrow books

THE NEW ALEX CROSS NOVEL

I, Alex Cross

James Patterson

Alex Cross must battle against the very people he works for to catch a sadistic killer with powerful contacts . . .

Detective Alex Cross is celebrating his birthday when he receives an urgent call from work. An all-too-regular occurrence for Cross. There's been a homicide, nothing new there either. But then comes news Alex wasn't expecting – this time the victim is his niece.

Devastated and grief-stricken, Cross vows to track down the killer. Although, as he investigates he discovers far more than he would wish to know about his niece – she was a high-class prostitute at a very expensive and very exclusive club located just outside of Washington DC. It is clear that this case will test Cross as he never has been before.

As more women working at the same club disappear, it becomes obvious that there is more going on at the sordid mansion than illegal prostitution, and Cross will stop at nothing to solve the mystery of these brutal murders. But he is being foiled at every turn by bureaucracy and a cover-up that stretches as far as the White House. But what are they hiding? And why? Alex can trust no one and will have to do this alone.

Century · London

A NOVEL BY ALEX CROSS

Alex Cross's Trial

James Patterson

**Alex Cross writes a story, passed down through his family,
of one of the biggest trials in history . . .**

Ben Corbett is a brilliant young lawyer in early-twentieth-century Washington
DC. Yet he is a disappointment to his wife and father who believe he
wastes his talents by doing poor-paying and thankless work helping the poor
and downtrodden.

One day, out of the blue, he receives a private invitation to the White House.
President Theodore Roosevelt has personally selected Ben to help him
investigate rumours of lynchings and a re-emergence of the outlawed Ku Klux
Klan in Ben's own hometown of Eudora, Mississippi. Ben accepts the mission
handed to him and is given the name of a man in Eudora who will help him in
this covert operation – the man's name is Abraham Cross, great-uncle of Alex.

As Ben delves into the murky depths of racial hatred that hide beneath the
surface of this seemingly sleepy Southern town, people become suspicious
of what he is trying to do, and make it very clear to Ben what he is risking
if he continues. Ben must decide if he is willing to lose old friends, his family,
maybe even his life for the cause he believes in.

In his quest to bring about justice for the tortured and tormented black
community of Eudora, Ben will have to take on the biggest, most difficult,
and most dangerous trial of his life. But can one man fight an entire town,
an entire state that is stuck in the past and willing to go to any lengths to
halt change and the coming of a future that they desperately fear?

Century · London

THE *SUNDAY TIMES* NO. 1 BESTSELLER

Sail

James Patterson
& Howard Roughan

A family under threat. A killer ready to strike.

As Peter Carlyle, a smooth-talking, super-successful lawyer, waved his family off on a sailing holiday, all they had in mind was lying back and relaxing. But when a violent storm broke out, an explosion caused the boat to vanish without a trace and the family were lost, presumed dead.

Until now. When a message in a bottle is found, it becomes apparent that there must have been at least one survivor.

The race is on to rescue the family, but does everyone looking for them really want to find them alive? Was the explosion the accident everyone assumed it to be? Survival may be the least of their concerns. In fact, being found may be the last thing they should be hoping for . . .

'This gripping novel by the world's bestselling thriller author will have you on the edge of your deckchair.'
Daily Express

arrow books

Swimsuit

James Patterson
& Maxine Paetro

Perfect models, beautifully executed

A breathtakingly beautiful supermodel disappears from a swimsuit photo shoot at the most glamorous hotel in Hawaii. Only hours after she goes missing, Kim McDaniels' parents receive a terrifying phone call. Fearing the worst, they board the first flight to Maui and begin the hunt for their daughter.

Ex-cop Ben Hawkins, now a reporter for the *LA Times*, gets the McDaniels assignment. The ineptitude of the local police force defies belief – Ben has to start his own investigation for Kim McDaniels to have a prayer. And for Ben to have the story of his life.

All the while, the killer sets the stage for his next production. His audience expects the best – and they won't be disappointed. *Swimsuit* is a heart-pounding story of fear and desire, transporting you to a place where beauty and murder collide and unspeakable horrors are hidden within paradise.

'Patterson's annual summer thriller is another exceptional treat'
Mirror

'The thriller genre's leading goal scorer . . . Pulp fiction at its most moreish' *Shortlist*

Century · London

James
Patterson

**To find out more about James Patterson
and his bestselling books, go to
www.jamespatterson.co.uk**

We support

National
Literacy
Trust

I'm proud to support the National Literacy Trust, an independent charity that changes lives through literacy.

Did you know that millions of people in the UK struggle to read and write? This means children are less likely to succeed at school and less likely to develop into confident and happy teenagers. Literacy difficulties will limit their opportunities throughout adult life.

The National Literacy Trust passionately believes that everyone has a right to the reading, writing, speaking and listening skills they need to fulfil their own and, ultimately, the nation's potential.

My own son didn't used to enjoy reading which was why I started writing children's books – reading for pleasure is an essential way to encourage children to pick up a book. The National Literacy Trust is dedicated to delivering exciting initiatives to encourage people to read and to help raise literacy levels. To find out more about the great work that they do visit their website at www.literacytrust.org.uk.

James Patterson